Praise for Jacqueline Grima

'A wonderful twist-filled thriller! . . .
I couldn't turn the pages fast enough.'

'A **masterclass in storytelling**! I literally read this in one day.'

'What an absolute grip of a read . . . I was hooked from the
start and this was **a one-sit read.**'

'A gripping read that had me on the edge of my seat . . .
Full of twists . . . **I was hooked.**'

'A book with a real **"sting in its tail"** . . . A really
good psychological thriller . . . Certainly fooled me!'

'**Masterful storytelling**, highly recommended
if you like Adele Parks and B. A. Paris.'

'A **fast-paced and incredibly gripping read**.
I could not put it down.'

JACQUELINE GRIMA has been writing since she was very young, her first experience of rejection when she submitted a short story to her namesake *Jackie* magazine in her teens. In 2015, after deciding to take her writing more seriously, Jacqueline embarked on a Creative Writing MA at Manchester Metropolitan University, graduating with a distinction as well as the 2018 Janet Beer prize for outstanding contribution. Her work has since appeared in a variety of publications, both in print and online. Jacqueline writes in the living room of the home she shares with her three grown-up sons and an even more grown-up black Labrador called Taz. She spends a lot of time dreaming of having her own office.

Also by Jacqueline Grima

The Weekend Alone

My Daughter's Killer

JACQUELINE GRIMA

ONE PLACE. MANY STORIES

HQ
An imprint of HarperCollins*Publishers* Ltd
1 London Bridge Street
London SE1 9GF

www.harpercollins.co.uk

HarperCollins*Publishers*
Macken House, 39/40 Mayor Street Upper,
Dublin 1 D01 C9W8

This paperback edition 2023

1
First published in Great Britain by
HQ, an imprint of HarperCollins*Publishers* Ltd 2023

Copyright © Jacqueline Grima 2023

Jacqueline Grima asserts the moral right to be
identified as the author of this work.
A catalogue record for this book is
available from the British Library.

ISBN: 9780008581329

*For Taz, who we sadly lost during the writing
of this book, and all the canine and feline companions
who keep us company.*

And for my boys, and girls.

Chapter 1

Claire now

'Please don't hurt me.'

'Please don't hurt me . . .' He curls his lip, sneering at the snivelling mess in front of him. 'Have you any idea how pathetic you sound?'

'Why are you doing this?'

He scoffs. 'Do you really need to ask me that?'

'Please think about this.' Crying now, snot and tears dripping down pale skin.

'Think?'

'It doesn't have to be like this. There's a way out. There's always a way out. For me and for you. We can talk, work it out. Go back.'

He shakes his head. 'There's no going back. Not now.'

'I know you. I know you don't really want to do this . . .'

He raises an eyebrow. 'You think you know me? Believe me, you have no idea what I'm capable of . . .'

I blink as I try to push away the images that filled my mind last night as I tossed and turned. The dreams are back: the ghostly, tall figure, ready to strike, who makes me curl into an anxious knot when I should be resting. Who causes me to jerk awake in the

1

dark, early hours of the morning, to gasp for breath and scan the shadowy corners of the bedroom. Every night for the last week, I've slept restlessly and woken suddenly, scenes from the past sticking to me as much as the sheen of sweat that covers my skin.

And now, in the daytime, more thoughts haunt me, as brutal when I'm awake as when I'm asleep.

All I can think about is my daughter.

In my mind, I see Sarah now, begging for her life, her face pale, eyes wide. Pleading with the man towering above her not to hurt her. How must it have felt to be so vulnerable? To know that someone else gets to decide your future? Whether you live or die?

If only I could have looked ahead and seen what was going to happen. Saved her before she got to the stage where she couldn't be saved. Did her father and I fail her? I wonder. Or did we do everything we could, the two of us simply as helpless as she was? At a loss as to what more we could do?

Looking up at the first-floor walkway of the block of flats in front of me, I see again the blood in the hallway of number twenty-three, the small, spattered stains on the beige carpet I caught sight of from the doorway, closed off with blue and white crime scene tape, before the police ushered me and my husband away. My daughter's blood. As dark as the red wine Sarah and I used to share on a Saturday night, drops forming a neat circular pattern. Just inside the door, not far from where I stood outside, lay one of her shoes. A black suede ankle boot from a pair she loved, its sharp heel pointing upwards. Next to it, the silver chain Guy and I gave Sarah for her sixteenth birthday, snaked across the floor, broken. The letter S that once hung from it was nowhere to be seen.

When I caught a glimpse of the red stains, the shoe, the necklace, that night, in the cordoned-off flat, I'd almost vomited. A nearby police officer advised me to move away from the scene, go downstairs, so that I didn't contaminate the area with my own DNA. Of course I'd obliged. Did as I was told. Perhaps I should have screamed at him. Told him that what I was seeing was all that was left of my only child. Asked him how he might feel in such circumstances.

Instead, I dutifully walked with Guy, his arm around my shoulders, to the mobile police van the detective sergeant in charge of the crime scene led us to. Away from the journalists and the nosy neighbours who'd gathered around, even though it was the early hours of the morning by then. Inside the van, the detective had lowered his head as if we were in church. *I'm so sorry,* he'd said to us quietly, respectfully. *It seems . . . Please accept my . . .*

Now, I lift the bunch of flowers I've brought to my nose, the dozen carnations, wrapped in cellophane, smelling sweet and oily. Carnations were Sarah's favourite. Looking down at the foot of the concrete stairwell that leads up to the flat, I see that someone else has left a bouquet, a wilting bunch of freesias lying next to a damp yellow teddy bear with glassy eyes. Perhaps one of Sarah's friends brought them. Soon, both bunches will be withered, I think. Beaten down by the December weather. Left for dead.

I swipe at a tear on my cheek. How much pain she must have been in, my beloved girl. Even now, all this time later, it hurts to think about it.

'Granny?'

I blink again and swallow heavily.

'Granny?'

I look down at my grandson, standing next to me with his small hand in mine. On his head, the red and green Christmas bobble hat my ex-husband recently bought for him sits slightly cockeyed. A thick scarf covers the lower half of his face. 'What is it, Dylan?'

'Can we go to the park now?'

'Of course we can, sweetheart.'

'Where are we?'

I shake my head, looking up again at the first floor. 'Nowhere, honey.' *Only the place where your mother was last seen alive,* I think, but don't say. *Where her blood was spilt like common water, where her screams were heard loud and clear by the neighbours. The place where all of our lives – mine, yours, your grandfather's – were turned upside down.* 'Nowhere special.'

Dylan doesn't ask again. He's a good boy, even now, at four and a half years old, waiting patiently while Grandma has done nothing more than stand and stare at a building with a bunch of cheap flowers in her hand. He's too young to remember our other visits here, at the same time each year.

I take a deep breath and lay the flowers at the bottom of the concrete stairs. 'Come on, let's go.'

We head back to the car and I strap Dylan into the back seat. He chatters as I drive, twisting his favourite toy, an old grey bunny that used to belong to Sarah, between his fingers. His speech is well developed for his age. It's an achievement, the professionals tell me, considering what he's been through. Considering what he's missed out on.

I pull the car into a space and climb out, making sure we're both well wrapped up against the chill wind before we head out into the green space of the park. The weather forecasters are predicting snow over the next few days: Dylan's first white Christmas perhaps. Another milestone that won't be shared by his mother.

I sit on a bench, the iron seat cold beneath my thighs. As I pull my scarf more tightly around me, I watch my grandson scramble around the playground, his body stiff in his winter duffel coat, as if the many layers he's wearing are stopping him from moving his arms. He looks at a glove he's dropped for a second before picking it up and clumsily pulling it back onto his hand. As independent and determined as his mother when she was the same age.

'Claire, hi . . .'

I look up, startled by the voice. I spend so much time in my own head these days. So much time with just a young child for

4

company, that when someone speaks to me, my responses seem slower, my thought processes delayed. I take a breath, shielding my eyes from the low winter sun. 'Amy, hello. What brings you here?'

'Just out walking. Blowing away the cobwebs.'

'It's cold.'

'It is.' She sits down next to me and pulls her thin jacket around her. It doesn't look adequate for this time of year, especially if the predictions for the weather to come are accurate.

'You don't have a hat?'

She shakes her head. Her bleached blonde hair is very short, a ragged pixie cut that looks as if she's done it herself, styling it as best she can. Her head must be cold.

'I'll see if I can dig one out for you. Will I see you tomorrow?' In the ten years or so that I've been working at Gilbert House – a place of safety for the local homeless community, somewhere they can get a hot meal, a shower, access to a doctor – I've helped many people like Amy get off the streets and into shared accommodation, or hostels like the one she lives in now. Since she was rehomed, she's been *paying it forward*, as she calls it, by volunteering at Gilbert herself. I've kept in touch with quite a few of the clients I've supported, often visiting their new homes to make sure they aren't struggling to keep their lives on track. Amy is one whose progress I'd like to follow for as long as I can. 'At Gilbert?'

She nods. 'Probably. It'll be nice to get out for a while.' She looks at Dylan and clears her throat. 'He's grown. Your grandson.'

'He has. He's running around everywhere now. I can barely keep up with him.'

'Is he looking forward to Christmas?'

I shrug. 'He doesn't completely understand it yet, but I'm sure he'll be excited when the day comes.'

'I bet you've got him lots of pressies.'

'A few, but we try not to spoil him. He has all he needs.'

Amy looks at me. 'It must be difficult. Looking after a little one again.'

'It can be, sometimes.'

'You must get tired.'

Another shrug. 'It's not so bad.'

Amy lets out a small gasp as Dylan loses his balance and almost falls. She rises slightly from the bench. It's not the first time she's met my grandson. There've been times when, with no alternative childcare, I've had to take Dylan with me when on duty. Sometimes, he chats to her, offering her his toys to look at or telling her about his escapades at nursery. Today he's too absorbed in his park adventure.

'Don't worry.' I put an arm out to stop her. 'He's fine. He'll sort himself out.' I watch as he rights himself and carries on playing. His chatter carries towards us on the breeze.

She looks at me. 'It was all over the local news this morning. The anniversary.'

I nod, picturing Amy listening to the little battery-powered radio I gave her. She can't afford a television, or the licence to watch it. I've never commemorated the day, not with anything more than a quiet trip to the flat and flowers, not publicly as other bereaved families often do. It doesn't seem right somehow. 'I can't quite believe it's been three years.'

'You're so strong. After everything you went through, I don't know how you haven't just fallen apart.'

Everyone at Gilbert House knows exactly what happened to my family. It was all over the news, my colleagues sometimes switching off the old TV in the lounge room as I arrived for my shift. So I wouldn't see any more of the story than I had to. Little did they know, I couldn't tear myself away from it at home. It was as if I were an addict, my eyes following the words on the screen as if I'd die if I didn't absorb them, my fingers switching channels to see if the story was any different on another station. Perhaps I was hoping it would be somehow. That, with a simple press of a button on the remote control, my daughter would suddenly be back with me. 'I cope.'

'It's not just coping. It's . . . It's more than that.'

I take a deep breath before fishing in my pocket for my car keys. Short conversations on this subject are about all I can deal with. 'We should go. It's getting cold and I'm on duty tonight.'

'The helpline?'

I nod. The telephone line I set up for women walking home alone, after I lost Sarah, is just one of my many commitments, alongside my job and bringing up my grandson. Despite my good intentions when I had the idea, my constant efforts to keep my mind centred on the here and now, I know doing so much isn't good for me. I try not to let Dylan see how overtired and grouchy I often am.

'We could stay and chat a little longer? If you want to.'

I smile at her. I know Amy gets lonely – who wouldn't in her circumstances? – but, as much as I'd love to spend more time with her, I really do have to be going. The afternoon is darkening and I have to feed Dylan and settle him before I step into my other role. I also want to get home before the weather turns.

I look at Amy. 'Get yourself inside before the bad weather arrives. It's going to snow, they're saying. Stay warm, won't you?'

She nods.

'I'll bring you that hat tomorrow.'

I watch her walk away before coaxing Dylan back towards the car with a promise of fish fingers for tea. When we reach the car park, I notice a small red Citroën is blocking mine, the driver's face invisible through a very dusty window. Whoever it is inside seems to be staring at my grandson. Focusing on him in a way that doesn't seem quite right. Suddenly, a mobile phone appears behind the glass, as if the person in the car is taking a photograph.

I grab Dylan's hand, thinking about the number of times his grandfather and I have warned him about strangers, both of us trying to instil in him a lesson he doesn't yet understand. *Always stay close to Granny*, I've said numerous times. *Don't ever stray too far.* There are too many people in this world who can't be trusted.

Just as I'm about to approach the car and ask for it to be moved, demand to know why someone appears to be taking pictures of us, the driver revs the engine loudly and drives away. Dust from the ground rises in the air and hovers before falling again.

I turn and head back to my own car, thinking about the words Amy said to me just a few minutes ago. *It's more than coping.*

I close my fingers more tightly around my grandson's. *She has no idea how wrong she is*, I think. *I'm nowhere near as strong as anyone thinks.*

Because the man who took my Sarah away from me, who took Dylan's mother from him, changed who I am forever.

Chapter 2

Sarah before

The airport was busy, despite the early hour, even the staff milling around the baggage carousels looking bleary-eyed, as if they were coming to the end of a long shift rather than just starting one. Sarah yawned as she watched the first suitcases appear through the plastic flaps. Their flight had been full and no doubt there'd be many bags coming through before theirs appeared. She was looking forward to getting out of there and flopping into bed.

Drew touched her elbow. 'You wait here; I'll get the cases.'

Sarah nodded. She was grateful not to have to move. On the flight, her legs had been squashed to one side due to the larger gentleman sitting next to her and now they were aching. She knew Drew was tired too. When they'd come through security – trying not to move while they were scanned with a wand or roll their eyes while they waited for their hand luggage to go through the scanner – he'd looked twitchy and nervous. As if he'd rather be anywhere but there. She sighed as she watched him approach the baggage carousel. Despite the fantastic holiday they'd had, she didn't blame him for being a bit grouchy. The experience of a long-haul flight home and then trying to get through the strict airport protocol at the other side was enough to test anyone's patience.

She glanced at her phone, wondering if she should message her parents again, to let them know they were almost through to arrivals. Just a few more minutes, hopefully. Mum and Dad would have been waiting a while now and they would both be worried about getting to work. Dad would no doubt be feeling impatient at the thought that he still had to get through the morning traffic that always filled the motorway between Manchester and Warrington and that he might be late to the office. Perhaps she and Drew should have just booked a taxi, but, even though it was a lot to ask them to come to the airport so early, Sarah had really wanted to see her parents as soon as she got off the plane. She wanted them to be the first to hear all her news.

She lit up her phone screen and found the WhatsApp chat she shared with her mother. The last message Mum had sent had been to ask about their arrival time and Sarah had replied with all the details. She typed out another message now:

Just waiting for our bags. Not too much longer, fingers crossed!

She remembered when she'd first told her mum about the holiday Drew had booked for them both as a surprise.

'*America*? Isn't it a bit early to be going so far with him? And for *ten* days? You've only been together a couple of months.'

Sarah understood what her mum was saying. She herself had been surprised when Drew had presented her with the tickets. It hadn't even been a special occasion: her birthday, or Valentine's Day, for example. He'd just said afterwards that he'd felt like being spontaneous. Treating her.

'I've been away with Keeley loads of times and you've never had a problem with it.' Sarah's mum and dad had brought her up to be a confident traveller, her first holiday abroad just after she and her best friend had completed their A levels and wanted to do something to celebrate. Her parents had checked everything before they went. Made sure the hotel was safe for two eighteen-year-old girls travelling alone, made sure they both had adequate insurance, had photocopies of their passports and spare money hidden in their luggage. They'd covered every eventuality.

'That's different.' Mum had looked doubtful. 'You two are practically like sisters, you've been friends for so long. What if you and Drew find you don't get on once you're together twenty-four hours a day? It's only been dates and the odd night together before now. Can Drew even afford such extravagant surprises? What does he do for a living?'

'He's self-employed. He owns that big gym in town, as well as an online health and nutrition company.'

'Wow.' Her mum had looked impressed. 'Maybe you *have* picked well this time.'

'He comes from quite a well-known family, apparently. His dad was a very well-respected senior police officer and local councillor, before he died.'

Her mother raised an eyebrow at that. 'Not *Donald* Allison?'

'That's him.'

'Double wow.'

Sarah sighed now as she watched Drew locate the first of their cases and deftly pull it from the conveyor. She couldn't imagine, even in the early days, ever not getting on with him. From the beginning, they'd simply clicked, seemed to have what all the social media posts called *chemistry*. And the holiday had gone so well. Even better than she'd expected. She was sure her parents would like Drew as much as she did once they got to know him better. Her dad was always twitchy when a new boyfriend came on the scene. She'd always been his little girl and probably always would be.

She smiled to herself as she noticed an older woman openly admiring Drew's physique as he caught hold of the second case. He was a handsome man. Seven years older than she was, something else that had concerned her mother a little when they'd met for the first time. Every time Sarah looked at him, she had a funny feeling in her tummy, as if her insides were doing the forward rolls they used to have to do in PE at school. Not only was Drew good-looking, he was also a complete romantic, sending her a dozen roses after just their second date, and another dozen after their third. Then there were the chocolates and wine and the meals at high-end restaurants, where he'd recommend dishes and order for her, so she'd be surprised. Mum had thought it was a bit over the top, rolling her eyes as both Sarah and Keeley enthused and gasped over every delivery, every gesture. Such attention from a man was like a dream come true.

Surely her mum understood the feeling of just knowing something was *right*? Had perhaps felt similar when she'd first met Dad? Although Sarah couldn't imagine her dad ever going to the same lengths Drew had been to when it came to romance.

He wheeled both cases towards her.

'Shall I help?'

He shook his head. 'I've got them. You lead the way.'

As they made their way towards the arrivals hall, Sarah felt another flutter in her stomach. Nerves this time. Part of her was so looking forward to telling her parents all about her trip, but another part of her was reluctant to tell them exactly how well it had gone. What if they really did think that her and Drew's relationship was moving too quickly? Should they still be meeting up in bars and restaurants at this stage, like she had with her other boyfriends, rather than travelling thousands of miles together? She fiddled with the letter S at the base of her neck.

She tried to focus as she followed the other passengers through the double glass doors. The time difference between the two countries meant she and Drew had been catapulted forward by eight hours, their journey beginning a whole day ago, and she was really starting to feel a bit unbalanced now, when it should have still been night-time for her. She smiled as she spotted her parents at the far end of the hall, behind a barrier. At least they didn't look too agitated by their early morning trip.

She lifted her hand in a wave before jogging over to where they were waiting. She put her arms around her dad's neck before hugging her mum. 'Thanks so much for coming. I know it's super-early and you both have work. We would have booked a taxi, but I just really wanted to see you.'

Her dad shrugged. 'Well, I could have done without such an early start, but you know we'd rather make sure you get home safe than be worrying.' He glanced at Drew as he spoke, as if to say, *I hope you've taken good care of my precious daughter over the last ten days.*

'Thanks, Dad.'

Her mum gestured over her shoulder. 'Come on, let's get out of here. The poor dog is waiting for his breakfast, not to mention the fact that the car park is costing us a fortune. You can tell us all about your trip when you get home.'

Sarah felt her heart thud. 'Hold on a sec, Mum . . .'

Her mum was already on the move. 'I know you're keen to tell us everything, Sarah, and I can't wait to hear all about it, honestly, but we really should go. You need to get some rest if you're going to be ready to go back to work tomorrow. I've changed your bedding and put out some clean pyjamas if you want to get some sleep for a little while. Maybe Drew could come round for supper tomorrow and we could . . .'

'Actually, Claire . . .' Drew came up from behind Sarah, still wheeling the cases. It seemed strange, hearing him call her mum by her first name. As if they were old friends.

Sarah's mum turned back, frowning. 'What is it?'

Drew glanced at Sarah before continuing. 'Well, Sarah and I were hoping you could drop us both off at my place? If that's not too much trouble?'

'Both of you?' Her mum looked at her dad and then back at Drew. 'But Sarah has work tomorrow, Drew. Her boss won't take

13

kindly to her having any more time off, especially as she didn't give much notice before jetting off to the States with you. She'll want to shower and unpack . . .'

Sarah suddenly felt nervous, much more so than she had when she was coming through from baggage collection. She felt much the same way she had when she'd had to tell her parents she'd decided to switch subjects just a few months after starting her degree course. Or when she'd overspent on her account and gone overdrawn. She felt her cheeks flush as she touched her necklace again. It was a habit she often turned to when she was anxious.

'Sarah?'

Sarah looked back at her mum.

'What's going on?'

Sarah took a deep breath and tried to smile. She held up her left hand, waggling her fingers in an exaggerated backward wave. 'Mum, Dad, you know what often happens when people go to *Las Vegas* . . .' She crossed the fingers of her other hand. She was so hoping her parents' reaction wasn't the opposite of what she wanted it to be.

Her mum's eyes widened as she put her own hand to her mouth. 'What? You mean?' She looked at her husband as if to check he was following her train of thought. To confirm she wasn't imagining the rose gold ring she was seeing on her daughter's finger. 'Are you kidding?'

Sarah shook her head and laughed. 'No joke. Drew and I got married. Can you believe it? I'm *Mrs Allison*.'

Chapter 3

Claire now

I stand at the living room window and look out across the darkening space at the back of the house. It's much colder now than it was this afternoon, but the heating is on and the Christmas lights I hung on the tree just a few days ago make the inside of the house seem cosy. I think about Amy in her tiny room in the hostel on the other side of town. The opposite of cosy, as I've seen on the many occasions I've visited her there, taken secondhand clothes and toiletries. I hope she can afford to switch on the two-bar fire I recently found for her. It's not great, a donation left outside Gilbert House, but it's better than nothing.

The garden is covered in a light layer of frost now; icy crystals sparkle on the grass. Sarah loved being outside, I remember, as I look up at the clear moon, the thousands of stars gathering around it. Autumn and winter were her favourite seasons, one racing into the other in a flurry of leafy walks and garden tidying and building snowmen. Will Dylan be the same? I wonder. A lover of nature like his mother? If Sarah were still here, would she be teaching him about plants? Encouraging him to love and respect what grows around us, as we did with her?

I remember the night our daughter decided she wanted to camp out with Keeley, when the two of them were eleven or twelve. Guy had been all for it. Children needed to be able to spend time outdoors without fear, he'd said. He'd done it frequently when he was a child and look at him now. He'd made it through unscathed. In the end, I'd bought an old baby monitor, much like the one I use for Dylan now, and set it up between the tent and our bedroom. The girls had eventually got cold and migrated inside. Their giggles made me smile as they reached me over the airwaves.

Sarah always made a point of saying what good parents we were, Guy and I. Easy-going, laid-back, compared to her friends' parents. Always willing to let her enjoy her adventures, never too serious. We were the best role models, she'd say often. A compliment we'd wave away but secretly enjoy.

Sometimes, I wonder if my daughter ever really knew me at all.

I hesitate as I grab the curtains on either side of me, about to pull them closed. In the darkness, beyond my reflection, I'm certain I can see a slight shadow, flickering between the trees at the end of the lawn, gone before I can ascertain if it really existed, or if it was simply a figment of my imagination. It wouldn't be the first time I think I've seen someone lurking around the house in the eighteen months or so since Guy and I split up. My nerves are often heightened these days, my imagination in overdrive, as must often happen to people who mostly live alone. Especially those who have been through a trauma.

I stare though the window. There it is again. Something moving. Perhaps it's an animal, I think. A fox or one of next door's cats, who never seem to stick to their own territory. It suddenly makes its way behind the shed and towards the back gate, gone again. I swallow heavily and close the curtains to shut out the night.

I switch on the TV, always tuned in to my preferred news channel when I'm in the house. Even Dylan has got used to the constant drone of the newsreader. As I flop onto the sofa, the lights of the baby monitor on the side table next to me flashing briefly

16

as my grandson settles to sleep in Sarah's old room, I hear my ex-husband's voice in my head, as clear as if he still lives here. As if he never left. *Aren't our lives difficult enough without subjecting ourselves to this onslaught of misery, day in, day out?*

Guy never did understand my need to watch the news constantly. I struggled to explain it to him that it's like a compulsion. Like the need for a cigarette or alcohol or a chocolate bar. As if the constant grim, often macabre, storylines are feeding something inside me, like I'm a snake swallowing mice. Other people's misery assures me that I'm not alone, that I'm not the only person to have been through such upheaval.

I quickly scan the headlines at the bottom of the screen, black letters on a white background: a little girl who has wandered away from her family in Scotland; a prisoner on the loose somewhere, a few cities away; another parliamentary scandal. I think about the little girl's parents. How strange it must be for them to tune in to the news and see themselves as the focus. Everyone in the world able to see what they're going through, suddenly an audience to their distress. It's not easy.

I jump as my mobile rings, the dog pricking up an ear from his usual place on the hearth rug, watching me. *Poor Boswell*, I think, as I scrabble around the sofa for my phone. He misses Sarah as much as I do.

'Hi.' I don't need to look at the screen to know who's calling.

'Just checking in before I settle. You okay?' Guy sounds tired. Neither of us has a great sleeping pattern lately. Quite often I doze on the sofa on and off for days at a time, without ever making it upstairs to my bed. I suspect my ex is the same.

'I'm okay.' I glance at the clock on the mantelpiece, an old carriage my ex-mother-in-law gave me when we got married, that I've always hated. Almost eight-thirty. Next to the clock, my daughter stares out at me from the picture taken on her wedding day. Sarah is smiling widely, her face freckled and golden from the American sun, her long hair looking a little lighter than its usual dark brunette shade. The left side of the original print has been cut off, the image made smaller. Only Sarah's face is showing now. I avert my eyes and glance down at the laptop next to me on the sofa. 'I don't have much time to talk. The first calls will be coming in soon.'

Guy yawns loudly. 'That helpline. You know I'm really proud of you for setting it up and everything, *really* proud, but couldn't you leave someone else to take the reins on the odd occasion? It's Friday night. You should be getting some rest after a week of working and looking after Dylan. When do you get any time to yourself?'

I imagine him in the bedsit he's lived in since we split up, not far from the big roundabout that leads into town. No doubt he'll now be in front of the TV, his eyes not quite focused on some nature documentary or motoring programme, his hand clutching a tumbler of whisky. He and I talked a lot about the pros and cons of founding a helpline after we lost Sarah. I knew what I was committing to, how much work it would be. But what would I be doing at the weekends, once Dylan was asleep, if I didn't have the calls to occupy me? Also sitting drinking whisky?

'It's our busiest weekend of the year.' *Mad Friday*. Two weeks until Christmas and the world and his wife are out celebrating. As I might have been if I were still living a normal life. If I were still married, not estranged from most of my friends. If it weren't the anniversary of losing my daughter. 'Besides, it helps keep my mind off things.'

Guy sighs. 'It doesn't get much easier, does it? Every year, it feels the same.'

I glance at the TV again. On the screen, officers in high-vis vests seem to be searching hedgerows and woodland for the missing little girl. 'No, it doesn't get easier.' I change the subject. 'Are you still okay to collect Dyl in the morning?'

'Yep. I'll be there, usual time. Tell him I've got ice cream in for him. And fish fingers of course.'

'That'll be fish fingers two days in a row then.' I try to feed my grandson as healthily as I know his mother would like me to. But what are weekends for to a four-year-old, if not treats? I jump as the doorbell rings, the sound seeming overly loud. 'I'll have to go. Someone's at the door and I don't have much time.'

'Are you expecting anyone?'

'I don't think so.'

'Put the chain on.'

'I'm fine, Guy. I'm sure I can cope with answering the door by myself.' Ever since he moved out, my ex has been protective of me, jittery about me being in the house alone with Dylan. Part of the territory for a family like ours, I guess.

'Just humour me.'

I end the call and head down the hallway, Boswell at my heels. I hope I can get to the door before the bell sounds again. I don't want Dylan to wake up. Despite Guy's warning, I forget the chain and swing the door wide open, ready to send whoever is calling on me at this time of the evening on their way.

My heart thuds. I know as soon as I look across the threshold that I've made a big mistake.

Chapter 4

Sarah before

Sarah looked down at the table she'd set. It didn't look quite as good as her mum's tables, when she and Dad threw dinner parties for Dad's work colleagues or hosted the family Christmas. Some of the cutlery didn't quite match, two of the forks from a different set, and she'd accidentally chipped one of the plates as she was getting it out of the cupboard. One of Drew's plates. She was proud of it though, and the way she'd draped the napkins mostly hid the tiny chip. She hoped. 'What do you think, Mum?'

Her mum smiled at her. 'It looks lovely, sweetheart. Doesn't it, Guy?'

Her dad nodded. 'Really nice, love.' He gestured to the kitchen. 'I'll go help Drew with the wine.'

Sarah looked down at the table again, just to make sure everything was in the right place. This was the first dinner she'd hosted as Drew's wife and she wanted everything to be as perfect as she could get it. It had taken some getting used to, living in a new place, trying to treat it like her own. She'd been in the same house all her life, apart from her brief spell at uni, and now, since moving into her husband's flat, she felt almost like a stranger.

She'd packed up all her stuff in such a hurry after they got back from their holiday that she'd ended up leaving half of it behind: her make-up and childhood journals, some of her most treasured possessions. Maybe it would have been different if they'd found somewhere completely new together after they'd got married, but that wouldn't have made any financial sense. Not when Drew had a place that he'd already been living in for years. Even if the area it was in wasn't quite what she'd been used to growing up. She looked up as her mum spoke again.

'I love those napkin rings. Very trendy.'

Sarah smiled. 'We got them with the John Lewis vouchers you got us after the wedding. Drew really appreciated you getting us something. He said you really didn't need to. Especially as you weren't there.'

'No, well.' Her mum's smile slipped a little. 'We couldn't not get you anything, though, could we? Our little girl just got *married*.'

Sarah chuckled and wiggled the fingers of her left hand again. She was struggling to get used to wearing the ring. Sometimes it felt heavy and cumbersome and, on the odd occasion in the couple of weeks they'd been home from the US, she'd slipped it off when Drew wasn't looking. Just to give her finger a break. It probably wasn't the type of ring she'd have picked herself – she'd have preferred something daintier – but she loved it, nonetheless.

'I guess we should have had an idea, in hindsight. You did go to *Vegas*, after all. Obvious really.' Her mum looked thoughtful for a second. 'I just wish . . .'

Mum stopped talking as Drew and Sarah's dad came in from the kitchen, carrying bottles of wine. Drew seemed relaxed as he chatted to her dad about a recent football match. He'd welcomed both of her parents warmly when they arrived, complimenting Mum on her outfit and thanking her for the expensive chocolates she'd brought. It was exactly the scenario Sarah had been hoping for when she'd suggested a dinner party to celebrate their wedding with everyone who hadn't been there.

When Drew had first met her parents, a couple of weeks or so after they started dating, he'd been quiet and reserved, and Sarah had warned her dad beforehand not to make any of his stupid jokes. Drew wasn't like the immature boys she'd gone out with in the past. He didn't drink a lot or have any desire to smoke weed. Nor did he like fast food or going to burger joints. He liked to eat healthily and work out. When she'd introduced him to her parents, she'd kind of felt like she was back in the days of her parent–teacher conferences at school. When Dad had shook her teacher's hand and made some comment about the premier league to break the ice. She was glad the atmosphere seemed a little more relaxed tonight.

She looked back at her mum. 'Wish what?'

'Nothing, it doesn't matter.'

Drew put the wine on the table and came over to where Sarah was standing. He draped an arm around her shoulders. 'The table looks great, doesn't it, Claire? Your daughter's worked really hard on this dinner. She's been cooking all day. You should be proud of her.'

Sarah felt her cheeks flush. She hadn't told her husband about the frantic call she made to her mother early this morning, when he was still in bed. She'd woken up in the small hours sure that the whole dinner party was going to be a disaster because she'd chosen lamb for the main and had never cooked it before. She didn't want Drew to see her in such a state. Luckily, Mum had patiently talked her through every step of what she needed to do and the smells now coming from the flat's kitchen seemed right.

'I'm sure it's going to be delicious.' Her mum winked at her discreetly.

'Definitely.' Drew looked at her and lowered his voice. 'Though, don't think I didn't notice the little accident you had with the plate.' He chuckled. 'I guess you owe me a new one, *clumsy*.'

'I'm sorry . . .'

'I'm just kidding.'

Sarah smiled. She'd thought she'd managed to hide what had happened.

They all looked up as the doorbell rang, Drew rubbing his hands together as if the sound signalled the beginning of the party. 'Great, more guests. I'll get it.'

Sarah watched him leave the room before straightening the napkin in front of her for what must have been the twentieth time. She had butterflies in her tummy. She didn't want to let Drew down, especially after he'd noticed the plate. 'What were you going to say, Mum?'

Her mum shook her head. 'Nothing important. Only that I wish Dad and I could have seen you. On your wedding day. If you'd told us beforehand, perhaps we could've done some last-minute rearranging. So we could have come over and seen what a beautiful bride you were.'

Sarah smiled. 'I was hardly that. I was wearing shorts and a T-shirt, with sun cream across my nose. Besides, we didn't know ourselves before we went. We only started discussing it after we got on the plane.'

Her dad began to pour wine. 'So, whose idea was it, in the first place? To get married?'

Sarah frowned. 'Well, it was both of ours, I suppose.'

'But someone must have brought the subject up first?' Her mum picked up a glass of wine and took a gulp. 'I guess it must have seemed romantic, being spontaneous like that. Weren't you bothered about Keeley not being there? I'm sure she would have loved to be a bridesmaid. Plus, both your grandmas might have enjoyed investing in new hats.'

Sarah shrugged. She felt confused. Part of her *had* wanted her friends and family to be at her wedding, especially her parents and Keeley. She was close to them and knew it would have meant a lot to have them there. But when Drew had suggested they get married, just the two of them, when he'd said the time just felt right, he'd been so enthusiastic, she couldn't help but get swept

23

along with the idea. She remembered how he'd leant towards her on the plane, a mischievous look in his eye.

'I have an idea.' He'd wiggled his eyebrows.

'Please don't tell me you want us to join the Mile High Club.' Sarah had laughed.

'More than that. How surprised do you think everyone would be if we came back from Vegas as *man and wife*?'

She hadn't thought he was serious at first, but he'd soon persuaded her he was. Did she regret it now? Only sometimes, briefly, when Mum seemed sad at having missed out. How could she ever regret having married a man like Drew? Who'd paid for her to fly to America and barely let her spend a cent while she was there? Who opened doors for her and pulled out chairs and helped her into her coat?

She looked towards the door as her husband came back in, the rest of their guests trailing behind him. Keeley and her partner and Drew's mum and brother all seemed to have arrived at the same time.

He gestured ahead of himself. 'Come on in, guys; grab a seat. I'll get some more wine. Guy, Claire, this is my mum, Audrey, and my brother, Dan . . .'

As he disappeared into the kitchen again, her mum and dad introducing themselves to Drew's family, Sarah headed towards Keeley and her girlfriend. She was so glad to see her best friend at last. They'd barely spoken since Sarah came back from the US and it seemed ages since the two of them had spent any real time together.

'Hi.' She briefly kissed Alice before enveloping Keeley in a hug. 'I'm so glad you're here.'

'Me too.' Keeley grabbed Sarah's left hand. 'Let me see it then. Oh my goodness, wow, it's stunning. I'd never have imagined you picking something like that.'

'Drew picked it. Got my size right and everything.'

'How lovely. He's a man who likes to surprise you, I'll give him that.'

'Definitely. Can you believe it? Me, *married*?'

'I'm not sure I can. It's like one of those whirlwind romances you hear about.' Keeley smiled and hugged her again. 'I'm so excited for you.'

'Me too.'

'What about your mum and dad? Have they got over the shock?'

'I think so. They seem to be coming to terms with the idea. I'm not sure about Drew's mum though. I mean, I barely know her, to be honest. I've only met her once before and she scared me. She's so *posh*. And I haven't met his brother at all before tonight.' She grimaced. 'Maybe I should go and say hello.'

She headed over to where her parents were chatting to her in-laws.

'It's a lovely flat, isn't it? I like what Drew has done with it.' Her mum looked around her at the small space. Drew's flat was very different from the house where Sarah had grown up. Her childhood home had always been kind of chaotic, her working parents not having much time to commit to household chores. It had been a fun place to live, she'd always thought, and all her friends had seemed to think the same. When Sarah had visited the flat for the first time, when she and Drew had been out on just three or four dates, she'd been amazed at how tidy it was. Every possession had its place and her husband liked to keep it that way. She was trying her best to change her way of living to match his.

She wondered what her mum thought of the area the flat was in; the estate's reputation for being a little rough was a stark contrast to the expensive décor inside where they lived. Surely Mum and Dad would have noticed the graffiti on the walls, the vandalised cameras, as they came in? All of the surrounding security measures seemed to be broken, the run-down wasteland that surrounded their block a little scary to walk around after dark. Sarah hadn't mentioned anything to her husband, but she sometimes wondered why he'd chosen to buy property there above other nicer places in the town. It wasn't as if he had any money worries. As far as she knew anyway. He was quite a private person, even with her.

She smiled at her mother-in-law before nodding at Drew's older brother. 'Thank you both for coming. Nice to meet you, Dan.'

'You too. Thanks for inviting us.' Dan's smile was hesitant, almost shy. 'Nice to see Drew settling down at long last.'

Dan couldn't have been more different from his brother, Sarah found herself thinking, both in looks and temperament, if her instinct was right. Although Dan was a little older, his skin was less weathered than Drew's, his whole demeanour more relaxed, as if he were simply strolling through life without too many worries. Whereas Drew liked to dominate a room, Dan seemed quite content just to blend into the background.

She tried to focus as she heard her mum chuckle.

'Well, with this place being so tidy, I guess it's a good job Sarah hasn't brought the dog here to live with her. It's a shame though. Boswell is really going to miss having her around. He was her dog, originally. A present, after her A levels.'

Audrey grimaced. 'Oh, Drew would never put up with a dog.'

'Yes . . .' Sarah's mum looked at her. 'Sarah was telling us how she thought about bringing Boswell but unfortunately she couldn't, because of Drew's allergies.'

'Allergies?' Audrey glanced at Dan who raised an eyebrow.

Sarah frowned. 'He was telling me how you had a family dog when he was little, but you had to rehome it because Drew discovered he was allergic?'

Dan's eyes widened. 'I'm not sure you've got that right. We got rid of that dog because Drew hated it. My brother whinged and whined from the minute we got it to the minute Mum took it back to the shelter. I remember it clearly because I'd loved that mutt myself. I was gutted when it had to go. I'm afraid Drew isn't a big lover of *any* animals. He seems to think their main purpose is to provide food.' He shrugged.

Sarah felt confused. Surely there was some mistake? Drew had definitely talked about allergies when she'd suggested bringing Boswell to visit to see if he might settle in at the flat. Hadn't he? She missed her dog and was sure Boswell missed her. Even if he could've come overnight on the odd occasion, it would have been better than not at all. She remembered how Boswell had growled the first time she took Drew home, her then-boyfriend laughing it off and keeping his distance.

She was about to ask Dan more when she was interrupted by Drew coming in from the kitchen again. He was tapping the corkscrew on the side of the bottle of wine he was carrying.

'Before we sit down and eat the delicious meal, my *wife* has been preparing all day – I still can't get used to calling her that – I'd just like to say . . .'

Sarah pushed thoughts of the dog away and smiled as she tried to focus on what her husband was saying.

Chapter 5

Claire now

As soon as I open the front door, I know that the person on the other side of it is a journalist. It's after dark on a Friday evening, but I shouldn't be surprised. To the tabloid press, no day or hour is sacred or off-limits. There was a time, during the months our family was making the headlines, when Guy and I couldn't step out of the house without planning our outing with military precision. Despite pleas from the police to let us grieve in peace, reporters and photographers would fill our driveway almost every day, crowding us as soon as we tried to go anywhere, bombarding us with questions. Sometimes, we would sneak out of the back gate to avoid them. Guy would go first into the alley behind the garden and gesture me forward only when he knew the coast was clear.

'Please go away.' I try to close the door again.

The woman on the step puts her hand out. 'Please, Mrs Wallace, just a few words about . . .'

'I said, *go away*.'

She's almost in my home. The place where my husband and I raised the daughter we lost. The house where our beloved Sarah grew up. Boswell puts his head between my ankles and grumbles at her; he has a natural instinct for people who don't mean well. I attempt again to close the door, but her hand is flat against it. She's a petite woman but is obviously stronger than she looks.

'With it being the third anniversary today, I just wanted to ask about your current feelings towards your daughter's killer? Will you ever forgive him?'

I stop and look at her. '*Forgive* him? That man took my daughter away from me. If it was *your* daughter, would you forgive him?' I purse my lips. 'You people are brutal, do you know that? Was it one of your team who was taking pictures of my grandson at the park this afternoon? Was it?'

She shakes her head. 'I have no idea.'

I don't know why I'm even talking to her. I remember how difficult it was, in the early days, to ignore the reporters' questions, or reply with a simple *no comment*, as the police advised us to do. Sometimes, it was tempting to engage with them. To set them straight on the mistakes they were making in their accounts. When they questioned if Sarah could have avoided what happened to her. If it was her own fault. 'I'm going to close the door now, so you'd better move your foot away from it, if you don't want to lose a couple of toes.'

Boswell barks sharply as I push against it from the inside with all my strength.

'Just one more thing, Mrs Wallace . . .'

I try to close my mind off to what she's saying. Like Sarah used to do when she was little. When she put her hands over her ears and sang to block out anything she didn't want to hear. What would I look like if I did the same?

'Do you think he'll ever reveal what he did with Sarah's body?'

I gasp, the door moving inwards again as I take my weight from it. I look at this woman. This person who has no right to be saying such things to me. No right to be invading my space the way she is. To be speaking my daughter's name. I see again what I could see in my mind as I stared up at the block of flats earlier today, Dylan next to me: the dark-red blood; the shoe; the necklace that is now fixed and around my own neck, ever since the police gave it back to us. It's the only thing I have, besides my grandson, that makes me feel close to her. That keeps her here with me.

I grit my teeth. 'If you do not leave my doorstep right now, I'm going to call the police.' I give the door one last push and slam it closed, not caring now if I hurt her.

I stand for a few seconds, trying to control my breathing. I know journalists have to make a living, that they're simply doing their job, earning a wage to feed their families, but no matter how many times I experience their invasion of my privacy, it never gets any easier. Why can't they leave us alone?

As I head back to the living room, I hear her words over and over in my mind:

Do you think he'll ever reveal what he did with Sarah's body?

If I'd answered her, opened up my home, given her the interview she so desperately wanted, what I would have said is *no*. No, I don't think the police will ever find my daughter. Not now. Not after all this time. But the thought that they might, one day, is always with me. It never leaves.

I scan the news headlines as I sit back on the sofa. Nothing seems to have changed in the few minutes since I went to answer the door. The little girl in Scotland still hasn't been found; the prisoner is still on the loose somewhere; an MP is refusing to resign. I glance at the closed curtains, thinking about the shadow I saw flitting around the garden when I pulled them across the window. How it slinked between the trees before disappearing in the direction of the back gate. Nausea rises from my stomach to my chest. Could it have been the same journalist, sneaking around the back of my home? Trying to get a picture of me through the window? The very thought of it makes me seethe.

Bracing myself, as I often have to do, I look again at Sarah's wedding photo on the mantelpiece. At the edge that's been cut by scissors. I'm trying not to cry. The experience on my doorstep, the thought of someone perhaps in the garden, beneath the upstairs window of the room where Dylan sleeps, has shaken me. Just getting through the anniversary is difficult enough without having to be reminded of what *that man* did to us.

Drew Allison. Sarah's husband.

The man who has been in prison for the past two years after being convicted of her murder. The same man I cut from her wedding picture before reframing it. Whose image I hacked at in the same way he hacked my daughter from my life, imagining myself hacking at him for real. At his flesh and bone. Ending his existence, the same way he ended mine.

I shake my head to clear it. I can't think about him now. About the things he did. Or about shadows in the garden. I have too much to do, an obligation, one I committed to at a time when I needed to find a purpose in my life. When I felt so lost, I thought I'd never function normally ever again.

I pull on my headset and click on the green icon on my screen.

Chapter 6

Sarah before

Sarah sat still in the passenger seat of her mum's car. She felt her stomach flip. During the ten-minute journey to Warrington town centre, she'd barely said a word, putting off what she needed to say. She already knew how her mother was going to react. Perhaps she should just wait, tell her another time. Sarah had had a lot to cope with over the eight weeks or so since she'd come back from Vegas – adapting to a new way of life, a new routine, learning how to be a wife – and she was beginning to feel a little tired. Not to mention the fact that she'd been up early this morning to make Drew's breakfast before he set off for work. She'd never been too fussy about what her porridge looked like, but her husband liked his just so.

She waited while her mum pulled the car into a space.

'Thanks for coming with me today, sweetheart. I like it when you volunteer at Gilbert House. It means we can have a good catch-up. We should do it more often.'

Sarah climbed out of the car. In front of her, the tall, Gothic former church building where her mum worked kept the strong summer sun from blinding her. She often felt proud of what her mother did. For as long as she could remember, her mum had been feeding those who didn't have the means to feed themselves, whose home was the very streets that surrounded them, or, at best, barely adequate housing. Sarah had started coming in with her on the odd occasion at the age of sixteen. She found the people she served lunch to chatty and amicable. A far cry from the stereotypical so-called vagrants they were often made out to be by those who were quick to judge.

She hoisted her bag onto her shoulder as they walked from the car park and through the narrow alley that led to Gilbert's front entrance. It was a place the town's regular shoppers often avoided. Sarah had noticed on many occasions how parents often pulled their children back if they strayed too close. As if they were approaching a busy road, or quicksand. She took a deep breath. 'Mum . . .'

'Hmmm?'

'I think I'm going to give up my job.'

Her mum stopped walking. 'What?'

Sarah looked at her feet. 'It's not permanent. It's just going to be for a little while, I think. While I figure out what I really want to do.'

'Want to *do*?' Her mum turned to face her. 'But you love your job. At least you did when you landed it. Didn't you tell your dad and me that this was your dream role? We took you and your friends out to celebrate and everything, spent a fortune on that fancy meal.'

'I know, and I appreciated it. Of course I did. And you're right, I was happy when I got the job. It was a fantastic opportunity, especially for someone my age, but now . . .'

'Now, what?' Her mum's eyes widened. 'You're not pregnant, are you?'

'Of course I'm not. We have plenty of time ahead of us for that. I just need some space to figure out if the path I'm on is really the one I want to take. If I really want to work my way up the marketing ladder. Drew thinks . . .'

'Drew?'

Sarah swallowed and nodded. 'He thinks now is the ideal opportunity for me to take some thinking time. About what I really want to do with my life. He said he's happy to support me until I figure everything out.'

Her mum looked confused. She stepped back as one of Gilbert's regulars shuffled between them, a middle-aged man, in a hefty anorak despite the warm weather, making his way to the entrance. 'But Sarah, Drew doesn't need to support you. You can support yourself. Don't forget how important it is to have your independence. Your dad and I have always taught you that. A woman should always have her own money to fall back on.'

Sarah scoffed. 'I've told you. It's not going to be forever. It's just for now. And why shouldn't my husband support me? Drew and I are a couple. We're one and the same. Are you saying you don't think we'll last? That we'll end up splitting up?'

'Of course that's not what I'm saying.' Her mum's expression softened a little. She put a hand to Sarah's arm. 'I'm just saying I want you to always be the feisty, independent daughter I've raised, that's all. The one I know will always be able to look after herself, who knows her own mind. Wasn't your boss talking about the possibility of early promotion just recently?'

'That was just speculation. Nothing definite.' Sarah wasn't quite telling the truth. She'd been pretty sure the promotion was on the cards, but she wasn't going to tell her mum that. Her husband had just made her think, that was all. Helped her to see things from a different angle. He did have more experience than she did in the world of work, after all. He'd been running his own business for years. 'Drew has opened my eyes to the fact that there are other opportunities out there for people with my qualifications. He's made me realise I don't have to stick to the same role for the rest of my life just because . . .'

'The rest of your life? You've only been there five minutes.' Her mum looked around the alley as if thinking before turning back. 'Have you told your father?'

'Not yet.' Sarah sighed and raised an eyebrow. She wasn't sure if her dad's reaction would be any easier to cope with than her mum's. 'I don't suppose you'd tell him?'

Her mum rolled her eyes before chuckling. 'Leave it with me. I don't think he'll be entirely pleased though. Dad bent over backwards to get you that interview. Just don't rush into anything, that's all I ask. Maybe you and Drew could come over for supper at some point and we could talk about it some more?'

'Maybe. He's really busy at the minute though. I'd have to see if he's free.' Sarah linked her arm into her mum's as they made their way to Gilbert's entrance. 'You know I appreciate everything you've done for me. You're the best parents ever, you really are. Even Drew has said so on more than one occasion.'

'He has?' Her mum looked surprised.

Sarah nodded. 'He's always complimenting you. He says it's no wonder I've turned out like I have.'

'What a charmer. Come on, let's get inside. We've still got lots to do before lunch service.'

They skipped up the steps, Sarah waving to Billy on reception. She felt a lot lighter now she'd spoken to her mum, even if Mum didn't quite agree with her plans. 'Morning, Billy. It's a lovely day out there. You should get out for a walk when you can.'

Billy scowled. 'Far too hot for me. No chance you'll get me out there without factor fifty and a wide-brimmed hat.'

Sarah giggled. Billy had been volunteering at Gilbert House for as long as her mum had worked there, after he'd been through a period of homelessness he'd been determined to get out of. He usually kept himself to himself, often sarcastic or morose, but he was well liked by the rest of the team. Sarah enjoyed coming to help out. Like her mum had said, it was a chance for them to spend time together and she enjoyed talking to the regulars, finding out what was going on in their lives. She was always happy when she learnt that someone had managed to find decent accommodation or a new job.

She thought about her husband. Perhaps Drew would like to join her and her mum at some point. Do some volunteering, get some satisfaction from helping out those who needed it. It would be something they could do together. She'd mention it to him when she got back to the flat. Got *home,* she reminded herself.

They dropped their bags in the staffroom before making their way into the dining hall and behind the counter. While Mum went into the kitchen to help organise the food, Sarah grabbed an apron from a hook on the wall, slipping it over her head and tying the strings around her back. She looked around the dining room. A few regulars were milling around already. Some sat alone, staring into space; others chatted to each other. It was still an hour or more until lunch was served, although Sarah imagined that perhaps they simply found the smell of cooking meat and vegetables nourishing. Took comfort from it, made the most of it while they could.

She thought about the Sunday dinners they'd always had when she lived at home. She and her dad would often spend all day in the kitchen, digging out recipe books, listening to music, chatting. She supposed she'd taken that time for granted, didn't always think about what it must be like not to have good food to look forward to. To not know where or when she'd get her next meal. Sarah looked across the room at a girl about her own age, sitting in a far corner, her head resting on one curled fist. The girl looked pale, even though it was summer. Her clothes were faded and her blonde hair greasy. Sarah wondered when the last time might have been that this girl had eaten, or enjoyed a warm shower. Curled up by a radiator with a good book. Lunch at Gilbert House was probably the one constant she had in her life. The one thing she could rely on.

Sarah sighed heavily. She was very lucky, she thought to herself, as she began to organise ladles and serving spoons on the stainless-steel counter. Two great parents who had given her everything she could have asked for. A decent education, a lovely group of mates, including the best friend she'd known forever. And now, a wonderful husband.

She pulled her phone from her pocket as it vibrated, Drew's name filling the screen. She smiled. She liked how he called her frequently during the day. How interested he was in who she was with and what she was doing. Sarah thought it was sweet that he took so much interest in how she was spending her time.

'Hi.' Her stomach flipped at the thought of hearing her husband's voice, even though she'd only spoken to him a couple of hours before. She hoped she'd always feel like this when she spoke to him.

'Hey, what are you up to? Are you with your mum?'

'How did you guess?' Sarah frowned. She hadn't decided to come to Gilbert until the last minute, when Mum called after Drew had gone to work and asked if she wanted to spend her day off helping others.

'Just lucky, I suppose. I presumed you wouldn't want to sit around the flat all day when you're not working.'

'I might be doing that a lot if I give up my job. Mum has mixed feelings about the idea.'

'With all due respect, it's not your mum's decision.'

'I know that.' Sarah glanced at the pale girl in the corner, now with her head on the table as if she couldn't keep herself awake. She thought again how lucky she was. Her husband had offered to support her while she worked out what she wanted to do with her life. Drew didn't have to do that. 'I was thinking, when I do leave work, I may end up volunteering a bit more here, to occupy me while I think. Maybe you could come too one day?'

'Me?'

Sarah felt another flip low in her stomach. Not quite as pleasant this time. 'Only if you're not too tired. It doesn't matter if you think it would be too much. It was just a thought.'

'Hmm.' Drew was quiet for a few seconds. 'Will you really have time to be doing more volunteering yourself? I mean, you have a lot of decisions to make. Plus, I hate to sound misogynistic here, but, with my long workdays, you'll have to take on the majority of the cooking and the cleaning in the flat. That's just the way it is, I'm afraid. And if we want to start a family . . .'

'A family?' Sarah looked behind her, to make sure her mum wasn't nearby, listening.

'Well, I'm not getting any younger, babe. If we want kids, we're going to have to think about it pretty soon. I don't want to be too old to kick a football around, do I?'

Sarah suddenly felt very young. Being married was one thing, but the idea of becoming a mother was altogether different. If someone had asked her a year or so ago if she could see herself becoming pregnant any time soon, she'd probably have laughed. Kids had always been something way ahead in her future. But if it was what Drew wanted . . . As he said, he was older than she was. She had to take that fact into consideration. 'I suppose. I hadn't really thought about it. I presumed we'd discuss it first.' Perhaps it would have been a good idea to have this conversation before they spontaneously decided to get married in Vegas.

'That's what we're doing now. Anyway, gotta go, babes. Work calls. Enjoy your volunteering while you can. You might not have much time for it in the future. Love you.'

Sarah said goodbye and ended the call. As she put her phone back in her pocket, she reminded herself again how lucky she was. Drew was always there, at the other end of the phone when she wanted to speak to him. He always told her he loved her, no matter how many times he'd said it already that day. She seemed to be always on his mind, no matter where she was, what she was doing.

What more could she ask for?

Chapter 7

Claire now

I mute the television before taking a deep breath, reminding myself that I have to be professional. That I'm in work mode now, that I need to put my personal life to one side. Now is not the time to let my emotions get the better of me. When I had the idea of founding a helpline – almost a year after we lost Sarah, the trial behind us – it had seemed like an impossible concept. Now, on our busy days, we take as many as seventy or eighty calls a night. Sometimes more. The other operators on my team are no doubt going to be as busy as I am over the next few hours.

I clear my throat and speak as clearly as I can into the microphone. 'Hi, you're through to Claire at *Walk Me Home*. Can I take your name?'

'I . . . It's Jess. I'm walking home on my own and I didn't realise it would be so dark at this time. I'm nervous. I've never been so keen on being out on my own at night.'

'Okay, don't panic, Jess. I'm here to help.'

'Thank you.'

I begin to type. 'Can I check the number on my screen is the one you're calling from?' I give her the last three digits.

'That's right.'

'And you say you're alone at the minute?'

'Yes.'

'Okay. So, the next thing I must ask you, Jess, is if you feel you need immediate police assistance?'

'I . . . I don't think so. I got spooked because I thought someone might be following me. He came right up behind me but now he's crossed over the road. I'm actually beginning to think that he was trying *not* to scare me.' She laughs shakily.

'Okay, well, remain vigilant.' Glancing over the top of the laptop screen, I scan the news headlines again. It's a habit I find difficult to break. The newsreader looks slightly comical as her mouth moves but no sound comes out. 'If you think you need the police at any point during our conversation, I can help you with that, all right? Have you been out somewhere?'

'Yeah, I went out for after-work drinks with my colleagues. One of them offered me a lift home, but, stupid me, I said I'd be fine.'

'We've all done it. Don't be too hard on yourself. And how far away from home are you?'

'About ten or fifteen minutes.'

'Okay. Is there any sign now of the man you thought might be following you?'

A slight pause. 'No, he's gone. I think I was definitely mistaken. It's just so dark, hardly any lighting at all on this route.'

'That must be scary.' I try not to think about my daughter, how scared she must have been that night we lost her. How soon she must have realised there was no going back. I close my eyes briefly before pushing the thought away. 'We've started a campaign to get street lighting improved in the local area, but it's slow going. If you like, I'd be happy to send a pair of our volunteer walkers out to accompany you home?'

'You can do that?'

'Of course. Just give me your exact location and I'll try and find who's nearest.'

She describes a street on the outskirts of town, an isolated area not far from where Sarah lived with Drew. Like Jess said, it's dark and not the best place to be walking alone at night, even if it is still early. I doubt there are any security measures in place.

'We have a couple not too far away from there. They'll be with you in just two or three minutes.' I quickly type out instructions and send them to my volunteers. The pair I'm asking to help Jess are efficient and enthusiastic; they won't hang around. 'Their names are Annabel and Kye and they'll be wearing bright yellow *Walk Me Home* sweatshirts and coats and will have ID with them.'

Jess sounds relieved. 'Thanks so much.'

'You're welcome. In the meantime, I'm happy to stay on the phone with you until I know you're safe. Just be aware of your surroundings until the walkers get there.'

'This is a great idea, by the way. The helpline. I saw a flyer in a bar I was in just a week or so ago and I put it in my bag. It didn't occur to me then that I might need it so soon.'

'We're happy to help. Feel free to spread the word about us. We'd like to assist as many women as possible in not feeling so scared when they're out at night.'

'The walkers are here now, I think.'

I let a breath out, as I always do when I know someone is going to get home safely. 'Take the time to check their ID, Jess, then you know they're authentic. I'm happy to wait.'

The line goes quiet for a few seconds as a message comes onto my laptop screen. It confirms that my walkers are where I want them to be.

'Everything seems to be in order.'

'Great, have a safe journey home and feel free to call anytime.'

'Thanks, Claire. Night.'

'Goodnight.'

I end the call and log the outcome, as I always do, on the *Walk Me Home* portal. As I type, I can see that the other operators are getting busy, over half of them now tied up with their own calls.

The team is bigger this year than it's ever been, our experiences of the past two festive seasons prompting me to apply for more funding long before this Christmas approached. The number of volunteer walkers we use has doubled and I have no doubt we're going to need them this weekend. I suspect tonight is going to be a long and tiring one.

Taking advantage of a quiet moment, I head into the kitchen to put the kettle on before walking down to the front door and letting the dog out. Boswell likes the front of the house when it's quiet, his walks fewer now than they were when he was younger, when Sarah still lived here. He noses in the shrubs that line the drive before cocking his leg, once and then again. As I watch him, I fish in the pocket of the old hoodie I'm wearing for the emergency pack of cigarettes I bought when I took Dylan to the shop on the way home from the park. Sarah would hate it that I'm occasionally smoking again so I try to limit myself, but I figure today, the anniversary, might be exactly one of the *emergencies* I had in mind.

I light it and smoke quickly, squinting as the bright security light on the front of next door's house comes on. Peter and June are good neighbours, members of the local neighbourhood watch and always looking out for those who live around them. When Sarah was born, they were the first to knock on our door with offers of food and babysitting. Later, they offered food again, along with their condolences.

I can't help but smile as I remember the chicken fricassee: meat and cream and mushrooms dripping down the wall of the hallway behind me, pooling on the carpet. At least I'd waited until my neighbour was safely back in his own house before snatching the dish from my husband's hands and throwing it with all my strength. I was so angry. Am I still? I wonder. Most likely.

My heart begins to thud as I look up at the illuminated pavement in front me, not sure at first if what I'm seeing is a trick. The shadows playing games with me. On the other side of the quiet street, a tall figure is standing just out of reach of the light, arms bent, hands in the front pockets of what look like faded jeans. I can't tell if it's a man or woman. The figure's build is lean and slim and their face is shadowed and mostly hidden by the hood that's pulled low over their eyes. Just a sharp chin juts out at the bottom.

I straighten in the doorway, thinking about the journalist, the car that blocked me in at the park, the shadow I saw from the back window earlier, as it moved behind the shed and towards the gate. I remember Guy's words when I spoke to him on the phone: *humour me*. He'd told me to put the chain on the door before I answered it, but I'd ignored him. And now, here I am again, casually smoking a cigarette out in the open, making myself vulnerable in the very way I advise all the women who use the helpline not to. *You're your own worst enemy*, my ex-husband has said to me numerous times since the day we met when we were both still in uni. Perhaps he's right.

I throw my half-smoked cigarette to the ground, my eyes still on the figure. The person is standing perfectly still and watching me, as if they're rooted to the ground. Is it the same reporter? Perhaps now changed into more casual clothes, bundled up against the cold, still hoping to persuade me into an interview? Or is it a different one, perhaps the person in the car at the park, here for the same reasons?

My heart speeds up as I wonder if I should just call the police. Rush back inside and get my mobile and ask them to come. Yet what would I say? That there's a person in the street, simply standing on the pavement, apparently not causing any harm to anyone? On what is most likely the busiest weekend of the year, not just for the helpline, but for the emergency services too? It seems too soon to panic. Perhaps the person who seems to be watching me is someone entirely innocent. Someone who's simply stopped to admire the Christmas lights that decorate the houses on either side, or who is waiting for their own dog to catch up. That wouldn't be so strange, would it?

I take a step outside, not wanting to stray too far from the door, squinting through the darkness. 'Can I help you?'

The person doesn't reply. They simply continue to stare, eyes still hidden by the hood.

I decide to throw myself in at the deep end. 'If you're looking for a story, you're not going to get one, so you might as well just . . .'

The figure turns and walks quickly away.

I let out a shaky breath and pat my thigh. 'Come on, Boswell. Time to come in.'

The dog cocks his leg one more time and has a last sniff of the ground before scampering back up the driveway. Before he comes into the house, he turns back towards the street, his hackles risen. He growls deeply. It's the second time I've heard him make the same noise today.

I usher him inside and close the door, making sure it's locked and the chain is on, as my ex-husband advised.

I fill a mug with black coffee and two heaped spoons of sugar – another habit I'm sure Sarah would be unimpressed with – before heading back into the living room. As I pass the bottom of the stairs, I pause and listen for any sounds of Dylan stirring. I'm getting used to it now, having my grandson living here, but for a time I was filled with a sense of anxiety that almost disabled me. A constant fear of the *what if*. Of not being able to look after him properly, to replace the mother he barely remembers. The father who destroyed his life before he'd even learnt to walk. Hearing only silence, I go back to the sofa and take a sip of hot coffee before pulling my laptop back onto my knee. The dog lets out a sigh as he settles in front of the fire.

I put my headset on and make myself comfortable, trying to dismiss thoughts of dark figures outside. Most likely I'm just being paranoid, I think, shaken by my earlier visitor, today of all days. As I look at my screen, I see that a queue of calls is beginning to form, much earlier than it normally would. I click on the green icon to accept the first call that's waiting.

'Hello. You're through to the *Walk Me Home* helpline. My name is Claire. How can I help?'

The words that come down the line cause goose bumps to form all over my body and the hair on the back of my neck stands up.

'You can help me by listening very carefully to every single word I say, Claire. Because I know where Sarah is.'

Chapter 8

Sarah before

The flat's kitchen felt a little crowded when Sarah's mum and dad came to visit. The room wasn't huge and, with Drew's minimalist lifestyle, any extra people felt like a lot. She was used to visitors when she'd been at home, her friends often calling on her with no notice, at all times of the day and night, persuading her into movie nights or a pampering session, or taking over the kitchen while they experimented with new recipes. The flat was different though. Drew had said, just a few days ago, that it might be a good idea if her mum and dad let them know in advance if they wanted to call round. Gave them a bit of notice. Just in case she and Drew had any plans, or simply wanted some time to themselves. She wasn't sure how her parents would feel about that. They'd always been spur-of-the-moment kind of people.

Mum sat at the breakfast bar and sipped the coffee Sarah had made her. It had taken her a while to work out Drew's coffee machine, but she thought she was getting there with it now. Her husband was quite particular about his hot drinks.

'This is lovely, sweetheart. Maybe *we* need to get a coffee machine.'

Mum looked at Dad. 'What do you think, Guy? You could get me one for my birthday?'

Sarah's dad raised an eyebrow. 'As well as the new handbag you wanted? We'll see.'

Sarah chuckled. 'Drew says he couldn't live without his proper coffee. He says it sets him up for the day.' She glanced at the kitchen door, wondering when her husband was going to join them. He'd said he had some paperwork to do in the small office down the hall, but her parents had been here for twenty minutes or so now and he still hadn't appeared.

'So . . .' her mum took a biscuit from the packet she'd brought with her '. . . are you looking forward to Keeley's engagement party? I can't believe she and Alice have finally decided to tie the knot. It's so nice to see her happy with someone after some of the other characters she's been out with. What happened to the two committed singletons you and your best friend were when you were teenagers? Wanting to travel the world and see the sights before either of you settled down?'

Sarah shrugged. 'We grew up, I guess.' She leant against the counter and looked down into her mug. She still wasn't sure she'd got the coffee quite right; she'd have to try harder. 'I'll have to see what Drew's doing. I don't know if he's working the night of the party. Running the gym means he often has to work late.'

Her mum frowned. 'But that doesn't stop you going, does it? Drew working?'

Sarah shrugged again. She was beginning to wonder if Drew was right. If it might be better if her parents gave her some notice before visiting. She knew they meant well, but sometimes she felt as if all they did was ask her questions. As if they were questioning her relationship with her husband. The way she lived her life now. It didn't seem fair. 'Drew just gets worried if I'm out after dark. He doesn't like the idea of me walking home by myself when he's not around.'

Her dad shrugged. 'I could pick you up? It's not like it would be the first time I've stayed up late to make sure you got home. I've picked you and Keeley up enough times in the past. Even when you were very, very drunk.' He rolled his eyes.

'Dad wouldn't mind at all, sweetheart. Keeley would be gutted if you weren't there. The party wouldn't be the same without you.'

'I said I'll see.' Sarah tipped her coffee down the sink; it definitely wasn't right. She wanted it to taste how it did when Drew had shown her how *he* made it. 'Can we just leave it at that?'

'Of course.' Her mum glanced at her dad. 'Just let us know.'

Sarah glanced up as Drew came into the room. She loved it when he was at home with her, casually dressed in an old band T-shirt and chinos, instead of his more formal work gear. He was completely right about not wanting visitors invading their privacy on the rare days they got to spend together. Her mum and dad could come round when he was at work. Maybe once she'd finished her chores and started preparing the evening meal. She was so busy in the flat, she really didn't miss work at all. Or her friends. She didn't have time to.

'Sorry I've been so long. Any coffee going?'

Sarah shook her head. 'It doesn't taste right. I'm going to make another pot.'

He kissed the top of her head. 'Ah, don't worry, you'll get there in the end.' He turned to her mum and dad. 'Claire, Guy, good to see you. I didn't know we'd have the pleasure of your company today.'

'We were just passing.' Her mum gestured towards Sarah. 'We were just talking about Keeley's engagement party next week. Guy would be more than happy to pick Sarah up and bring her home if you're working. Then you don't have to worry about her having to walk.'

Drew was quiet for a second before speaking. 'Worrying about my wife is what I do best, isn't it, babe? It's completely up to Sarah what she does, Claire. If she wants to go to the party then, of course, that's her decision. I wouldn't dream of making it for her.'

Sarah felt her husband's eyes on her as she fiddled with the coffee machine again. Her hands felt unsteady and she was being more than a little clumsy. Having so many people around her was making her nervous and she was frightened she was going to break something. Like when she'd chipped the plate at the dinner party, the one she had actually replaced in the end. Drew had said it didn't matter but his comments afterwards about his favourite dinner set not being complete had made her feel guilty. Why did the kitchen seem so crowded now? It wasn't like she wasn't used to having her parents around her.

'Anyway . . .' Drew clapped his hands together '. . . I really hope you don't think I'm rushing you off, but I'm afraid Sarah and I have plans for this afternoon.'

Sarah looked around and saw her mum's eyes widen.

'Oh, you never said, sweetheart.'

'I . . .' She looked at Drew.

'That's because Sarah didn't actually know. I was going to surprise her with lunch out.' He shrugged. 'I guess the surprise has been spoilt a bit now, but never mind. Better run and get changed, babe. I'll see your parents out.'

Sarah kissed her mum and dad goodbye before heading down the hallway to the bedroom. She'd had no inkling that Drew had been intending for them to go out today, otherwise she would have said something to Mum and Dad as soon as they arrived. She wouldn't have gone to the trouble of making proper coffee. Or eating any of the biscuits they'd brought, her husband often telling her that eating between meals wasn't a good habit. But that was Drew all over, she thought, as she rifled through her wardrobe for something to wear. Always catching her off guard. In a good way, of course.

She jumped as she realised he was standing in the bedroom doorway behind her. 'What about this?' She held up a dress she'd pulled out. It had always been one of her favourites. 'Good for a lunch out?'

Drew screwed up his nose. 'I've never been so keen on that one, to be honest.'

'Oh, okay.' Sarah was surprised. He'd never said. She pulled out another. 'How about this one then?'

Drew came further into the room. 'You know . . .' he grimaced '. . . I'm not sure I'm that hungry anymore. If your parents hadn't arrived, we could have gone earlier, made a day of it. Maybe you could just whip us something up for lunch instead? There's plenty of stuff in the fridge. Is that okay, babe?'

'Of course.' Sarah turned and faced him. Drew always seemed so tall when he was standing over her. 'Is something wrong?'

He moved his head from side to side, as if weighing up his answer. 'Hmm, I think it was just all that talk about the engagement party, to be honest. It's kind of dampened my mood. You know how much I worry about the idea of you going out without me there to look after you. To make sure you get home safely. It doesn't feel quite right letting your dad have that responsibility anymore, does it? I mean, *I'm* your husband. It should be me making sure you're safe.'

Sarah thought for a few seconds. She really should be more sensitive to the fact that Drew worried about her so much. 'Well, I just won't go then. I'm sure Keeley won't miss me. All our other friends will be there to make sure she has a nice time.'

Drew smiled. 'That's my girl.' He wrapped his large hand around the top of her bare arm as he leant in and kissed her. 'Think I'll just nip into the gym for an hour while you sort lunch. You don't mind, do you?'

Sarah shook her head. 'Of course not.'

She watched her husband leave the room. When he'd gone, she looked down at her arm and saw the imprints of his fingers just beginning to fade away.

Chapter 9

Claire now

The police searched for Sarah's body for weeks, but they never found her.

Concentrating on the wasteland surrounding the flat where she'd lived with Drew, teams of officers dug and dug. Searched in shrubs and bushes, beneath piles of rubbish, at the base of trees. With no working CCTV in the area, they could only guess what might have happened to her, where she was. Samples taken from both Guy and myself told them, through DNA testing, that the blood found on the hallway floor, as well as spotted on the walls above, had to be Sarah's. Could only have come from a child that my husband and I had created together.

Our daughter had been attacked in what was supposed to be her own home. She'd just got back from Keeley's wedding.

She'd chosen to walk home, despite her friends trying to persuade her to share a taxi with them. Sarah hadn't wanted to wait around. She'd wanted to get home, telling Keeley she was anxious that Drew would probably already be back from his late shift before her. Sarah had promised her husband she wouldn't stay late, that she wouldn't drink too much or dance with anyone. That she'd keep herself to herself.

She'd called me as she walked, to check on Dylan. Drew had been reluctant to have us look after his son. *Dylan might get distressed*, he'd said – our grandson didn't know us that well then – but Sarah had persuaded him that it was for the best, while she was out and he was working. She really wanted to go to the wedding and she couldn't very well take a little one with her.

'How's he been?' Her voice sounded shaky, as if she were shivering.

'Perfect,' I remember telling my daughter. 'As good as gold. Just like his mum was at the same age. You really shouldn't be walking home on your own at this time though, sweetheart. Dad would have come for you if he wasn't feeling so awful. This nasty bug has really knocked him for six.' Guy had been in bed all day, a particularly virulent strain of winter flu that had been circulating his office finally making it to his desk.

'I'll be fine. Honestly, it's not far.'

'Will Drew be there when you get back?'

'I expect so.'

'If he were any kind of husband, he'd have come to pick you up himself.'

'Mum . . .'

'Okay, okay, I'll keep my opinions to myself. Have you got your keys ready?'

'Yep. At the door now.'

It was at that moment, as my daughter let herself into the flat that our lives changed forever. I'd still been at the end of the phone; I'd heard everything before the call was cut off.

I'd called the police.

They told us to stay at home, so they'd know where to get hold of us, so they could do their job without interference from distressed relatives. Like the good citizens we were, we'd done exactly as we were told. I distinctly remember the chill air that hit my face when I opened the door to the two young officers who first came to break the news to us.

Are you the mother of Sarah Allison? one of them asked as I stared at him, slightly breathless and conscious of the old dressing gown I'd just put on before I answered their knock. I'd stuffed my hands into the pockets and nodded, in shock.

May we come in?

When he'd told us what had happened, we'd insisted on going to the site ourselves, Guy dragging himself down from upstairs, looking even paler, greyer, than he had before. It was when we got there, up to the walkway, that I saw the blood in the hallway, the shoe, the broken necklace. The blue and white tape.

They'd found the missing letter S in Drew's car. In the same search, just hours after Sarah went missing, they also found blood on the lip of the boot as well as inside, as if someone had been hoisted up and thrown into the well. Fibres that matched my description of the dress my daughter had been wearing that night – a silver and black shift that was one of her favourites – were also found in the car. Drew's bank records proved he'd bought cleaning materials just a few days before, including a mop, disposable cloths and bleach. He'd also, rather stupidly, it seemed, tried to delete a search he'd done on his laptop about disposing of a body.

Around three weeks later, a dog walker stumbled across a bundle of clothes in an isolated wood approximately five miles away: the silver and black dress, the other ankle boot, also with spots of blood on them. They were wrapped together in a bin bag along with Sarah's underwear and a strapless bra and stockings. The bin bags were the same type Drew always had in the flat. I remember how Sarah had told me that her husband was quite particular about his shopping. He liked to buy the same brands week in, week out, in the same shop, fussy about the quality of what he spent his hard-earned money on. The police told us very gently that they wondered if he'd removed her clothes to make the task of dismembering her easier. They later found a hacksaw. Also with Sarah's blood on it.

When he was arrested, Drew's face was covered in scratches, as if someone had been trying to defend themselves against him. He didn't have an alibi.

My son-in-law was convicted of murder ten months later, on circumstantial evidence.

The trial lasted twelve days, Guy and I telling the jury about Drew's relationship with our daughter, all the things she'd been through since he entered her life. Some of Sarah's friends sat in the public gallery as we talked to the court, Keeley often wide-eyed and frowning in disbelief at what she was hearing. After we'd had our turns, a witness, a young man who'd been sheltering from the cold beneath the block's stairway, stated how he saw Sarah letting herself into the flat that night, how she'd seemed to be arguing with her husband in the doorway, as if Drew didn't want to let her in. It was the last time she was seen. An elderly gentleman who'd lived in one of the neighbouring flats near Drew for many years also spoke quietly and politely to the courtroom about the loud scream he'd heard. He'd been too frightened to investigate but, like me, had called the police.

Now, I sit as still as stone on the sofa as I listen to the sound of deep breathing coming into my headphones. I glance at the baby monitor next to me, making sure there are no flashing lights, that Dylan is still settled. 'Who is this?'

Trying to remain calm, I scan the computer screen in front of me, looking for information about the person who's calling. Whoever it is has blocked their number. The laptop can't tell me anything about their identity.

'That would be telling, Claire.'

The voice at the other end of the line belongs to a woman, but it's muffled, as if it's a bad connection or the person speaking is perhaps covering her face with a scarf or something similar, to keep herself warm if she's outside. Her accent is what we used to call *Queen's English*. I search my brain; it's difficult to tell, but I'm certain this person is someone I haven't spoken to before.

'How do you know me?'

'*Everyone* knows you, Claire. You're the mother of Sarah Wallace. The woman who disappeared. Or Sarah *Allison*, I suppose I should call her. You've been in all the papers, haven't you? All over the news. Those pictures of you, standing at the edge of that wasteland, looking on while the police searched for Sarah's body? They really tugged at my heartstrings. You're so brave, so *strong*. A real role model to women everywhere.'

Her words make bile rise in my throat. The long days of the police search were some of the worst of my life. I look at the computer screen, see that the queue of calls is getting bigger. Should I message one of my team? I wonder. Let them know I have a nuisance caller? We've done training about this, when I first founded the helpline. We've all had them: men calling, late at night, pretending to be frightened, laughing with their mates, or irate at the flyers that insist *Walk Me Home* is for women, or anyone who identifies as a woman, only. The rule seems to rub some people up the wrong way.

I try and remember the voice of the reporter who came to my door earlier, who prevented me from shutting it with the flat of her hand, who I thought might be lurking across the street just a short time ago. 'Were you just outside my house? Because if you're a journalist after an interview, you need to be aware that all you're succeeding in doing now is blocking our system, preventing vulnerable women from getting through.'

'Ah, Claire, it's not like you to be reticent. You've given plenty of interviews before, haven't you? All those heart-wrenching words about what you've been through. How you lost your precious daughter. How it inspired you to help others.'

'*Enough.* I'm not giving you a story. In fact, I'm going to end this call now . . .'

'Except, I'm not a journalist, Claire.' The line fades out, then back in again, the signal weak. 'That's not what I am at all. Believe me, I already have enough of a story. I don't need you to tell me anything. I know it all already.'

I swallow heavily. On the hearth rug, Boswell turns and looks at me, as if he can sense my building distress. I think about the words the caller first said to me when I answered: *I know where Sarah is*. It's impossible. No one knows where my daughter is. Not even the police, despite their extensive searches, which went far and wide before they eventually gave up. Before they told us they didn't think they'd ever find her. Or what was left of her. 'I don't believe you.'

'Please yourself. But I'm telling you, Claire. I know what no one else does. I know where your daughter is. Where she ended up, what happened to her. Maybe, just maybe, if the police had carried on searching, just a little bit longer, they might have eventually found her.'

I think about the cold and desolate wasteland. The patches of soil and dirt and garbage the search teams rifled through. The wild animals who no doubt roam there at night, looking to feed. On flesh and bone if they're lucky. I close my eyes briefly. 'Tell me what you know.'

'I'm afraid that will have to wait until next time . . .'

'What?' I sit up straighter. I have a queue of calls waiting – women needing my help – but suddenly, I don't want this unexpected caller to go. I need her to give me the information she has. To tell me what she thinks she knows about my daughter, my only child. 'No, wait.'

'Be sure to expect my call, Claire. Speak soon.'

The line goes dead.

I put the laptop and headset to one side and stand up, aware I have calls waiting but barely able to breathe. As I stand, bent at the waist, hands on hips, I feel the eyes of both the dog and Sarah on me: Boswell watching me from his position on the rug and my daughter from the picture I keep on the mantel. I turn and rush into the kitchen where I vomit into the sink. After rinsing my mouth, I open the back door. I need to feel the night air on my flushed face, no matter what shadows or figures, what dangers, may be lurking around me.

As I take deep gulps of low-lying mist, the dog hovers behind me, seeming reluctant to leave the house this time. Somewhere, not too far away, I can hear someone singing a Christmas song, out of tune and mixing up the words in the same way Sarah used to when she was very young and tried to sing about elves and reindeers. It seems surreal somehow, hearing this joyous sound when I feel so sad, so anxious. Next door, Peter is shuffling around his own garden, his slippered feet skimming his flagged path. The lid of his wheelie bin bangs open, a plastic bag rustling as he puts out his day's rubbish.

He speaks to June who must be waiting in the back doorway. 'Such a sad affair. All this time not knowing. Maybe we should do something. Get a card maybe or some flowers. Let her know we haven't forgotten it's three years.'

June whispers back. 'I hope they threw away the key when they locked that man up.'

I feel my skin prickle as I clear my throat loudly. So much talk about my family, my private affairs, so many people invading my life. My neighbours mean well, I know that, but I can't bear to hear any more of their conversation. Not now, when I've had such a shock. Peter and June say nothing more and, within seconds, I hear their back door close quietly.

I look out across the dark garden, the silence eerie now as the first flakes of the predicted snow begin to fall from the blue-black sky. Ever since Guy moved out, I've cared little for the outdoor space we once paid a fortune to maintain. I no longer worry about the dog doing his business on the grass or scraping up the blades with his back paws afterwards. I remember how disappointed Guy looked last time he visited, eyeing up what used to be our dream space, the place we used for relaxing. For entertaining our many friends and work colleagues. I can't imagine entertaining anyone ever again.

When Guy and I first got married, we swore that if, *when*, we had children, they wouldn't change our lives completely. That we'd still travel and have a social life, enjoy a dinner party or a glass of wine with friends at the weekend. Too many couples we knew had seemed to make being parents the sole focus of their lives. Given up everything that had gone before. That wouldn't happen to us, we said and laughed. We knew better.

Then Sarah came along.

The minute I looked at my daughter, as I lay exhausted in the hospital bed, I knew she was my *everything*. That I would never again put anything or anyone before her. Looking up at my husband, I saw the same in his eyes. We were parents. It was the role we'd play first and foremost for the rest of our lives.

In my mind, I hear again the muffled words the strange caller said to me on the phone just a few minutes ago. *I know where Sarah is.*

The dog scurries around me in a panic as I fold in on myself in the doorway, my knees giving way beneath me, the air leaving my lungs as suddenly as if someone has punched me in the stomach. Boswell tries to lick my face, his tongue rough on my skin. I've had emotional outbursts before, many of them over the past three years – screaming fits and bouts of complete irrationality, blaming Guy for everything that has happened to us, not able to process a coherent thought – but none of them have been as sudden, as physical, as this tidal wave of grief that has swept my feet from under me.

I miss my daughter so much.

As my surroundings darken, my vision shutting down, as thoughts of my lost child overwhelm my mind, the last thing I'm sure I see is another shadow flit across the bottom of the garden. It heads in the direction of the back gate and disappears.

Chapter 10

Sarah before

Sarah slipped her arms into her coat. It was getting chilly outside now that summer was coming to an end and, from what she'd seen from the flat's window, there was a brisk wind blowing. Just a few minutes ago, she'd watched somebody walk across the car park, the man's head bowed, hands clutching the thin scarf at his neck. Seeing him had prompted her to dig out something a bit more substantial than a denim jacket.

She looked at her reflection in the hallway mirror, smacking her lips together to smooth out the nude lipstick she'd chosen. Even though she'd given up work and now spent much of her time indoors, she still wore make-up most of the time. Drew liked her to look nice, even when he wasn't there. Some days, it seemed a bit of an effort, doing up her face when she had cleaning to do and dinner to cook; she liked everything to be perfect before her husband came back from work. But if that was what he wanted, she was happy to oblige.

Most days, Drew FaceTimed her because he said he wanted to see how pretty she looked. He'd called her three or four times most days since they got married, asking her what she was wearing and how she was spending her time. What she'd decided to do for dinner that night. He did the same even when he was working late at night, the gym open twenty-four hours. His calls sometimes woke her up if she'd gone to bed, but Sarah didn't mind. She liked how he wanted to check on her, make sure she was safe while he wasn't there.

She rubbed at a stray smudge of mascara, thinking about how she and her friends used to get together in her old bedroom at the weekends and try out the cosmetics she used to get for free through her marketing job. She and Keeley would laugh as they painted each other's faces, styled each other's hair. It seemed silly now, what she used to spend her time doing. A little immature, maybe. Since she'd married Drew, she felt more like a grown-up. She wanted to do more grown-up things. The things a wife would do.

It would be nice to see her best friend today though. Sarah had missed her, the two of them only having met up once or twice, that she could remember, since she and Drew had come back from Vegas. She thought Keeley might have been a bit upset when Sarah had missed the engagement party, but she'd assured her friend she wouldn't miss the cake tasting and wedding open evening Keeley wanted all the girls to accompany her to in a few weeks. To help her decide between various invitation designs and flowers and favours. Drew wouldn't object to Sarah wanting to support Keeley a bit more with her wedding arrangements, surely? Even though she hadn't had a big wedding herself, with hers having been a last-minute decision, her husband would understand how important the run-up to someone's big day was.

She tucked a stray hair behind her ear before pulling her phone from her pocket and taking a selfie, pouting the way she used to when she and her friends were on a night out. She smiled as she looked at the picture. She'd post it on Instagram and tag Keeley. Maybe her friend would then post one of herself getting ready.

She frowned as she clicked on the pink and orange icon.

Her account didn't seem to be coming up. Perhaps the site had crashed. She'd have to try and sort it later. She needed to get going, otherwise she'd be late to the pub Keeley had picked for their lunch date. Sarah didn't eat much pub food these days. When she and Drew ate out, it was usually in an upmarket restaurant, one that Drew had already been to and wanted her to experience. It had taken Sarah a while to get used to all the fancy food, not to mention the extravagant prices – she was much more used to home cooking – but she could see why her husband liked visiting those types of places so much.

She put her phone back in her pocket and picked up her bag, taking one last glance around the flat to make sure it was in order before she went to pull open the front door, realising that Drew would have locked it when he went out to work. She looked around for her keys. They didn't seem to be in their usual place on the hallway table. The ceramic dish she and Drew both dropped them into when they came home was now sitting empty.

Sarah rooted in her bag. She'd had her keys the day before, she was sure. She hadn't been out at all, but she remembered dusting around the hallway – Drew liked her to dust at least three times a week – and they were there, in the pot, like always. Where could they be now? She went into the kitchen and looked around before heading into the bedroom and looking there too. No keys.

Sarah began to feel a little panicky. Last time she and Keeley had arranged to meet for lunch, Drew had surprised her with tickets to a theatre show that he'd picked up at the last minute and she'd had to let her friend down. The tickets had cost her husband a lot of money so she could hardly say no. She'd promised Keeley that nothing would stop her turning up this time. Drew was at work, the flat was tidy and her husband's evening meal was in the fridge, ready to be reheated later. All she had to do was make sure she got home before Drew did so he could put his feet up after his long shift and she'd dish up. Now she was frightened she was going to be late, and that Keeley would think she'd let her down again. That she didn't want to see her.

She pulled out her phone and scrolled though her contacts list. As she pressed her thumb on Drew's name, she felt a little nervous about bothering him at work. He was usually the one who called her, not the other way around. She hoped she wasn't disturbing him.

'Babe? Everything okay? I'm a bit busy at the minute. You know I can't really answer while I'm working. That's why *I* call you.'

'I know, I know, I'm sorry.' Sarah felt silly, as if she was being a pest. 'I was just wondering, have you seen my keys? They're not in the pot and I'm on my way out to meet Keeley. We've had this lunch date planned for weeks.'

'Oh shit, yeah, I forgot . . .'

'Forgot what?'

Drew cleared his throat. 'Well, I picked your keys up with mine, this morning. Just grabbed the whole bunch from the pot without thinking about it. I was running a bit late, so I didn't really have time to come back in once I'd realised what I'd done.'

'You took my keys?' No wonder she hadn't been able to find them. At least she wasn't going crazy.

'I did. I'm sorry, babe. Stupid, eh? I'll bring them back tonight and put them in the pot. No harm done.'

'But . . .' Sarah looked at the clock on the wall. It was getting late. 'How will I get out to meet Keeley?' The flat had no other door apart from the front. There wasn't even a window that was big enough for her to open and climb through.

'Hmm. I guess you might have to rearrange? Keeley won't mind, will she?'

'Can't you nip home?'

A note of irritation entered Drew's voice. 'Babe, I'm at a meeting in another gym at least twenty miles away. I can't just *nip* home. Maybe you'd understand that if you worked yourself.'

'But it was you who . . .' Sarah stopped herself. It *was* Drew who'd first suggested she might want to take some time out from work, but it was she herself who'd made the decision to leave her job in the end. She had to take responsibility for that. It was funny how what she thought was going to be just a few weeks of thinking about her career had now stretched into months. There just always seemed to be so much to do in the flat. 'I just feel like I'm letting her down. We haven't had lunch together for ages. I miss her.'

'You do? Well, I'm sure Keeley doesn't miss *you*. Not anywhere near as much. If she did, she'd have been a bit more persuasive about you going to the engagement party, wouldn't she? Didn't she just accept quite quickly that you weren't going? Maybe she doesn't want to be friends with you so much, now you're married. Who knows how people think?' His voice softened. 'Look, why don't you just call her now and explain what's happened? You can blame me. After all, it is completely my fault. I'll bring your keys home and then you can meet with Keeley whenever you like. If she's any kind of friend, she'll understand. Won't she?'

'I suppose.' Sarah didn't feel sure. This wasn't the first time she'd let Keeley down. Sometimes she felt as if she'd totally abandoned her friends and family since she got married. 'I'm not sure it's safe though. Being trapped here in the flat on my own, with no way to get out. I mean, what if there was a fire or something?'

Drew chuckled, the sound drowned out by what sounded like a passing car. 'I'm sure there's not going to be a fire, babe. Don't you think you're being a bit overly dramatic? I'll be home in a few hours. You'll be fine.'

Sarah hesitated. Drew was probably right. Still, that didn't stop her from feeling a little helpless. She wondered whether she should have another key cut and give it to her parents, just in case. 'Okay. I'll call her now.'

'That's my girl. Gotta run, babe. Maybe you could do a couple of those jobs you've been meaning to get around to while you're stuck inside? Weren't you going to clean the bedroom carpet at some point?'

Sarah looked down at her outfit. It had taken her ages to get ready, but now she'd have to get changed. 'Maybe. I suppose it would make more sense than sitting around.'

'See you later.'

She sighed as the call ended. So much for the nice day she was looking forward to. She hoped Keeley wouldn't be too cross with her and that they'd be able to rearrange without too much hassle. She lit up the screen of her phone and scrolled down her list of contacts once more.

She frowned again, thinking about the trouble she'd had accessing her Instagram account before she rang Drew.

Now, Keeley's number had completely disappeared.

Chapter 11

Claire now

I down a glass of water before hobbling into the living room. My legs feel weak and my mind is disorientated. It's been a long time since I've fainted. The last time I went so dizzy was when Drew was sentenced and Guy had to help me out of the courtroom. I need to get myself together. There are women out there right now feeling scared, needing to reach out to someone. *I* founded the helpline. It wouldn't be professional of me to let them down. No matter what's going on in my private life.

I pat the dog on the head to calm him and encourage him to settle in front of the fire. My episode has frightened him and I remind myself again how confused he must be by the events of recent years. First, he lost Sarah, the person who looked after him, played with him, fed him, since he was just a puppy. Then Guy moved out. I wouldn't like him to think he might lose me as well. I take a deep breath as I sit back on the sofa. The phone call I received earlier, the fainting spell, have thrown me completely and I still have a long night ahead of me. I have to get it together.

I put on my headset and take a few seconds to fully calm

myself, trying not to think about the shadow I'm sure I saw again in the garden, before clicking on the icon to accept the next call.

'Hello, you're through to Claire at *Walk Me Home*. How can I help?' I'm aware my voice is shaky. If Guy were here, no doubt he'd insist I leave the helpline to the other phone operators and have a proper break. I haven't eaten much today and slept little last night, the approaching anniversary on my mind. When he still lived here, my frequent refusals to spend a whole night in our bed asleep were just one source of the arguments between me and my husband. Before we lost Sarah, we barely spoke a cross word to each other. We shared everything, even our deepest secrets. We were as close as two people could be.

The girl at the other end of the line is one of my regular callers. I recognise her voice immediately, feeling glad that talking to her will give me a chance to get my breath back. Becky is on her way home from a late shift at the coffee shop where she works. She often has to walk home by herself in the dark, her boss refusing to pay out for a taxi for her, and she's said to me numerous times that the helpline has been a *godsend*. Just having someone on the other end of the line as she walks makes her feel safer, not to mention the fact that she knows there's always a pair of walkers nearby, if she's feeling especially vulnerable.

I wait until she's inside her house and has locked the door behind her.

'Thanks, Claire. I hope tonight isn't too busy for you.'

'Oh, I'm sure it will be. Goodnight, Becky. Stay safe.'

The next two calls I take are also fairly straightforward. The first is from an older lady, waiting for a taxi that doesn't seem to have turned up. Frightened her violent ex-husband might be lurking somewhere nearby, as he often does, she doesn't especially want to walk by herself. She was married for thirty-six years, she tells me, before she had the courage to leave, her daughters supporting her afterwards in finding alternative accommodation, as well as financial and emotional support. Now, as she tries to build a new life, make friends, the only obstacles on her path are the constant attempts by her ex to do what he sees as making amends, trying to convince her to give the marriage another go. Not to mention her constant visits to the court to enforce the restraining order he keeps breaking. I leave her in the company of a pair of my most trusted walkers.

The next call I take, just a few minutes later, is from a trans woman, making her way home from an early Tinder date, a taxi out of the question for her after she spent almost a week's wages on a new outfit. She tells me about her experience of being heckled while she shopped earlier in the week. It's a regular occurrence in her life, she says, even in the daytime. Sales assistants look at her suspiciously; dressing rooms are often out of bounds. No wonder she feels so vulnerable after dark, I think. I stay on the line with her until I know she's safe.

In between calls, I pop upstairs to check on Dylan. In the bedroom that used to be my daughter's, my grandson is sleeping peacefully, a soft snore and occasional mutter, as he turns over beneath his cartoon-filled duvet, the only sounds in the room. We redecorated it when he moved in, Guy and I, filling the room with everything our grandson loved – helicopters and aeroplanes and rocket wallpaper – so that he'd feel at home. Our marriage was still intact then, the two of us unaware still of how what happened to Sarah would soon pull us apart. How our differing feelings would destroy what we'd always treasured. Our love for each other.

I sit at the edge of Dylan's bed and examine his face. His Cupid's-bow mouth is almost an exact replica of his mother's when she was the same age, the freckles across his nose and cheeks a little paler than hers. Only occasionally do I see his father, the man I loathe, in his features. When Dylan frowns at the meal I put in front of him or pouts at not getting his own way, a flash of consternation crosses his face like the light from passing traffic. It's only a fleeting glimpse of Drew, but it's there. I try to ignore it, to think that Dylan takes only after Sarah, that he has inherited all of her good qualities: her kindness and consideration of others; the way she always put others' needs before her own. Someone like Drew should not have had any part in creating this totally innocent little boy.

I pull the bedroom curtain to one side and make sure the window is locked before heading back down the stairs. In the kitchen, I make fresh coffee and give Boswell a treat. I feel a little better now after my fainting spell. My head is a little less fuzzy and my legs slightly stronger. I'm fully aware that the anniversary, as it always does, has made me jittery and anxious, the visit from the reporter, the strange phone call earlier, only exacerbating the feeling. Perhaps once today is over, once I get some sleep, I'll be able to relax. Enjoy the festive season with what's left of my family. In the same way everyone else does.

I go back into the living room and settle on the sofa. On the TV, the newsreader is still talking about the child in Scotland, who has apparently been found in the house of a relative. Police are investigating. The headlines at the bottom of the screen have changed little since I last checked them. Next to the television, the lights of the Christmas tree illuminate the room. Sitting beneath it is the present for my daughter that I bought a few days ago and wrapped up in red and gold foil paper. I've bought her a gift every year since we lost her. Guy says it's silly, that I need to accept that our daughter isn't going to be here for Christmas, but it makes me feel better if I include her when I'm buying for my grandson. It makes me feel closer to her somehow. I touch the letter S at my neck, trying not to picture it covered in blood. It rested against her skin once, as it rests against mine now. The necklace was a part of Sarah and deserves to be looked after in the same way she looked after it for so long.

I pull my laptop onto my knee and slip on my headset. The clock on the mantel says it's just past eleven. The next few hours will no doubt be our busiest of the night, call after call likely coming in. When I started the helpline, it took a few months to work out when we might be most needed. Now, we operate only on a Friday, Saturday and Sunday night, or special occasions, and all calls stop at four in the morning. Otherwise, the chance to snatch even the shortest of naps before Dylan wakes would be beyond me.

I accept the first call in the queue.

'Claire?'

I feel my heart thud. '*Keeley*? Is that you? What on earth . . .?'

'I'm so glad I got through to you. I thought one of the other operators might pick up.'

'Why are you ringing the helpline?' It's been a while since I've spoken to Sarah's best friend. After the trial, we swore we'd keep in touch, but, as often happens, life – working, running the helpline, looking after Dylan – has got in the way. Sometimes I feel guilty that I don't try to contact her more. I feel a sudden rush of anxiety. Keeley is the last person I expected to hear speaking over my headset. Does she need my help? Is she in danger? 'What's the matter?'

'I tried to ring your mobile, but you didn't answer. I didn't know what else to do.'

I look at my phone on the sofa next to me. *Shit.* I should've kept it with me at all times. Stuffed it in my pocket as I wandered the house. The call from the strange woman who claimed to know about Sarah, plus losing consciousness at the back door, has led me to not be quite as organised as I usually am. 'I was upstairs, checking on Dylan. Keeley, what on earth is going on?'

I look at the queue of calls building on my screen. Sarah's friend is yet another caller who wants to speak to me personally, who is preventing other women from getting through, but I can't ignore her. If anything happened to Keeley, I'd never forgive myself.

'I . . .' She sounds out of breath, panicky. 'I left town about twenty minutes ago. I'm heading home after a few drinks with the girls. We had such a lovely time, Claire, talking about Sarah, how we wished she could be with us. How much we miss her. I know we didn't speak quite as much after she got married, didn't do as many things together as we did before, but we still all remember her, you know?'

I frown. Surely Keeley hasn't called me simply to be sentimental? To trawl over memories of my daughter? I glance up at Sarah's picture again. I love to talk about her, I always have, but now is most certainly not the time. 'And? Are you in some kind of trouble, Keeley?'

Keeley sounds as if she's sobbing now. As if she's taking great gulps of air in the same way I did when I opened the back door earlier. 'It was when I got to the quiet streets, Claire. Someone was following me. I'm sure of it. I could hear their footsteps, after I left the main road and there was no traffic.'

I sigh. 'Then you did the right thing by calling the helpline. We're here for you as well as everyone else. Now, would you like me to send a pair of . . .'

'No, you don't get it.'

'Don't get what?'

She hesitates, the line going quiet, just for a second or two. 'Claire, it was Drew. I'm certain of it. *Drew Allison* was following me.'

I suddenly feel dizzy again, as if the blood has drained from my head and puddled at my feet. I look up at the TV, my heart thudding as I see a headline that wasn't there before. New information about an earlier story, the details, apparently not quite clear when they talked about it previously, now updated. The words *Breaking News* fill the bottom of the screen.

I feel bile rise in my throat again as my mobile phone begins to ring loudly.

Chapter 12

Sarah before

Sarah stood in the flat's kitchen and gazed out of the window. Below her, she could see crisp November leaves, swirling around on the grey ground, the breeze picking them up and dancing with them before dropping them again. It had been a while since she'd been out for some fresh air. She'd loved it when she and her mum used to go for autumn walks when she was younger, the two of them laughing and chatting, sometimes for hours. Drew had told her that spending less time with her parents was simply a part of growing up. She needed to be more independent. He hardly ever saw his family these days. Since his dad had died, they hadn't been as close, he and his mum and his brother. Such was life, he'd said.

Just that morning, her mum had called her and asked if she wanted to meet up for a coffee, perhaps do some shopping afterwards. Along with walks in the countryside, shopping used to be their thing. The two of them would joke that Sarah's dad wasn't allowed to join them. *Girls only,* her mum would say with a laugh. *We'll bring you a present, so you won't feel left out.* Was that the kind of mother Sarah herself would be eventually? she wondered.

Close to her child? The ideal role model, like her own parents had been? She hoped so.

She'd put her mum off, feeling guilty but like she didn't have any choice. She wanted to focus on creating a nice meal for her husband, wanted tonight to be special. 'Could we leave it until next week? I'm trying out a new recipe for dinner and it's likely to take up most of the day.' Not to mention the fact that, if she wanted to get to town, she'd have to take the bus. Drew had recently persuaded her that running two cars was far too expensive. What was the point if she was no longer working? They could easily manage with just one and, if Sarah needed to go anywhere, he could take her on his days off, he'd said.

'You seem to spend a lot of time in the kitchen, sweetheart. I mean, I know cooking can be fun and all, but wouldn't it be nice to just get fish and chips one day? Does *Drew* ever cook?'

'Of course he does.' Sarah felt a surge of irritation. She stared at the wedding ring she'd slipped off her finger and left at the side of the sink, making a mental note to put it back on before Drew came home. Why did she always seem to have to defend her husband? Surely wanting to treat him to a nice dinner wasn't so unusual? 'He works hard, don't forget. Besides, he cooked me three courses just last week. A starter, dessert, wine and everything. It was really special.'

What she didn't mention was that she'd barely seen Drew that day, even though it was his day off. He'd stayed in the kitchen for hours, not letting her in because, as he said, he didn't want to spoil the *surprise*. While she was waiting, she hadn't had much choice but to clean the bathroom and bedrooms. She could hardly swan off out somewhere, or sit around watching TV, while Drew was working so hard to please her, could she?

'Hmm, okay. I'm sure it was lovely. I just miss our days out together, that's all. It seems like I have to make an appointment to see you these days. Dad misses you as well. And Boswell.'

Sarah had felt her stomach drop. She had to admit, she'd missed her family as well recently. As much as she'd thought before that she didn't have time to think about her life before she got married, part of her would have liked to revisit it *occasionally*. Yet wasn't Drew right? That breaking away from them was natural at this stage in her life? She had to put her husband first.

She turned away from the window and picked her phone up from the counter. Perhaps she'd text her mum now. Just so Mum knew that she still wanted to keep in touch, wasn't trying to avoid spending time with her. She barely used her phone at all these days, not like she used to. Ever since Drew had persuaded her that social media was for immature attention seekers, she hardly picked it up, apart from when she wanted to search for the odd recipe. She'd been surprised when she couldn't access her Instagram account, that day when she'd been heading out to meet Keeley, only to find that Drew had taken her keys by mistake, but she later found out that it was her husband who had closed the account.

Sarah didn't mind that he knew her log-in details. After all, they were husband and wife – they weren't supposed to keep things from each other – but she'd thought he would have spoken to her first, before he made all the pictures she'd taken of herself and her friends over the years disappear. Still, she supposed he was right. It didn't seem proper for a married woman to spend so much time online, posing and being silly. That stuff was for young girls. Shortly afterwards, she'd deleted her Facebook and Twitter accounts as well. Anyone who wanted to get in touch with her would have to simply text or send a WhatsApp message.

She clicked on her mum's name and typed out a quick message:

Let's take a rain check on that shopping trip, shall we? Soon, I promise! Give Dad and Boswell a big hug from me xx

She followed it with a picture of the ingredients she'd carefully laid out on the counter. Hopefully that would stop her mum from worrying so much. As she put the phone back on the table, she reminded herself to ask Mum for Keeley's number the next time they spoke. She had no idea how her best friend's details had disappeared from her contact list. Drew had told her he wouldn't dream of deleting it and Sarah believed him. Of course he wouldn't do something like that. Why would he? Most likely, it was just some kind of glitch.

Her stomach lurched as she heard Drew's key in the front door lock. He was home early today. Sometimes he did that, she'd noticed. Told her he'd be late back from work, only to arrive home at lunchtime. At other times, he did the complete opposite, heading out for what he claimed to be a short meeting, only to reappear a full twelve hours later, claiming he'd not had time to let her know. He liked to surprise her, he often said. So that their relationship would stay interesting and they wouldn't ever take each other's presence for granted. She could see his point, she supposed, although it was sometimes difficult to appear presentable, to be dressed in the clothes he preferred her to wear, refresh her make-up, if she never knew when he was going to show up.

She always tried her best to look good for her husband. Sarah had heard about women who let themselves go after they got married, who no longer made an effort once they had their man. She herself still spent time on manicures and pedicures. She topped up her fake tan every few weeks, as she always had. If Drew came home unexpectedly and she was still in her pyjamas and dressing gown, she'd quickly rush to the bedroom to get changed. She didn't want him to think she was slovenly.

She checked her hair and face in the oven door before busying herself with chopping the vegetables she'd got out of the fridge. She hoped her husband wasn't hungry just yet, as the meal was nowhere near ready. She'd wanted to take her time preparing it, so it was just right.

She smiled as he came into the kitchen. 'You're early.'

Drew shrugged. 'Is that a problem?'

Sarah swallowed. Sometimes Drew was so busy at work that he came home a bit grouchy. She understood. He had a lot of responsibilities. 'Of course not. Would you like a snack? Dinner will be a while.'

Drew reached over her shoulder and grabbed a carrot from the bag. He began to chew loudly. 'A proper meal would have been nice. As soon as I come in, I mean.' He glanced at her phone on the counter. 'Too busy talking to your mum to cook? Or texting your friends?'

Sarah frowned. Her husband always seemed to know what she was doing, even when she was in the flat alone. She wasn't sure how he managed it. 'I haven't spoken to anyone.' She had no intention of telling him how her mum had suggested they go shopping. She didn't want to make his mood worse by giving him the idea that Mum wanted her to ignore her duties as a wife while he was working hard and keeping a roof over their heads.

'Sure?'

She smiled as she turned to face him. 'I'm sure.'

Drew looked down at her left hand. 'Where's your wedding ring?'

Sarah felt a rush of anxiety. With Drew being home early, she'd completely forgotten to put it back on. She took it off a lot these days, when she was cooking or cleaning. The ring was uncomfortable, but she wouldn't ever dare tell her husband that.

She snatched it up from the counter. 'I took it off while I was washing my hands, just a few minutes ago. Just before you walked in the door, actually.'

'Is the ring I bought not good enough for you? Or do you like to pretend you're not married when I'm not here? Swan around *my* flat, acting like you're young, free and single?'

'Of course I don't.' Sarah thought that what Drew was saying couldn't be further from the truth. She never forgot she was a married woman. How could she? 'I love being your wife – you know that.'

'Do you? How much?'

She tried to smile again. 'Lots. Look, why don't you go and have a soak in the bath and I'll get the food sorted as quickly as possible. Then we can eat together. I'll set the table.' She was quite hungry herself, she realised. Since she'd married Drew, he'd persuaded her that she didn't really need to eat both lunch and dinner. With not being especially active at the minute, she'd be prone to putting weight on more easily. Normally, these days, she just had a very light breakfast – some fruit or a protein bar – and then ate with her husband later. Drew knew how the body worked as well as anyone.

He threw the carrot back onto the counter before nodding and heading for the door. She seemed to have appeased him, for now at least.

'By the way,' she called after him, sensing his mood had softened. 'Would you be okay to give me a lift next week? To the wedding open evening I'm going to with Keeley? It's a bit far for me to walk from here to the far side of Penketh.'

Drew stopped in the doorway, his back to her. For a full five seconds or so, he stood, not speaking. The only indication he'd heard her was the twitch of his shoulders. Up and down.

Sarah hesitated. Had she said the wrong thing? 'It . . . It doesn't matter. Really, forget I said anything. I'll get a taxi, or ask Dad to take me. I know you're . . .'

Suddenly, Drew flew at her.

Sarah gasped. She wasn't sure she'd ever seen anyone move so quickly. It was as if her husband hadn't actually run at her, but that he was one second in the doorway, the next, directly in front of her, with his hands at her throat. She felt his fingers tighten. The letter S from her necklace dug into her skin.

'So, you expect me to be running you here, there and every-where after a hard day at work?' He growled the words. A fleck of spit left his mouth and landed on his bottom lip. 'Is that what I am to you? Nothing more than a chauffeur? Someone who drives you to places where you can take off your expensive wedding ring and flirt with people?'

She shook her head. 'Of course not. Really, it's fine. I'll just . . .'

'Just what? Get *Daddy* to take you? When are you going to stop behaving like a child, eh, Sarah? Stop running to Mummy and Daddy every time you need something?'

Sarah squeezed her legs together, her bladder threatening to empty itself down her clothes. Surely she shouldn't feel so frightened? This was her *husband*. 'Of course. You're right. I'll just . . . I'll make my own way . . .'

'Will you, now?' Drew squeezed her throat again, harder this time, but not quite enough to cut off her air supply. It was as if he knew exactly how much pressure he needed to use, to scare her without causing actual damage to her neck. 'Do you think I haven't done anything like this before, Sarah? That I couldn't kill you, right now? Right this very second?'

Sarah felt a tear wet her cheek. 'What do you mean? Drew, please . . .'

'*Please* . . .' He mocked her, smirking.

She shook her head again. She needed to get herself out of this situation. 'I won't go.' She struggled to get the words out, make herself clear. 'You're right. Totally right. My place is here. At home. With you. I'll tell Keeley I'm not going.'

Drew looked at her for a few seconds. Just when Sarah thought he was going to let go, say he was sorry, that he was tired and didn't know what he was doing, his face changed. His eyes darkened.

He let go of her of her throat. 'Out.'

'What?' Sarah felt panic bubble in her stomach.

'I said, *out.*' Drew pushed her towards the kitchen door. 'If you don't appreciate the home I've provided for you, been generous enough to let you move into, not to mention the ring I bought, then you can leave.'

Sarah braced her bare feet on the floor, trying to stop herself from moving forward, but her strength was no match for her husband's. Before she knew it, she was in the hallway and at the front door. 'But, Drew, please. It's cold. I'm not wearing any shoes . . .'

'Then maybe you'll learn to be a bit more grateful.'

He opened the door and shoved her out, the flat of his hand on her back.

Sarah stood on the walkway, turning to face the entrance of what was supposed to be her home, the railing that guarded the steep drop to the car park at her back. She was crying now. She was cold already, the stiff wind penetrating her thin sweater and leggings. 'Please, don't do this. *Please.* At least give me my coat, my shoes . . .'

'You don't deserve them.'

She braced herself for what she was going to say next. She didn't want to tell her husband her news like this. She was going to tell him tonight. Light candles and serve a special dinner before smiling across the table at him, taking great delight in the look on his face when he found out what was going to be happening in their immediate future. She took a deep breath. 'Drew, I'm pregnant.'

He stopped in the doorway and looked at her.

'I took a test this morning. I'm already six weeks gone.'

Her husband stared at her, his eyes narrowing.

Then he turned away and slammed the door in her face.

Chapter 13

Claire now

My hands are shaking.

'Keeley, tell me exactly where you are. I can send a pair of walkers to you. They'll be quicker than the police.'

My mobile stops ringing, unanswered.

'Claire . . .'

'Just *tell* me your location.'

Sarah's friend describes a street not too far away and I type as quickly as I can. One of my walkers answers me immediately, perhaps sensing the urgency in my words.

'They're on their way. Can you still see him?'

The line goes quiet for a few seconds, as if Keeley is maybe turning in circles where she stands, looking in every corner, every nook and cranny, for potential danger. 'No, no, I don't think so. But it was *him*, Claire. I'd know him anywhere.'

She could be mistaken, I think. Despite our lack of contact recently, Keeley went through everything with us. She was as much a part of our family as Sarah, Guy and myself. She lost her best friend. I'd have thought, as she says, that she would recognise the man who caused all our misery, even at a distance. Yet she's a young woman, out on her own after dark. I decide to deal with the most important thing first. 'Keeley, is there a restaurant still open nearby? Or a pub?'

'Yes.' She sounds scared. 'There's a takeaway, just across the road. That one that opened not so long ago. There are people inside.'

'Go there. As quickly as you can. Go inside, where people can see you.' I type out another message, updating my instructions to my volunteers. 'Wait there until you see the walkers. They'll be with you in less than a minute.' I hope they're walking quickly, running even, despite the busy shift they've had.

'I'm inside now.'

'Okay, don't move.' I take a breath, trying to calm myself, thinking again about the figure, the shadows I've seen outside my own house tonight. 'When you get home, lock the door and all the windows. If you think there's a problem, call the police.' Although they may take a while to get there, I think. No doubt, my team are not the only ones with a lot on their plate this weekend.

'I can see the walkers. They're here.'

'Okay, good. Keeley, I'm going to hang up now, but if you need me, call my mobile immediately. You were Sarah's best friend and I'll always be here for you, okay?'

'Okay, thank you. And, Claire?'

'Hmm?'

'Be careful.'

'I will.'

I end the call, seeing a message on my screen to confirm that my walkers have reached their destination. At least Keeley is safe. For now.

Please let this be a false alarm, I think.

I pick up the remote control and turn the TV's volume back on. The newsreader is still talking about the developing story, her tone sombre, as if she's issuing a warning to everyone who's listening.

Residents are warned not to approach the man who is considered dangerous and possibly armed . . .

The escaped prisoner. The one who made the headlines earlier in the night, apparently having broken out of a prison somewhere far enough away from here not to cause me to worry.

Except the information was wrong. And the escapee was imprisoned much nearer to my home town than I thought. Less than twenty miles away in fact.

My mobile rings again and I glance at the screen, recognising the number. I look at it for a few seconds. I don't want to answer, but I know I have to. This is something I can't pretend isn't happening.

'Hello?'

'Claire? It's Jane Fellows.'

The family liaison officer who has dealt with Sarah's case from the beginning. Who has always been the one to call when the police need to tell us something, to give us information. Sometimes *urgent* information.

'I'm here.' I don't know what else to say.

'I'm sorry to call you so late and I'm very, very sorry for what I'm about to tell you. Your family has been through so much already . . .'

'Just tell me, Jane.' I stare at the picture of my daughter as I speak, taking comfort from her presence, feeling again the shock of how life can change from one minute to the next.

'Claire . . .' Jane seems to be bracing herself '. . . he's out. Drew Allison has escaped from prison. We don't know how, or what exactly happened, but I *promise* you, we're going to get every single spare officer we have on getting him back where he belongs. He won't get far.'

I want to vomit again. Was it Drew outside my house a short while ago, watching me? The person who I thought was a reporter looking for a story? Was Sarah's best friend right that

81

he was following her? 'When? When did this happen? When did he get out?'

'A few hours ago, it seems. Earlier this evening.'

So, not the person in the car at the park, who seemed to be taking pictures of Dylan. Was that a journalist after all?

'It's the anniversary.' My voice doesn't sound like my own, as if I'm listening to it from somewhere very far away. 'Is that why he's picked today?'

'I don't know, Claire. Who knows what his thought processes are? But obviously, there is a risk that he might be looking for some kind of revenge. That he'll target you and Guy for testifying against him. We're doing a risk assessment as we speak and we figure the best initial plan is to send a team to both yours and Guy's houses, to install panic buttons, as well as having a patrol car pass by on a regular basis.'

I wince. Dylan has been through so much already. I hope he doesn't wake to find an influx of strangers in his home. 'Okay. You said *initial* plan?'

'Yes. If it becomes more obvious what your son-in-law's intentions are and we feel that he actually poses a direct threat to your family, then the next step is to move you all to a safe house. I'm afraid we won't have a choice.'

Tears prick at my eyes.

'If it's any reassurance, Claire, I have no doubt that we'll catch up with Allison soon. He won't be able to get far. Not with half the force on his tail.'

Who is she trying to convince? I wonder. Me or herself? I picture myself, standing in the front doorway earlier, smoking a cigarette and watching the dog as he peed. Standing at the back before that, listening to Peter and June talk. Vulnerable.

'Thank you for letting me know.'

I end the call before she can say anything else. Jane is more than used to it, my tendency to hang up on her when she's given me news I don't want to hear. I know she won't take offence.

For a minute or two, I simply sit and stare at the picture of my daughter on the mantelpiece. My beautiful Sarah. Her life, her future with her son, taken away from her far too soon. Part of me feels as if I can't move. As if I might sit here, on this sofa, the laptop on my knee, the dog watching me with one ear pricked, forever.

He's escaped.

Drew Allison, the man we worked so hard to put behind bars for the murder of our daughter, has somehow managed to get out of prison.

When he was sentenced, we thought it was over. At least, in as much as it could be. Guy and I could get on with our lives, despite the fact they were very different from before. We would never be the same, but we could move forward, albeit slowly, hesitantly. Painfully. Raise our grandson in the same way we raised Sarah. Even if we eventually had to accept we'd be doing it as a divorced couple, a fractured family.

When our son-in-law was arrested, my husband and I had stood together, in the car park below the flat. Three figures had appeared in the stairwell, two of them police officers, Drew in the middle. He was negotiating the steps carefully, his gait, the swagger I normally associated with him, not as confident as every other time I'd seen him. His chest protruding like a pigeon's, he was holding his hands in an awkward position behind his back. The officer on his left had her hand to his elbow, guiding him. They'd handcuffed him, like someone who might have been a danger to the public.

Guy and I had watched as the police led Drew to an awaiting police car, the officer who'd been holding his elbow now putting her hand to the top of his head. Before he climbed inside, Drew had turned and looked at us. He'd looked very different, his face pale and scared. For the first time in a long time, he wasn't smirking. His power over everyone around him seemed to have disappeared, like smoke into the air. As I watched him get into the back seat, I'd wanted to storm over to him, to push the officers around him to one side. To lean into the car and spit in his face.

Now, as I contemplate the news I've been given, one thought runs through my mind:

If Drew is out, then we failed. Sarah, Dylan, still asleep upstairs. We failed them both. All our hard work, all the stress, the anguish, was for nothing.

Suddenly, I jump up and cross the room, grabbing the string of lights that circle the Christmas tree as if I have no control over my own body. I can feel the dog watching me as I tear down the decorations I spent so much time putting up, pulling at baubles, at branches, at the star that sits on the top, until they're all lying in a heap on the carpet. Picking up the present I bought for my daughter, the one Guy told me I shouldn't have bothered with, I tear the neat wrapping from it and hurl it into a corner, the mini fragrance bottles spilling from the box as it lands. I put my hands to my hair, wanting to tear it out. Tears run down my cheeks and one of my fingers is bleeding after I caught it on the wiry end of a tree branch. One single spot of red blood drips onto the carpet at my feet, taking me back to the blood the police found in Drew's flat three years ago. My daughter's blood.

Behind me, I can hear my mobile ringing. I don't want to answer but, again, I know I have to. Guy will have heard, perhaps seen the news and come to the same conclusion I did. Possibly even had his own phone call. Jane Fellows is fully aware that we no longer live together.

I swallow down a sob as I put the phone to my ear.

'Is it him?' Guy doesn't even say hello.

'Yes.'

'Jane called?'

'Yes. Didn't she call you?'

A pause. 'Not yet, but I'm sure she will as soon as I've spoken to you.'

I look at the tree I've just completely wrecked. 'They going to come round and install panic buttons. Both here and at yours.'

'Okay.'

'And have patrol cars pass by.' We're quiet for a few seconds, both of us no doubt equally stunned. 'Shit, Guy, how the fuck could this happen?'

'I have no idea. We mustn't panic.'

I feel a surge of anger. '*Mustn't panic*? How can you say that?' I try to lower my voice; the last thing I want is for Dylan to wake up. 'Guy, he's *out*. After everything we went through. That *bastard* is out.'

'I know, but we don't know his intentions, not at the minute. Maybe he just wants to get as far away as possible. Go somewhere, abroad maybe.'

'And it just happens to be the anniversary? If that doesn't tell us his intentions, then I don't know what does.'

'They'll catch him, Claire. He might not even get so much as a mile from the prison. He's probably hiding out somewhere 'til he thinks the coast is clear. He's a murderer; they'll have every man and his dog out looking for him.'

Grabbing a tissue from the box on the table, I clumsily press it to my bleeding finger, trying not to think about the person I saw at the front of the house earlier. Maybe Guy's right. Maybe Drew *is* simply trying to get out of the country before the police catch him and the person I saw is completely innocent. Just a coincidence. The figure seemed slighter than Drew, thinner-framed, less bulky. Is it possible it was someone else? Or could my son-in-law have lost weight while he was in prison? 'What if he comes after Dylan?'

A pause, as if Guy is thinking. 'He won't. He's not that stupid.'

'He's not stupid at all; that's the point! Dylan is his *son*, Guy. In his eyes, we took his child away from him.' Like he took ours.

'He's not stupid enough to add kidnapping to his list of wrong-doings.'

85

Isn't he? I wonder. My stomach churns, the coffee I've drunk swirling around, as if it's in a washing machine. 'Let's hope so.' I sigh. 'I have to go. I'm supposed to be on duty. I have calls waiting. There'll be enough disruption when the tech team gets here, to install the panic alarm.'

'Keep your doors and windows locked. Don't answer the door to anyone except that team. And don't go outside, except to let Boswell out as quickly as you can.'

'Why would I go outside? It's freezing out there.' I know I shouldn't be, but a large part of me feels irritated with Guy, as if this is all his fault. Of course it's not.

'Don't think I haven't noticed the smell of cigarettes on you lately. Maybe go without for tonight?'

Even now we don't live together, he knows me well. 'I'll try.'

'If anything happens, anything at all, call me. Or the police.'

I say goodbye, standing in the same spot for a few seconds, not sure I have the strength to move. In front of me, the Christmas tree looks as if it's been battered by a hurricane. I'll have to put it back together before Dylan wakes up. I probably won't be able to sleep anyway.

I check the locks on both the front and back doors before sitting back down. As much as I don't feel up to it, I have to take some more calls. I have a responsibility.

I pull on my headset and accept the first call in the queue.

'Hello, you're through to Claire at . . .'

'Claire! I told you I'd call back!'

I sit up straight. With all the fuss about Drew, I'd forgotten about my strange caller. Now, here she is, on the line again. The same muffled, distant voice. The strange cut-glass accent.

'All those other blasted operators I've had to hang up on before I finally got through to you, so frustrating! So, have you seen the latest headline? I know you watch the news all the time. You might want to look up at your TV, right about *now* . . .'

As much as I don't want to, am desperate not to, I do exactly as she's instructed me to. I raise my head.

I feel tears begin to well again as I see another *Breaking News* headline, this time accompanied by a grainy picture of my son-in-law – his mugshot, his stare cold:

Escaped prisoner, now identified as convicted murderer Drew Allison, has been spotted in his local area.

Chapter 14

Sarah before

Sarah sat in front of the computer in the Gilbert House office, remembering a conversation she'd once had with her mum when she was around sixteen years old. The two of them had been clearing up together, one Saturday evening after supper, just a few days after Sarah had dumped her most recent boyfriend because she didn't think he was being romantic enough towards her. The guy had been solid, dependable, no doubt loyal, but ultimately, she'd found him boring.

'Romance isn't everything, you know, sweetheart. What matters more is trust, friendship. Look at me and your dad. We were friends for ages before we began dating. And when was the last time he bought me flowers or chocolates? Took me out for a surprise dinner? I'd say *never*, probably.'

Sarah sighed. 'But is it too much to ask to want someone special? Someone who treats you like you're the most beautiful person on earth?'

Mum had paused and looked at her, her hands still in the soapy water. She seemed to think carefully before she spoke. 'You know, I had a friend once, when I first went to uni. Part of the group your dad and I used to hang around with. She was a bit like you. She believed that one day a handsome prince would come along and sweep her off her feet. Just like in the movies.'

'And?' Sarah picked up a plate and dried it with a tea towel. 'Did she meet her *prince*?'

'She did.' Mum carried on washing. 'A few months after she started her course, she was asked out on a date by a very handsome, popular guy a couple of years above. Gorgeous, he was. All her friends were very jealous.'

Sarah was confused. 'So, that's a good thing, isn't it? She proved that it *can* happen, like it does in films?'

'Sure.' Her mum looked at her. 'Until he started abusing her.'

Sarah paused. 'You're kidding?'

'Nope. The guy was perfect, apart from one small thing. He was a complete and utter callous bastard who thought of no one but himself.'

Sarah remembered feeling shocked; she hadn't heard her mum swear before. 'What did he do, exactly?'

Mum shrugged. 'It started out just little things. Like wanting her to be with him instead of with her friends. Telling her they weren't good enough for her, getting upset if she wasn't free to spend time with him. Before long, she was spending practically every hour of the day at his beck and call. She even started missing classes. Her work began to suffer, as well as her prospects of doing well. After just a few months, this guy pretty much controlled every single thing she did. He told her what to wear, how to style her hair, who she could speak to and who she couldn't. Eventually, she could barely make a single decision without his say-so.'

Sarah frowned. 'That doesn't sound good, but are you sure he was controlling her? Maybe that was just how it looked to you? Maybe he was just looking out for her? Helping her? Just because he was advising her about her clothes or her hairstyle or whatever, that doesn't necessarily mean he was abusing her, does it? I mean, isn't abuse *violence*? Like punching and stuff?'

Her mum shook her head. 'Not always, sweetheart. Trying to *control* someone can be just as abusive as physical violence. It's about power. And no one person should have more power than the other when it comes to relationships.' She paused. 'Besides, he did hit her eventually. The longer she stayed with him, the more she turned up to lectures with black eyes and split lips.'

'So, why the hell didn't she leave him?' Sarah felt angry that the girl hadn't simply dumped this guy.

Her mum dipped her hands in the water again. She seemed to think for a few seconds, as if absorbed in the memory of her younger days. 'I guess we'll never really know. Sometimes, when you're in that situation, you can't quite see things for what they are. All her friends and family were worried about her. They tried over and over again to persuade her to get out of the relationship, but she thought they were all jealous of her, because she'd found someone who was a great catch. She thought that was why everyone wanted to split them up.'

'Are they still together now?'

Her mum went quiet again. When she eventually spoke, she sounded sad. 'No. One day, he beat her up so badly that he broke her jaw. So she ended it.' She cleared her throat and took the tea towel from her daughter to wipe her hands. 'And that was that. Anyway, come on. Let's leave the rest of this and go and watch some TV.'

Now, Sarah stared at the computer screen in front of her. She wasn't supposed to be in the office, not really. The equipment in there was for staff use only, but Sarah didn't want to use her own laptop, at the flat, or her mobile phone to look for what she wanted to find. Shortly after they'd got married, she'd told Drew all her passwords. He'd needed them, he'd said. So he could fix any problems with her computer if they arose. She hadn't minded. In fact, she'd been happy to hand over any problems she had with technology, relieved, at the time, that she would no longer have to deal with them herself. And, if she changed her passwords now,

Drew would want to know why. Neither could she have used her parents' computer, or the old one in Gilbert's TV room, that the visitors used to look for jobs and to write their CVs. Both were too risky. Someone might look at her search history and put two and two together.

She thought again about her mum, now on the other side of the wall, in the large dining hall, cleaning up after the lunch rush. Just a few minutes ago, claiming to feel nauseous, Sarah had said she needed to sit down, so Mum had told her to come into the office for a little while. Perhaps use the old sofa for a nap. She leant back in the desk chair and rested her hand on her rounded stomach. Ever since she'd told her parents about her pregnancy, they'd been so nice to her, looking after her as if she were a little girl again. As if she were so fragile, she might break at any moment. Is that what they thought of her these days? she wondered. That she was somehow not strong enough to cope with having a child? Were they right?

She sighed. Her parents' reaction to her baby news hadn't been exactly what she wanted. Sarah had hoped they'd be excited, even ecstatic, as grandparents were supposed to be, but Mum had seemed hesitant, unsure.

'I thought you were going to wait a while before you had children? Get your career sorted out first? Decide what you want to do with your life?'

As she seemed to a lot of the time lately, Sarah had felt irritated. Couldn't her mum see *this* was the life she wanted? To be Drew's wife and the mother of his child? It was enough for her. It really was. For now. 'I can go back to work later, Mum. It's important that I spend time with the baby first. Enjoy him or her while I can.'

In the end, Mum and Dad had both hugged her and told her that they were happy for her. That they would do as much as they could to help. Sarah appreciated their words, but she'd known they weren't entirely happy. She could see it in their eyes. She wished, more than anything, that they could at least *like* Drew more. That they could see him as she saw him. See how much he did for her, how he put her first. How he was going to be a brilliant dad. Because he really was going to be the best parent ever.

What no one knew, not even her husband, was that this wasn't the first time Sarah had been pregnant.

She'd been going to tell Drew, the last time, just a few months before she fell with this child. She hadn't long done the test and she was biding her time before she told him the news. Like with this pregnancy, she'd wanted it to be special. She'd wanted to create an atmosphere, make an occasion out of it that they'd always remember. But she hadn't got the chance. When Drew had come home from work, the day she'd done the test, he'd not been in the best of moods. There'd been no violence then, not really, just the odd snipe when he wasn't happy, the odd grumble.

Flopping down onto the sofa, he'd stretched his leg out at just the wrong time, as Sarah was walking past to switch the TV to his favourite programme, hoping to placate him. She'd fallen into the coffee table and had begun to bleed heavily later the same night. Her next pregnancy test, just to be sure, had been negative.

She was sure it had been an accident. Her husband had wanted a baby; he would never do anything to hurt her if he'd known.

She played with the letter S on her necklace, trying not to think about how it had dug into her skin when Drew had grabbed her, just before she'd told him she was pregnant with this baby. Drew had made mistakes, of course he had. Who hadn't? What he'd done on that day was something she'd never expected him to do, not in a million years, but ever since then he'd been so nice to her. She was sure he'd never do it again.

Until last night.

He hadn't hurt her. Not really. It had been more like another *accident*, like when she'd tripped over him. Sarah had been getting ready for bed, cleaning her teeth in the flat's small bathroom while Drew had a quick shave in the bathtub next to her. They'd been talking about the baby, Sarah telling her husband how she'd spoken to Keeley and found out that her friends wanted to host a baby shower for her in one of the local wine bars. Wasn't that kind of them? she'd said brightly. The next thing she knew a sharp pain had ripped through her bare calf. She'd gasped and looked down at her leg. Blood was pooling on her skin.

'Shit, I'm really sorry, babe. I was reaching to put it in the bin.'

'What?' Sarah had ripped toilet paper from the roll and bundled it against the cut.

'I was reaching over to put the razor in the bin and you stepped back and I must have caught you.' Drew was looking at her, as if he were somehow challenging her to question his account of what had happened.

Eventually, he'd climbed out of the tub and walked into the bedroom with a towel around his waist, leaving her to dress the wound using the small first aid kit from the cabinet. Neither of them had mentioned the baby shower again. Sarah thought it would be best to discourage her friends from the idea. She wasn't bothered.

She put a hand to the mouse on the desk, hovering the on-screen arrow over the search bar and remembering again what her mum had said about her friend at uni. It wasn't the same. Of course it wasn't. She and Drew were not in an *abusive* relationship. Were they? What had happened the night before had genuinely been an accident. Drew had no reason to want to hurt her. And the time before that, he'd simply made a mistake. He'd been tired after work and had lost his temper. When he'd eventually let her back into the flat, her bare feet cold from the concrete walkway, he'd simply gone back to treating her as he always did. Asking her about the meal she'd been planning on cooking. Admittedly, he hadn't apologised, but maybe that was a good thing. She'd heard about men who made gushing romantic gestures whenever they'd done something wrong, but the most important thing was, as her mum had said all those years ago, that she trusted him not to do it again. Which she did. Absolutely, she did.

She never did go to the wedding open evening. In the end, her morning sickness had left her feeling weak and a little fragile and Drew had suggested going out might be too much for her. Instead, they'd sat together in front of the television and he'd rubbed her feet. She was kind of glad she hadn't gone and, even though she hadn't let Keeley know, she was sure her friend would understand. Her husband and her baby came first.

Still, she clicked on the screen, figuring it would do no harm to look while she was here.

Feeling guilty, she typed two words into the search bar: *abusive relationship*. Her skin prickled as thousands of results came up straight away, some explaining the exact nature of domestic abuse, while others offered help and support. A way out. Sarah glanced at the office door to check no one was about to enter before she scrolled down a little. She wasn't sure exactly what she was looking for but wondered if maybe it was some kind of reassurance. Perhaps a website that could tell her that what she had experienced in her marriage, which was really hardly *violent* at all, was actually *not* abuse. Just the usual ups and downs of a married couple. Like everyone goes through.

She knew what her mum would say. Of course, Sarah hadn't said anything to her parents about what had happened the day Drew put his hands to her throat, or about the cut on her leg, even though she'd been trying to disguise the slight limp it had caused her today. She didn't think it was any of their business, not really. Not to mention the fact that she didn't want a fuss. Mum and Dad would just try and make her rethink her marriage, ask her if she thought Drew was really the man she wanted to be with for the rest of her life, no matter how much she thought she loved him. She could hear it all now: their shocked exclamations, the concern in their voices.

She winced as she felt the baby kick. Sarah wasn't stupid. She knew that what Drew had done was wrong. But he was her husband. And now they were having a child. A child she had no intention of letting grow up without a father. She couldn't think of anything worse. Surely doing that to her baby would simply be condemning it to a life full of challenges. To living below the breadline and having no access to the opportunities other children had. She didn't want to do that.

Besides, she knew full well that if she accused her husband of violence, she would ruin his life. Drew was a businessman, well-known in the area. He was the son of a prominent police officer, a local councillor who'd secured funding for many of the town's charities, possibly even for Gilbert House itself. If anyone ever found out that the online search she was conducting now was related to Drew Allison, his life, his family's reputation, would be left in tatters.

Did she really want to be responsible for opening such a huge can of worms? To have to cope with the fallout that followed her accusation? The possible press attention, the publicity?

No, she was being ridiculous, melodramatic, as her parents always told her she had a tendency to be when she was younger. Drew wouldn't hurt her again. And he would certainly never hurt their child. She knew that for sure. Call it instinct. It was silly for her to think otherwise. To even be sitting here, searching on the internet about abuse. Her husband didn't deserve that; he really didn't.

And she was positive he'd just been spouting nonsense when he'd put his hands to her throat and said something silly about having done this before.

She closed the browser just as her mum opened the office door. 'Feeling better?'

Sarah nodded. 'A lot better, thank you.' She was telling the truth. Giving herself a little talking-to had made her realise how lucky she was to have a man like Drew. Who worked so hard to provide a nice home for her. Always put her first.

'Good. I'll take you home now, if you like? I hope that husband of yours is going to look after you when you get there. Maybe he could cook dinner and let you put your feet up.'

Sarah hesitated, just for second. She thought about the meal Drew had suggested she cook tonight, an elaborate main and dessert that would likely mean she'd be on her feet for a few hours that evening. He wanted her to have a practice run before their upcoming Christmas dinner, so she'd get everything just right on the day. Sarah had been a little confused as to why Drew wanted everything to be perfect at Christmas. After all, it would only be the two of them. Her husband thought it would be too much for her, having friends and family around. He wanted them to spend their first festive season together quietly. Yet he still wanted her to produce a perfect meal.

She took a breath and smiled at her mum. 'I expect he'll do exactly that.'

Chapter 15

Claire now

'You really didn't know what I was capable of, did you?'

No answer. Just a gasp, a dribble of drool. Of thick mucus.

'Admit it. You thought I was one of the good guys when we first met. A real good egg. That I would never dream of doing anyone any harm.'

A fresh drop of blood rolls down flesh before hitting the ground. It spatters in a star shape.

'Funny how appearances can be deceptive . . .'

I drag my fingers through my hair as I make my way to the front door, Dylan behind me, the dog behind him. My two constant shadows when we're in the house together. As I open the door, my grandson squeals with delight. He's always excited to see his grandfather.

Guy sweeps Dylan into his arms. 'Hey, big guy, how's my favourite boy called Dylan doing?' He reaches down and pats the dog's head. 'And my favourite dog called Boswell.'

Dylan puts a hand to his mouth and giggles. His grandad greets him the same way every time they see each other and he loves the game.

Holding his grandson in the nook of his elbow, Guy leans towards me and kisses my cheek. 'You look tired.'

I nod. I've barely slept, apart from a too-short doze on the sofa, sometime in the early hours, when the dreams once again filled my head, refusing to be pushed away. By the time I'd finished up at the helpline, put the Christmas tree back together and waited for the tech team to install the promised panic alarm – now above the fireplace, next to my daughter's picture – it had been almost dawn. Even then, although I was exhausted, I was too wired to go to bed, too many thoughts competing for space in my mind. The news about Drew, as well as the calls I received from the girl who blocked her number had really shaken me up.

I look at my ex-husband, realising he looks like I feel. His skin is pasty, almost grey, fine lines spreading from his eyes and his mouth. Since we lost Sarah, Guy seems to have aged a million years. At least the anniversary has passed now, I think. Over for another year. Even if it did bring another challenge into our lives neither of us were ready for. 'So do you.'

We walk through to the kitchen.

'Any more news?'

I glance at Dylan. He may not even be five years old yet, and can hardly remember his father, but I don't want him to pick up on the fact that there's something wrong. A child of his age can only take so much trauma, no matter how well the professionals say he's doing. 'Not really. Jane called again this morning to assure me they're on his trail. There've been confirmed sightings that they're hopeful might lead to something. I presume you've heard he's been spotted? Not too far away?'

He nods. 'I saw the headline last night. Let's hope they catch him before long, then we can avoid putting a certain someone . . .' he gestures towards Dylan with his chin '. . . through the ordeal of having to go to a safe house when he should be enjoying the run-up to Christmas.'

I spread my hands. 'I still can't believe he managed to get out. What is he? An escape artist? A magician?'

'I heard it was a guard who helped him.' Guy shrugs, moving Dylan from one arm to the other. 'Some bloke who'd taken you-know-who under his wing. Thinks he's innocent and that he deserves his freedom.'

'Where on earth did you hear that?' I frown. Jane didn't say anything on the phone, but, then again, I hadn't asked her for details about the escape. What good would it do us now, to know how he got out?

'My mother.'

'Your *mother*?' I roll my eyes. 'The woman who thinks aliens are running the country?'

'She read it on Facebook. In one of her true crime groups.'

I shake my head and start to put the last few things in Dylan's brightly coloured rucksack. 'Anyway, I've put Grey Bunny in. He won't sleep without it. Plus, his favourite dinosaur pyjamas. And don't let him have too much ice cream.' I look at him. 'You've had your own alarm installed?'

Guy jigs Dylan up and down. 'Yep. And tell Granny there's no such thing as too much ice cream, is there, Dyl?'

Dylan giggles.

Guy grabs the bag from the table with his free hand. 'We'll leave you to it then.'

My stomach suddenly lurches at the thought of being in the house on my own. I have no intention of worrying Guy even further by telling him about my experiences over the past day: the car at the park, the journalist, the person outside the house. Not to mention, the unexpected phone calls. The second conversation I had with the strange, muffled, well-spoken girl who claims to know all about my family was short. After she'd told me to look at the news headlines, informing me that Drew was nearer to us than we thought, she'd hung up, just like the first time. The silence at the end of the line, the information on my laptop screen, telling me she'd blocked her number once again, had left me feeling more disconcerted than ever.

And still, I have no idea who this woman is. *Why* she called me. Whether she really does know anything about Sarah, or if it's all just some elaborate prank.

I swallow heavily, feeling a little nauseous again. All I've managed this morning was a cup of strong coffee. 'I'll walk you out.'

I follow them through the hall and watch as Guy lowers Dylan to the floor and slips his arms into his winter coat, wrapping a mini scarf around his grandson's neck before leading him out to the car. As I often do when I see them together, I feel sad. Despite the initial reservations we had about Sarah's very sudden marriage, our suspicions that all was not as rosy as it seemed in her and Drew's relationship, Guy and I had been excited about becoming grandparents. We'd talked about it when Sarah was younger, even before she met the man who turned her life upside down: how great we'd be, cool Granny and Gramps, who our daughter's children would always want to spend time with. Would look forward to, rather than dread, seeing. Now, look at us: grandparenting from different houses; Guy taking Dylan for alternate weekends. How different our lives could have been.

After securing his grandson onto his booster seat, Guy looks up and down the street before turning to look back at me. 'You're not going out, are you?'

I shrug, thinking again about the figure who stood on the opposite pavement last night. A light layer of snow has now settled on the ground where the person stood. The weather forecaster on the news this morning promised more to come tonight. 'I have to go to Gilbert. I can't avoid it; they're short-staffed. And I promised Amy I'd take her a woollen hat. She'll be cold without it.'

He grimaces. 'You'd be better off staying at home.'

'Where I'm a sitting target?'

'Where the police can keep an eye on you. Look, if you insist on going, lock the car door once you're inside it, and park as near to Gilbert as you can. And come straight home. Are you on helpline duty again tonight?'

'Yep. I've had to draft in a few more volunteers. We're expecting it to be busier than ever now there's an escaped prisoner on the loose.' I try to smile.

Guy rolls his eyes. Leaning forward, he kisses my cheek again, the smell of his favourite shower gel familiar and comforting. Should I have asked him to stay with me? I suddenly wonder. To bring over some of his stuff and bed down in the spare room, the three of us hiding from danger together? I push the thought away. Dylan is safer with his grandfather. Drew knows exactly where I live but Guy's new place will be harder to find. Our son-in-law may not even know we've split up.

'Go back inside and lock the door.'

I nod and, after waving goodbye to Dylan, head back up the path, the house looking bare compared to the others in the street that are heavily decorated with festive lights. Boswell waits for me in the doorway. Since last night, he seems skittish and restless, reluctant to go outside. It was all I could do to persuade him into the back garden to pee first thing this morning.

Keeping the door open just a crack, I watch Guy's car disappear down the road, the butterflies in my stomach doing a merry dance now. I look in one direction and then the other. Drew could be anywhere. Hiding behind the large oak tree a few houses away. Lurking in the shadows of someone's driveway. Perhaps he's waiting for this very moment, for Guy to drive away with Dylan so he is then free to launch an attack on the woman who was so determined to put him behind bars. Who will never, ever, forgive him for what he did to her daughter.

The promised patrol car slowly rolls by, the second time I've seen it this morning. I wave to the driver before going inside and engaging both the lock and the bolt.

Chapter 16

Sarah before

Sarah felt dazed. She'd never been in hospital before, not even as a child. She didn't want to be here now. Looking around the busy A&E department, she wondered if she could simply walk out. Find her shoes and try and get to the front entrance before anyone stopped her. The first doctor who'd assessed her had said she might be concussed, that they wanted to monitor her for a little while. Plus they wanted to scan her stomach, to make sure her baby boy – she knew it was a boy now, although Drew had told her not to tell anyone, that the gender of their baby was no one else's business – hadn't been affected by the so-called *fall* she'd had.

It was her neighbour who'd insisted on calling an ambulance. Old Frank, who lived two or three flats along, had found her on the walkway. Sarah had felt so stunned she didn't know where she was, or which way she had to turn to get home. Seeing the blood above her eye, Frank had taken her into his own flat and thought it might be *for the best* if he called for help. Drew was nowhere to be seen at that point. After doing what he'd done, *hurting* her, he'd run down the stairs to the car park and had driven away. She hadn't heard from him since. But then she didn't have her phone with her, did she? A few days earlier, her husband had hidden it somewhere, saying she needed a break from it. That too much screen time wasn't healthy. She'd looked in every corner of the flat but hadn't found it.

Had what happened been her fault? she wondered now. It was possible. She thought back to how their argument had started. Sarah had been feeling tired. The baby was kicking a lot and pressing on her bladder, so she'd spent the morning taking a long bath. She thought Drew wouldn't mind. When he had a day off, he was often more relaxed. Not so cantankerous as he could be when he'd been working. When she came out of the bathroom, she'd suggested they might get a takeaway that evening, remembering what her mum had said about fish and chips not doing any harm once in a while. Drew had seemed to be quite laid-back lately; it didn't occur to her that he'd object.

Not to mention object so *violently*. He'd practically chased her out of the flat, his face red with rage. Sarah wasn't sure what she'd done that was so wrong. As she'd tried to leave, to get away, Drew had grabbed the open front door and slammed it with all his might, before she'd had a chance to go through it. It had bounced back and hit her in the head.

When she'd found herself in Frank's flat, she'd told him she'd fallen. Sarah was in shock, not entirely sure what she was saying, but she'd been aware enough to know she couldn't tell the old man the truth. Instead, she'd said she'd been getting a bit of fresh air, but that she'd lost her footing, tripped over her own feet, and hit her head on the walkway railings. That Drew had gone out before it happened. She hadn't been able to think of anything better to say. She'd begged Frank not to call the emergency services. She'd be fine, she said, if he could just walk her back to her own flat. The old man hadn't listened. He'd seemed to think it was his duty, as an upstanding citizen, to help her. To do the right thing.

She was adjusting her position on the trolley when the curtain around her suddenly opened. Her mum stuck her head through, eyes wide.

'Oh, my goodness, Sarah, are you okay?'

Sarah felt panic flood through her as she noticed her dad, just beyond the curtain, talking to the nurse. She hadn't wanted her parents to know what had happened. Who'd told them? She tried to smile. 'What are you doing here? Who told you I was here?' She couldn't imagine that Frank would know how to get hold of them. Had Drew said something? Regretted his behaviour and contacted her mum and dad to confess what he'd done? She couldn't imagine it.

'We're still down as your next of kin. The hospital called Dad to let him know you were here, that you might be concussed. What on earth happened? They said a neighbour called the ambulance?'

She shook her head. She really wished her parents hadn't come. 'I'm fine, honestly. It's nothing. Just a stupid fall. I tripped. Frank shouldn't have called anyone. He was just being nosy, wanting to get involved in a drama. I'd have been perfectly all right if he'd just let me go home.' She played with the necklace at her throat. Her parents had always known when she was lying. Why couldn't she tell them what had really happened? Tell them the truth about Drew?

But she couldn't. The idea of anyone knowing what was going on in her marriage was horrifying. She was embarrassed that she'd got herself into such a situation. That it was her own fault. Wouldn't everyone say *I told you so*? Tell her she shouldn't have rushed into marrying someone she hardly knew? Probably.

Her mum sat on the edge of the bed as her dad came into the cubicle, sounding upset.

He kept his voice low. 'The nurse said they weren't sure she was quite telling the truth about just tripping. They think . . .'

'Think *what*?' Sarah knew her own voice was too loud. Since she'd arrived at the hospital, she'd tried to put what really happened to her out of her mind. She didn't want to think about her husband sending the door flying towards her; the way her head felt as if it had exploded when the wood made contact; the blood running immediately into her eye, blurring her vision. Now, her parents were making her see it all over again. Feel the pain, the fear that this could be how she was going to have to live her life from now on. 'Don't talk over me as if I'm a child! I'm an adult, and I'm quite capable of looking after myself.'

'We know that, sweetheart.' Her mum sighed. 'Look, Sarah, if you're having problems, if there's something we should know about, then just tell us. That's what we're here for. Are you . . . Have you been drinking?'

'Of course I haven't! I'm pregnant!'

'It's just that, this fall. We can't see how you could have just tripped. And your forehead looks so sore.'

'I'm *fine*.' Sarah said again. She couldn't bear the thought of the look of disappointment that would no doubt cross her mother's face if she knew the truth.

Her dad leant towards her. 'We just want to help, love. We're your parents. You know you can tell us anything.'

Putting a hand to her stomach, Sarah tried not to cry. She was so confused. Did her parents think she'd caused this herself? As much as she wanted to cover up what had really happened, part of her wanted to scream at them that it wasn't her fault, that it was her supposedly loving husband who had caused her injuries. But she was going to have a baby soon, and she wanted her little boy to have a father. She *needed* to make her marriage work. And she shouldn't have to feel judged because she wasn't ready to admit defeat.

Yet if this were happening to Keeley, she thought suddenly, if Alice were behaving the same way as Drew, what would she herself say to her friend? Would she tell her to stay with a partner who didn't treat her with the respect she deserved? Who tried to strangle her or caused doors to smash into her? Who treated her more like a servant than a wife? The idea of her best friend being hurt, treated like she was nothing, pulled Sarah up short.

She looked at her parents, seeing the sadness in their eyes. Would they really be disappointed in her, or would they simply take care of her, like they always had? Take her to her childhood home, where her dog would be waiting for her, tail wagging, and wrap her up in a warm blanket and feed her soup and cake?

She swallowed down a sob. 'Mum, Dad, he . . .'

The curtain suddenly opened again. 'Babe! What on earth have you done to yourself, you silly thing?' Drew's large frame filled the small space as he nudged her parents to one side and approached the bed. 'Thank God someone got you to the hospital. I dread to think what could've happened.'

Sarah flinched as he leant towards her and took her in his arms, her body reacting instinctively to his touch. She realised she was frightened. Frightened he'd hurt her again, even here, in the hospital, in front of everyone. But he wouldn't do that, would he? He wouldn't let anyone see what he was really like.

Leaning close to her, Drew whispered into her ear, 'You always have to be the centre of attention, don't you, my darling wife? Ever since you've been carrying that *brat* inside you.'

She began to cry.

Drew looked over his shoulder. 'Claire, Guy, thanks so much for being here, but as you can see, Sarah's feeling quite emotional, and who can blame her? I can take over from here.'

Her dad's eyes widened. 'But Sarah's our daughter, Drew, and she's hurt. We want to make sure she's okay.'

Drew straightened. 'And I'm more than happy to update you once I've spoken to the doctors.' He lowered his voice, as if trying to shield his wife from what he was saying. 'Since she's been pregnant, I'm telling you, Sarah seems to have become *so* clumsy. She can barely get out of bed without falling over.' He looked back at her and spoke more loudly. 'Must be the effect our little boy is having on you, eh, babe?'

Her mum put a hand to her mouth. 'It's a *boy*? Sarah, you never said.'

Sarah put her chin to her chest. She'd wanted to tell her parents, more than once, that they were going to have a grandson, but Drew had been adamant that he didn't want anyone to know. That they should keep it to themselves, enjoy having their little secret, while they could. She'd been looking forward to telling them the news herself. 'We wanted it to be a surprise.'

'Oops. I guess I let the cat out of the bag there, didn't I?' Drew shrugged. 'Anyway, thanks for coming, you two, but I'm here now and I'm sure the very busy doctors and nurses could do without so many people milling around Sarah's bed. I'll walk you to the entrance, if you like. I wouldn't want you to get lost.' He began to usher her parents out, as if they were unwelcome vermin.

Her mum didn't look happy. She spoke over her shoulder to her daughter as she left the cubicle. 'Call if you need us, Sarah.'

After the three of them had gone, Sarah lay back against the pillow. Before her husband had arrived, she'd been about to tell her parents the truth. Or some of it anyway. But, once Drew appeared, there was no way she'd have been able to accuse him of anything. He had a way about him, a way of convincing everyone around him that he was in the right, that his wife was simply clumsy, or nervous, or just plain stupid. She looked up as a nurse approached her bed.

The nurse smiled as she checked Sarah's wound. 'You're going to have a humdinger of a headache for a while.'

Sarah nodded. She thought again about how close she'd been to telling someone exactly what had happened that afternoon. Of confessing to what was going on in her marriage. What she was hiding. But then her husband had taken the chance away from her. Now, she was looking into the kind face of someone else who might be able to help her. Who might take her seriously in the few moments she had before Drew came back. Should she say something?

The nurse spoke again. 'Good job you've got that lovely husband of yours to look after you, isn't it? I wish I had someone like Drew Allison at home. I've been single for years. Ever since my divorce.'

Sarah wondered if she'd heard right. 'You know Drew?'

The nurse nodded, smiling again. 'Of course. We all *love* Drew here. His family have done so much for the hospital over the years. His dad was responsible for getting us the new wing. We were so grateful.' She pulled the covers further up the bed. 'I'll be back shortly.'

Sarah stared at her bulbous abdomen, thinking about the nurse's words. She'd missed her chance, not only with her parents, but also with a professional who might have been able to tell her what she should do. She might never get the chance to ask for help again. What was she going to do?

She gasped as a sudden sharp pain ripped through her stomach.

Chapter 17

Claire now

Guy and I met when we were just eighteen. Both of us freshers, my future husband hadn't long started a marketing degree, some of his classes crossing over with mine as I tried to get to grips with business and economics. The two of us took to each other straight away, laughing and joking, sharing the same sense of humour, from the day we met, but, as I'd often told my daughter, we were friends for a while before we went out on a date. What I hadn't mentioned to Sarah was that I already had a boyfriend when her dad and I were getting to know each other. A sports scholar called Tom, who I'd met on my very first day at uni and who hung around with the gang I'd become friendly with, Guy included.

Tom and I were together for a little under a year in the end, and I found his interest in me a constant source of surprise. He was good-looking and I suppose I'd always thought of myself as a little *ordinary*. An uninteresting girl, from an uninteresting small town. Guy didn't like him much, a sneer curling his lip every time he spoke Tom's name. He was glad when we broke up, despite the split leaving me feeling fragile, even shattered, for a while. In the aftermath, I found Guy's company comforting. Despite his apparent jealousy over my previous relationship, he was understanding and patient, and I began to feel drawn towards my friend in a way I hadn't before. I started to see him differently, to notice the way he looked at me. The way he made a beeline for me as soon as I arrived at any mutual social events, always asked if I was okay.

We'd been married almost thirty years when we split up.

We tried; we really did. For a long time, neither of us wanted to admit that our marriage wasn't working. That what we'd been through had taken away the joy that once bound us. We'd circle around each other in the house as if we were synchronised swimmers: Guy leaving the kitchen as I entered it; me migrating to the bedroom with a book if he sat down next to me on the sofa. How could we have broken the vows we'd made so determinedly at our own wedding? I often wondered, in the early days after he left. How could we no longer be prepared to stand by each other no matter what, until death parts us?

Of course, no one asked us when we got married, two naive twenty-somethings, how we might react if we were to lose the daughter we didn't even know then was going to exist. If that was a particular storm we'd be able to weather and still stay married. The priest hadn't included a vow that asked if we were willing to commit to forsaking all others *including our own child*, had he? Surely, we were allowed that one caveat? That one loophole in our solemn promises?

We told the police how ill Guy was, the night we lost Sarah. How he'd been confined to his bed by flu. Otherwise, he would probably have picked her up from the wedding that night, he'd said. Driven her home, like he always had when she lived with us, seen her into the flat. Would she still be alive, if he'd done that? he'd asked the detective in charge of the case, more than once.

I'll never forgive myself, my husband had said, again and again until he was hoarse. *Never.*

Thinking now about Guy's warning, his insistence that I don't make myself any more vulnerable than I already am, I park as near to Gilbert House as I can. Even after we've lived apart for a year and a half, he still worries about me, the same way I do him. I guess it's a habit we'll struggle to ever break.

I sit in the car for a moment and stare out of the windscreen at a small robin that has fluttered to the snow-covered ground, its tiny beak in search of debris. I remember how my mother used to say the appearance of the bird meant a loved one who'd passed had come to visit. An old wives' tale? I wonder. I listen to the radio, tuned in to a local station, and close my eyes briefly, hardly able to bear listening to the words of the presenter, but, at the same time, unable to simply reach down and press a button to cut him off. It's the same story that was all over the news last night, of course: the *dangerous escaped prisoner* who is believed to have come back to his old haunt on the third anniversary of his crime. The police have issued a warning to the public:

The prisoner is described as tall and well built, with thick, dark hair and blue eyes. He may still be wearing his prison-issue uniform of light blue tracksuit bottoms and a sweatshirt, but police believe he may have changed clothes at some point since his escape. They are advising residents of the town not to approach the man, but to call 999 immediately if they think . . .

Suddenly unable to stand hearing any more, I reach over and turn it off, the only sound in the car now the ticking of the cooling engine. Ever since last night all I've been able to think about is Drew Allison; thoughts of my son-in-law invade my brain like a virus during my every waking moment. When will we have any peace from this man? I wonder. When will we be able to get on with our lives without the constant anxiety of knowing he's still living on the same planet as us? Ever? Probably not.

I grab my bag and the old woollen hat of mine I've brought and climb out of the car, pulling my thick winter coat more tightly around me. The sky above me is grey and heavy and the weather forecast this morning predicted a substantial amount of snow later on. Much more, it seems, than the light layer we've had so far. I think about Dylan, how he's likely missing out on playing outside due to the potential danger. During so many winters, my daughter would come running inside the house, her bobble hat flecked with white flakes, wellington boots damp, and ask me if I had carrots for her sculpture's nose, buttons for his eyes. How she would have loved to have repeated the same experience with her own son.

I look over my shoulder, up and down the alleyway, as I climb the stone steps to Gilbert's entrance, my nerves heightened as I go inside, as if there's someone behind me. A shadow, that disappears whenever I turn around. The reception area is busy, a mixture of regular and new visitors crowding around Billy's desk as he hands out leaflets and winter survival packs. We always get busier when the weather turns cold. The demand for a hot shower is often more than our old water system can cope with. Just last year, we had no choice but to start a GoFundMe page in order to pay for a new boiler, our application for a grant turned down flat. Soon, we are going to have to replace the pipework in the small bathroom. We'll be lucky if it lasts another winter.

I dump my coat and bag in the staffroom before heading into the dining hall. Lunch service is going to be busy today and, with almost a quarter of our staff and volunteers off sick with flu, the rest of us are having to put in extra hours to make up the shortfall. It's not often I work weekends, but sometimes I don't have a choice. The welfare of the clients has to come first.

I grab an apron from behind the counter and put it over my head, aware, as I tie a knot behind my back, of the eyes now on me. Every other member of staff, every volunteer, seems to be watching my every movement. They've all seen the news, I assume. With my daughter's killer on the loose, they're no doubt concerned for my state of mind, my safety. I clear my throat loudly, as if to indicate that I have no intention of falling apart during my shift, that I intend to go about my work as usual. I quickly make a cup of coffee and a hot chocolate before heading over to the other side of the room.

Amy is sitting in a far corner. She's a quiet and reserved girl, who mixes little with the other Gilbert regulars, literally keeping her head down and barely talking to anyone during the time she spends here. Sometimes I watch her, as she creeps around the dining hall like a frightened mouse, piles up dirty dishes and bags up rubbish. As soon as she's finished her shift, she simply collects her meagre belongings and leaves without so much as a goodbye to anyone. The other volunteers and staff are used to her and leave her be. She's not the only one here who struggles with social skills.

I pull out a chair and sit down opposite her, moving the hot chocolate to her side of the table and taking the coffee for myself. We still have half an hour or so until the lunchtime rush and, since I'm one of the few people Amy welcomes into her space, I try to make sure we always have a little chat before we set to work. As I make myself comfortable, I try not to look at the scars on her forearms that are just showing, where the sleeves of her shabby sweater come to an end. I know she doesn't like anyone drawing attention to them.

'I've left a warm hat in the office for you. Make sure you grab it before someone else does. You're going to need it.'

Amy nods. 'Thank you.' She looks at me, her blue eyes wide behind the old-fashioned glasses that cover half her face and don't suit her. 'How are you doing, Claire?'

I shrug. 'I'm okay.'

She raises an eyebrow.

'Honestly, I'm fine.'

'You must be scared, knowing he's out.'

I look around the room. Some of the other members of staff are still looking at me, their brows creased with concern. Perhaps, like Guy, they think I shouldn't be here. That I should have stayed at home, behind a locked door. Can't they see that I'm probably safer here? With people? I suddenly wonder if my colleagues are worried for their own safety, rather than mine.

I look back at Amy. 'The police have installed a panic alarm. In the house. They've assured us they're doing everything in their power to find him.'

'Do you believe them?'

I nod. 'I have to. When they catch him and put him back inside, his sentence will be even longer because they'll add escape to his list of crimes.'

We sit quietly for a minute or two. Amy wraps her thin fingers around her mug of hot chocolate as I sip my coffee.

Eventually, she looks up at me. 'You're saying all the right things, but you don't sound completely convinced. You're worried. I can see it in your eyes.'

I sigh. Unable to talk to Guy, due to not wanting to add to his worries, I've been stewing on last night's events for hours; snippets of the news, as well as my conversations over the helpline, constantly come back to me the same way a song might get stuck in the head of someone who's been listening to it on repeat. I take another sip of coffee before putting my mug down and looking at Amy. 'Somebody called me, last night, on the helpline.'

Amy frowned. 'What do you mean? Someone wanting your help? Why has that bothered you?'

I shake my head. 'No, it wasn't the usual type of call.' I hesitate. 'It was a woman; she didn't tell me her name. She called twice, but she claimed . . . Her exact words were: *I know where Sarah is.*'

Amy sits up straight. 'Do you think she was telling the truth?'

I shrug. 'I have no idea.'

'Who was she?'

'I don't know that either.' I shake my head. 'It's not the first time.

Remember when that psychic contacted me and told me the same thing? And then there was that true crime fanatic who claimed to have worked out exactly what had happened? Neither of them actually knew *anything*. They were just looking for attention. I'm sure this woman is the same, whoever she is.' I purse my lips.

'And did she tell you? Did she say what she thinks happened?'

Another shake. 'No. She kept hanging up. Like she just wanted to string me along.'

'What if she rings again? What will you do? Talk to the police?'

'I'm not sure there'd be much point. She blocked her number each time, so I have very little information to give them. I'm sure they'd just think the same as I do. That it's a crank caller who'll get bored very quickly.'

'It must have unnerved you though. The idea that someone might know what happened.'

I wave her away. 'Please don't worry, Amy. I'll be fine. I'm pretty sure she won't call back.' Am I telling the truth? I wonder. Or is part of me hoping that my strange caller will contact me again, so I can find out if she really does know anything about where my daughter is? Would another call make me feel better or worse? Is being in limbo, unaware of the depth of my caller's knowledge, better than knowing the full truth of it?

Amy reaches out a hand and briefly touches mine. 'You need to be careful, Claire. Keep yourself safe. Where's your grandson?'

Looking up, I catch the eye of one of Gilbert's regular visitors, a young man who often entertains us with his guitar after lunch. He looks at me for a few seconds before giving me a sad smile and turning away. So many people, in such tough circumstances themselves, feeling sorry for me. I look back at Amy. 'He's with Guy.' I clear my throat. 'My ex-husband.'

She nods, frowning, as if she's worried. Part of me wonders if I've done the right thing by confiding in her about the calls I received. Amy is a fragile girl; she has enough problems of her own to worry about.

'Anyway, I'd better get back to work. Are you seeing your boyfriend tonight? How's it going with him?'

She shrugs. 'Maybe. It's early days.'

I gather our mugs together. 'Make sure you grab that hat and put it on when you leave. It's freezing out there.'

I make my way back to the counter, ready to throw myself into dishing up beef stew and vegetable curry, ideal dishes for a winter's day. As I sort out utensils and take the lids off the huge stainless steel serving vats, I become aware that someone has switched on a radio, an old transistor that one of the volunteers brought in to liven up the dining hall. The chirpy music that's playing stops suddenly and is interrupted by a sombre male voice:

We're interrupting today's lunchtime show to bring you some further breaking news . . .

I stand at the counter and listen, my limbs seeming unable to move despite the queue that is forming on the other side. Gilbert's regulars are keen to get their hot lunch on a day like today. The sound of the presenter's voice fades in and out as the radio's signal wavers, but I manage to catch most of his words:

The brother of the escaped convicted murderer Drew Allison has been found beaten and badly injured. Police believe that Allison, who has been on the run since . . .

Someone at the far end of the counter gasps and quickly flicks the radio off. It doesn't matter; I don't need to hear any more of the story.

The message my son-in-law is sending me couldn't be any clearer.

Chapter 18

Sarah before

Sarah twisted her wedding band around her finger nervously. Sometimes, recently, she saw the ring her husband picked for her in a completely different way to how she'd seen it when he first gave it to her. Then, she'd claimed she loved it. That it was perfect and exactly to her taste. Now, she often looked at the ring and saw its ugliness. It wasn't to her taste at all; she could see that. Did that mean Drew had never really known her? Or had he deliberately picked a piece of jewellery he knew she wouldn't like? Nothing would surprise her.

She smiled as the waitress put a large mug of herbal tea in front of her. She looked down at the hot green liquid, feeling guilty. Drew didn't like her spending money on what he saw as luxuries. In fact, he didn't like her spending money at all. Just the week before, he'd suggested he keep her debit card with him while he was at work, so she wouldn't be tempted to spend while they were supposed to be saving up, before they committed to having another child. He'd taken control of all their finances now, saying it was a husband's job to be the *man of the house* and pay the bills. She was only here, in the café, because she'd found a stray five-pound note in the pocket of the jeans she'd pulled on that morning.

She reached down towards the pram and pulled the woollen blanket further over the baby. Dylan was sleeping peacefully. As Sarah looked at him, she tried to imagine what her life might be like if she fell pregnant again. She really wasn't sure it was what she wanted, despite smiling at her husband when he'd talked about it. If it was what Drew thought they should do, did it really matter what she thought?

Looking around her, she studied the other customers: a man and woman sharing a cake; a group of forty-somethings enjoying afternoon tea. In the two and a half months since she'd given birth to her son, Sarah had barely left the flat. For the first few weeks after Dylan was born, she'd had an excuse: she was tired, still recovering from her difficult labour; Dylan was too young to go far just yet. But soon, her parents and friends had begun to notice how she declined every offer that came her way. Soon, she'd be running out of silly reasons to tell people she'd have to take a rain check. Even when her mum told her Keeley had said she'd come and watch the baby so Sarah could sleep, Sarah had waved the offer away. She was fine, she'd said to anyone who asked, too many times. She just wanted to spend some quiet time at home with her husband and child. Wasn't that every new mum's right?

No wonder most of her other friends had drifted away now, she thought as she emptied sugar into her mug, wincing as she heard her husband's voice in her head, warning her that it would make her fat. Only Keeley still made an effort to keep in touch, asking after her through her parents, despite the fact that Sarah never called her anymore, hadn't offered to help at all with the wedding. She never had got around to putting her friend's number in her phone again. What was the point, if Drew didn't approve of the two of them speaking, or meeting up?

Just a few days before, Keeley had turned up and knocked at

the flat door. The first thought that Sarah had when she'd opened it and saw her friend was: *thank goodness Drew is at work.* She had no doubt that her husband wouldn't be very impressed at Keeley turning up unannounced. He'd probably have said that Sarah was lying to him, that she'd encouraged Keeley to come and was now backtracking, making excuses.

As she'd stood in the doorway, she'd nervously looked up the walkway, to make sure Drew wasn't anywhere nearby, that he hadn't come home without letting her know. Keeley had been as bright and breezy, as friendly, as she always was.

'I was just in the area and thought I'd pop by on the off chance you were in. I feel like I haven't spoken to you for ages.'

Sarah had almost laughed. Where else would she be? She hardly ever went anywhere. 'Well, yes, obviously I'm here, but I'm a bit busy at the minute. I have a coffee cake in the oven. Drew's favourite . . .'

'Oh, I love coffee cake!' Keeley had smiled.

Sarah had immediately regretted saying anything about cake. She had no intention of inviting her friend in. Someone might see and tell Drew that she'd been entertaining visitors while she should have been doing other things. Besides, what she'd said was a lie. There was no cake. She'd just wanted to put Keeley off, get her to move on sooner rather than later. 'Oh, it's nowhere near ready yet.' She'd glanced over her shoulder. 'Um, the baby will be waking up soon. He's a bit fretful; he's had a bit of a cold.'

'I'm sorry to hear that.' Keeley had raised an eyebrow. 'I could come in and sit with him for a little while, if you like. So you can have a break, get some things done?'

Sarah had shaken her head. 'No, no, he just wants his mum at the minute.' Dylan didn't have any choice, she thought. He hardly knew any of the other adults in his life.

'Of course. It was just a thought. Are you okay, Sarah?'

'Oh, God, yes, fine. Never better.'

'Okay.' Keeley had shuffled her feet awkwardly. She looked

behind her at the car park before looking back. 'Well, I guess I'll go then . . .'

'Sure. Don't let me keep you.' Sarah had straightened, her hand on the door already, about to close it.

'Maybe we could . . .?'

'Yeah, maybe. I'll be in touch.'

She'd breathed a sigh of relief as she'd watched her friend disappear down the stairwell.

The truth was, she didn't want Keeley, *anyone*, to see the bruises.

She flinched now as she adjusted her position on the wooden chair beneath her. Of course, no one around her could see her injuries at the minute, the purple and blue skin that was hidden beneath her clothes, the dirty-coloured patches that dotted her arms and legs, that stopped at her wrists and ankles, but that covered her back and buttocks. There had been days when she could hardly sit due to the pain. Could hardly stand either. Drew wasn't stupid enough to hurt her in places the people around her could see. He knew how to hide his abuse.

And it *was* abuse; Sarah could see that now. Could clearly see that the way her husband was treating her wasn't right. Yet still, she hadn't left. Still, she stayed, hidden in the flat with the man who hurt her on a regular basis, didn't tell her loved ones the truth. Still, she made excuses to herself, every time he treated her badly. Grabbed on to the moments when he was nice to her, when he was romantic and seemed to love her the way he used to when they first met. Those moments seemed to be fewer and fewer recently.

Anxiety made her twitch. Drew wouldn't even like it that she was here, away from the flat. This morning, as her husband left for work, she'd told him that she intended to take their son to the park, so he could get some fresh air. Drew didn't much like her to go out without him these days, not even in daylight, but he knew Dylan needed to get out sometimes. That a young child couldn't stay cooped up all day. And she'd assured him they wouldn't go anywhere else, that they'd be back well before he got home. But on the way to the park, she'd walked past the coffee shop, remembering the money she'd found when she was getting dressed. Thinking about how nice it used to be when she met up with her mum or Keeley, ordered cake and frothy cappuccinos, she'd headed inside and taken a seat.

She'd drawn the line at ordering a milky drink: herbal tea was healthier, as Drew always pointed out to her.

'Hello, Sarah.'

She jumped at the sound of a deep voice, her heart starting to hammer as, just for a second, she thought it was her husband. That he'd found her, doing something she shouldn't be doing. When she looked up, she saw that it wasn't Drew at all. It was her brother-in-law. Dan was standing on the other side of the table, smiling down at her.

'Oh, hi.' She swallowed, not sure what else to say. In the past few months, she seemed to have lost the art of speaking to people, the skills that had once enabled her to easily have a conversation. Now, she barely spoke to anyone.

He gestured towards the window. 'I was just walking past, and I spotted you. Thought I'd come and say hello to my nephew.' He smiled again, this time at Dylan. 'He's grown.'

'He has.'

Dan cleared his throat, as if he felt a little awkward at the lack of spontaneous communication between them. He pointed at the chair in front of him. 'Mind if I join you?'

Sarah didn't answer for a few seconds. Would he think she was rude if she said no? If she claimed she needed to leave, that she had to be somewhere? She still had a full mug of tea in front of her. Wouldn't that look strange? Might Dan say something to Drew about seeing her here? Casually mention bumping into her, unaware of the problems he'd be causing? Eventually, at a loss as to what else to do, she shook her head. 'Of course not.'

He pulled out the chair and sat down before signalling to

the waitress and ordering a black coffee. 'So . . .' he adjusted his position '. . . how's things?'

Sarah looked down at her drink. She'd barely touched it, she was so uncomfortable. Not only was she somewhere she shouldn't be, but she was also sitting with a man. *Talking* to a man. Surely Drew couldn't be mad at her for chatting to his *brother*, could he? 'Okay.'

'Sure?' Dan bowed his head, as if trying to look into her eyes, perhaps read her expression. 'Life can't be too easy for you at the minute.'

Sarah looked up at him. 'What do you mean? Why do you say that?'

He gestured towards the baby. 'Well, you're looking after a baby, mostly on your own, I imagine, while Drew works long hours. As fantastic as my nephew is, I'm sure that can't always be fun. And I'm guessing my brother didn't take much paternity leave?'

She shook her head. In fact, Drew hadn't taken *any* time off after Dylan was born. Despite her having had a long and exhausting labour, not to mention numerous stitches, he'd gone back to the gym the very day she came out of the hospital. *The perils of being your own boss*, she remembered him saying. She'd been looking after Dylan on her own ever since.

'You know, if you ever need any help. Someone to watch the baby while you go shopping, or meet up with your friends, I'd be happy to help out. I've called Drew lots of times and offered my babysitting services, but he seems reluctant to take me up on it.' Dan sat back as his coffee arrived. He shrugged. 'Maybe he doesn't trust me.'

Sarah looked at him. She'd only met Dan twice before, once at the dinner party they'd held after their wedding, and again at the small christening service they'd had for Dylan just a couple of weeks before. The day hadn't been anything like she'd imagined. The so-called *celebration* of her own son's arrival into the world had been a sedate affair organised by Drew's mother. Most of the guests had either been Audrey's friends, or colleagues of her late husband. The only people Sarah herself had been *allowed* to invite were Keeley and her parents. Even the two people chosen to be her son's godparents had been complete strangers to her. She suddenly saw herself as the man opposite her must have seen her. Pathetic. Not even strong enough to be a parent to her own child. She mumbled her answer. 'He never said.'

'No.' Dan put his hand towards her, his fingers resting on the table between them. 'Sarah, are you okay?'

She felt her eyes sting, hoping she wouldn't start to cry. Not here, not now, when everyone in the coffee shop would look at her. She couldn't afford to draw attention to herself, not if she didn't want Drew to find out she'd lied to him about going to the park. 'I'm fine.'

'Only, you seem kind of low.'

Perhaps she should just leave now, Sarah thought. Dan's words were beginning to make her feel uncomfortable. All she'd wanted was a cup of tea. The chance to sit with her baby and while away an hour like other people did. *Normal* people. 'I really need to be going.' She pushed her chair back.

'At least finish your tea. I bet you hardly ever get to drink one while it's hot these days.'

Sarah didn't say that she hardly ever drank hot drinks in the flat anymore. Not since her husband had thrown a cup of coffee at her because she hadn't made it how he liked it, even though she'd tried her absolute best with that damned machine. She rubbed at her upper arm; the burn had mostly healed now.

She pulled her chair back in, not knowing what to do. Who was this person she'd become? she wondered. The person who seemed to doubt every single one of her own actions? Who couldn't make a simple decision by herself? Once she'd been what she supposed would be considered a high-flyer: a first-class honours student; an employee who would soon have her pick of positions. Now, she couldn't even order a hot drink without wondering if her husband would approve.

'Sarah.' Dan leant towards her, keeping his voice low. 'If there's something you want to tell me, something that's bothering you, I'd be happy to listen.'

She shook her head, feeling her bottom lip tremble. 'I told you, I'm fine. I just have a touch of the baby blues, that's all.' That's what her husband had told her, a few times over the past couple of months. That she was difficult to live with because she was depressed. As if he didn't have enough on his plate, he'd said.

'Shit.' Dan sighed and sat back in his chair. He hadn't touched his coffee.

Sarah frowned. 'What?'

'I should have done something.' He rubbed a hand over his face. 'I should have done something, as soon as Mum told me that Drew was planning to take you to Vegas. I knew you'd end up getting married there. I could see it in his eyes. How much he wanted you. How he wanted everything to go his way. But I was really hoping it would be different this time.'

Sarah didn't like what she was hearing. She remembered what Drew had said the first time he'd been violent towards her: that it wasn't the first time, not for him. Is that what Dan was referring to? She put her hands around her mug to stop them from shaking. 'What do you mean?' She wasn't sure she wanted to know.

Dan was quiet for a few seconds before once more leaning towards her over the table. 'I should have warned you, when you first started seeing each other.' He shook his head. 'I admit it, maybe I was just turning a blind eye because I didn't want to become involved. Again.'

'Again?' Sarah felt a flash of rage. 'You mean, you knew? Drew has done this before and you *knew*?'

She pushed her mug away and stood up, her chair almost toppling behind her. So much for not drawing attention to herself. Grabbing the handle of the pram, she tried to pull it out from between the tables, the wheels refusing to move as they caught on the furniture. 'Shit.'

'Let me help.' Dan stood and came nearer to her.

'What? Like you didn't bother to do before? When you knew what a bastard your brother was, but didn't tell anyone?'

'I'm sorry . . .'

Sarah pulled the pram free, frightened that Dylan would start crying with the jolting movement. She should never have come to the coffee shop. What was she thinking? She should have just gone to the park, like she said she was going to. Now, she'd have to get home and calm herself down, wash her face and brush her hair and redo her make-up, begin work on the evening meal, and look to her husband as if she were fine. 'I have to go.'

She hurried towards the door, the afternoon sun almost blinding her as she stepped outside. As she stopped briefly to pull the baby's sunshade over his face, Dan came up behind her.

'Sarah, wait.'

'Leave me alone, Dan. My marriage is nothing to do with you. It's mine and Drew's business and no one else's.'

'Is that what he tells you to say? After he's hit you?'

Sarah stopped. She looked at Dan, wincing as he put his hand to her arm. He was touching a particularly tender spot.

'I'm sorry. I shouldn't have said that. And you're right, I should've told you about my brother's behaviour in the past. I should've told *any* girl who got involved with him. But I really did hope he'd finally got his act together. That he'd changed. You seemed so . . . so *good* for him. I couldn't imagine him ever treating you badly. Ever *wanting* to. I was wrong. I truly am sorry.'

Sarah looked at him for a few seconds, before nodding. Was it Dan's fault that Drew was the way he was? Of course it wasn't. He wasn't responsible for his brother. The only person who needed to take responsibility for this whole mess she was in was her husband himself.

'Look . . .' Dan put a hand out '. . . give me your phone and I'll put my number in. You can call me.'

'I . . . I can't.' Drew had given Sarah her mobile back but, every time she used it, he seemed to know. Knew exactly who she was talking to or texting, even if she deleted the details. She still wasn't sure quite how he was managing it.

'Then I'll write it down for you.' He pulled a notebook and pen from the rucksack he was carrying and began to scribble. He seemed to sense what she was thinking. 'If you can't use your own phone, which I'm guessing might be the case, then find another way. Use someone's landline, reverse the charges. We can meet up and talk about this properly. I'll tell you everything I know.'

Sarah felt her stomach flip. If she couldn't manage to even go to a coffee shop without freaking out, how on earth would she meet up with Dan? Even the *idea* seemed ridiculous. She shook her head. 'Really, I shouldn't . . .'

Leaning forward, Dan tucked the piece of paper into the baby's pram, beneath the mattress. 'Just take it. If you can't meet with me, at least you have it if you ever need . . .' He paused. 'If you ever need help.'

Sarah looked at him before turning away, pushing the pram in front of her. She couldn't hang around any longer; she needed to get home. Her husband would be back soon, and she had no idea what he might do to her if she wasn't there when he came through the front door. She didn't even want to think about it.

Chapter 19

Claire now

The hospital is busy, what seem to be hundreds of people milling around its corridors, the tall Christmas tree in one corner looking out of place. As I make my way through the reception area, past the shop and coffee bars, searching the signs that point in all different directions, I feel a little sick. Who'd have thought that this would happen, after everything we've been through? When will it stop?

I head towards the ward I think is the right one, a phone call to the hospital's main switchboard from Gilbert House telling me where Dan would likely be. Amy had been upset when she'd heard the snatch of the bulletin on the radio, before the other member of staff had quickly switched it off. She'd tried to stop me from leaving.

'What if this is a trap, Claire? To lure you to the hospital?'

I'd looked at her. 'What?'

'Think about it. Drew knows exactly where his brother is now. He knows because *he* put him there. Has it occurred to you he could have just killed him? Why didn't he? What does he have to lose, after everything he's done? You need to be careful about what you're getting yourself into.'

I'd assured her I'd be fine, that I'd call the hostel later and let her know I'm safe. Despite my words, I knew that Amy was right in her concern: going to the hospital could be a very silly decision. A very *dangerous* decision.

As I drove the short distance across town, I'd listened to the radio again, the news on the hour telling me little more than I already knew. Only that Daniel Allison, son of the late councillor, Detective Chief Inspector Donald Allison, and brother of convicted murderer Drew Allison, had been found badly hurt just a few hours ago. It was suspected that his brother, recently escaped from prison, was responsible. It was all I could do to concentrate on the reams of traffic, the entire town seeming to be out doing their Christmas shopping despite the freezing weather. Images of Drew raining blows down on his older brother ran across my mind, as if I were watching some kind of horror movie.

My phone vibrates now as I head towards the lifts.

'Guy? Are you okay? Is Dylan safe?'

'He's fine. He's playing with his toys. Are *you* okay?'

'I'm okay.'

'Shit, Claire. This is getting scary.'

I stop behind an elderly couple who are standing in front of the lift doors. The display above tells us the car is heading our way. 'You heard about Dan.'

'Have you spoken to Jane?'

'No. I only know what I've heard on the news.'

'Where are you?'

I hesitate. The lift is nearly at the ground floor. I'm going to have to end the call very soon. 'I'm at Gilbert House. I'm fine, Guy, don't worry.' If I tell my ex-husband where I really am, he'll only have the same thoughts as Amy: that I'm putting myself in more danger than I need to. He won't understand that I can't just leave Dan alone and not let him know that I'm thinking about him. I have to see with my own eyes how badly Drew's brother is hurt.

'They'll move us to a safe house if this goes on much longer.'

'Maybe.' Part of me is furious that Drew Allison has us running scared. That man had such power over us for so long. Now, he's controlling our lives all over again. 'I have to go. Take care of Dylan. Don't let him out of your sight. Use the panic button if you have to.'

I end the call and enter the lift behind the elderly couple, trying to remain patient as the two of them are slow to enter and even slower to leave as we reach our destination. When I reach the ward I've been told that Dan is on, I mention his name to a young nurse and she looks unsure before she directs me towards a private room where a uniformed police officer is hovering just outside. The officer seems to recognise me and I suddenly remember how he was there, that night at the flat, the night Drew was arrested. He gestures at me to go in.

Once I'm inside, my heart hammers as I stand and look at Dan. Drew's brother looks ten times worse than I expected him to be. His right eye is almost closed, the skin around it swollen and purple, a huge gash splitting his forehead. Beneath it, his nose looks broken and his bottom lip is split and has scabbed over. One of his arms is in plaster, the other wrapped in a simpler bandage. There are ripe bruises all around his neck. Round and regular, they look like the finger patterns a child might make with paint.

He looks at me through his left eye. 'I wondered if you might turn up.'

I pull a plastic chair up to the bed and sit down. Like I have so many times over the past three years, I want to scream and cry, to destroy something, the same way I destroyed the Christmas tree in the living room last night. The same way Drew Allison destroyed my family. 'I'm so sorry, Dan.'

Dan licks his lips and swallows, even such a small movement seeming painful. When he speaks again, his voice sounds hoarse. 'It's not your fault.'

I pick up the tumbler of water from his bedside table and hold it to his lips for a few seconds. His injuries seem even worse now that I'm sitting more closely to him. I try not to imagine my son-in-law standing over him, the force he must have put into the attack. 'It's not yours either.'

Dan swallows and looks away. 'I offered to help Sarah. I knew what I was getting into. It was *my* choice.'

I nod. 'And now Drew wants revenge against anyone who turned on him. Who tried to stand up to him and make him accountable for what he was doing.' No doubt including myself and my ex-husband. 'Did he say anything?'

Dan winces as he attempts to shake his head. Obviously in pain, he closes his eyes briefly before looking at me again. 'It was all very quick. Put it this way, we didn't exchange any pleasantries.'

'Not a word? About what he's planning? Where he's hiding?'

'Believe me, Claire, if I knew anything that would help catch the bastard, I'd tell you. All I know is that I set off for work this morning, when it was still dark, and he was waiting for me as I wheeled my bike out into the alley behind my house. I don't remember very much after that.'

'But you're sure it was him?'

He tries to raise an eyebrow.

'Sorry, stupid question.'

A nurse comes into the room and checks the drip that's sending fluid into Dan's right arm. She fiddles with his tubes for a few seconds before glancing at me as she walks out again. No doubt she knows exactly who I am. Exactly what's going on here.

Dan waits until she's closed the door before he speaks again. 'Claire, my brother hasn't gone to the trouble of breaking out of prison just so he can get some fresh air. Drew is angry. Angrier than you can even imagine. Furious that he ended up where he did. That the perfect life he was trying to create was destroyed. His business was ruined, as was our family's reputation.'

I nod, but don't answer. I know all this.

'And it's *us* who are responsible. *We* put Drew behind bars, and he's never going to forgive us for that. Not *ever*. In fact . . .'

he tries and fails to adjust his position '... I wouldn't be a bit surprised if he comes back and finishes me off. Whether there's a police officer at the door or not.'

'Don't say that. If he'd intended to kill you, he would have done exactly that. Drew isn't stupid. He knows exactly how far to go and when to stop. Just like he knew with Sarah when he first started to abuse her.'

Dan grits his teeth, seeming angry suddenly, his already red face flushing further. 'If only I'd said something. Right at the beginning. I could have saved everyone so much pain. I'll never forgive myself for that.'

I put a hand to his arm. 'When I said it wasn't your fault, I meant it. You did everything you could to help her. You'll never know how much Guy and I appreciate that.'

We sit quietly for a few seconds, both of us no doubt thinking of what could have been. What might have changed if we'd each seen what was happening sooner. We'll never know. Eventually, I stand up. 'I have to go. I'll come back soon.'

Dan shakes his head. 'Don't. He'll be watching you. You know that, don't you?'

'They'll have caught up with him before that.'

'Don't count on it.'

I don't answer. As I turn to leave the room, Dan speaks again. 'Claire?'

I turn back to him.

'I'd do it again. Help Sarah, I mean. Even if I knew I was going to end up like this. I still would.'

I nod.

I head downstairs in the lift and through the long main corridor. When I exit the building, I see that the hospital car park is even busier than it was when I arrived. Crowds of people push past me with their heads down and hoods up, trying to protect themselves from the snow that's just started to fall again.

I light a cigarette and smoke it as I cross the narrow road, trying to get my bearings in the large space and remember where I parked. As I spot my car, my stomach lurches. The same red Citroën I saw at the playground yesterday is parked directly behind me, forming a T shape with my own car. I stand and stare at it, once again trying to make out the driver behind the glass. As I take a few steps nearer, the car begins to move. I watch as it exits the car park and quickly cuts into the traffic on the main road.

Could it be Drew this time, even though I know it can't have been before? That, according to what Jane Fellows told me, he wasn't even out of prison then? If not him, then who? Simply a journalist, as I previously thought?

Whoever it is, the fact that I've seen this car twice, when the man convicted of my daughter's murder has escaped, can't be a good thing.

Chapter 20

Sarah before

Sarah looked at the blood on the kitchen floor. Bright red and forming perfect circles on the ceramic tiles, the spots looked as if an artist had painted them. As if great care had been taken around their edges. Near to the table, one spot formed the shape of the sun, delicate splashes spreading from a central point. It reminded her of the paintings she used to do in primary school, she and Keeley sitting next to each other, happily creating idyllic scenes of family life: houses with four windows, mums and dads holding hands, children playing. How innocent she'd been then. How *unsuspecting*.

She swallowed, trying not to vomit. She didn't feel quite right. Her vision was blurry and her head was throbbing. Was the blood hers? Looking up, she saw her husband standing in the doorway, pressing a tea towel to his forehead. The towel was also stained red, the patches that were beginning to soak through from one side to the other looking less precise than the spots on the floor, as if these were part of an impressionist watercolour painting. Her stomach lurched as she realised where all the blood had come from.

It was Drew who was injured.

She'd hit him back.

Scenes from the past half-hour or so flashed through her mind as if she were looking through a kaleidoscope. Fleeting images of what had happened ran into each other: Dylan not feeling well, becoming grizzly as she tried to settle him in his cot; the thin shrill of the smoke alarm as the dinner she'd so carefully planned had started to burn; Drew coming through the front door to the chaotic scene, asking her why she was so disorganised. Where she'd been.

Sarah had been to the coffee shop again.

And Drew *knew*.

It was the one secret pleasure she'd kept from him. Every time she found a stray pound coin in the flat, she'd squirrel it away and, when she had enough, treat herself to a mug of tea and a biscuit. One time, she'd found four coins in an old handbag and had bought a cappuccino. It had tasted like heaven.

But it seemed that Drew had known all along. Where she'd been going when she'd said she was taking Dylan to the playground. She'd often wondered why her husband always seemed to be one step ahead of her. Why he always seemed to know what she was doing when he wasn't there. Who she was talking to.

Now she knew; Drew had been tracking her phone.

'No wonder my dinner is always burnt,' he'd said as soon as he came through the door and saw her struggling to remedy the situation. 'Do you think I don't know exactly what you're up to when I'm not here? That I don't know about your secret trips to that expensive coffee bar? What are you? A lady of leisure?'

'What?' Sarah had been confused.

'Don't you think I'd want to know if I suspected you weren't telling me the truth, lovely wife?' He'd grabbed her phone and held it in front of him. 'I put an app on it. So I could see all of your movements, know exactly where you go. And guess what, *darling*? Turns out you've been lying to me all along, when you've made out you were at home, caring for our son and lovingly making dinner for me after my hard day at work.'

To buy herself some time, to try and come up with an excuse, Sarah had gone to the little bedroom and busied herself with trying to settle the baby. Dylan hadn't been right all day. Usually, she had plenty of time to sort dinner when she got back, but today things hadn't gone quite to plan, Dylan needing a cool bath when his temperature had risen. She had no idea what she was going to say to Drew about where she'd been. Why she hadn't just told him the truth. He'd been *tracking* her? Her stomach churned as she made her way back to the kitchen.

Drew was leaning against the counter, one ankle crossed over the other. His foot tapped against the floor, up and down, up and down. He bit his bottom lip.

As soon as Sarah saw the look on his face, she'd turned and tried to run.

But she wasn't quick enough.

Her husband had flown at her, grabbing her hair from behind. The hair he'd once said was the most beautiful part of her, that he'd begged her never to cut. Had she screamed? Perhaps she had. Maybe more loudly than she'd intended. Now, as she stared at the red spots at her feet, she put a hand to the back of her head. Her scalp tingled, a small bald patch seeming to have formed in the area where Drew had grabbed her. She wondered if it would ever grow back.

She looked at him again and pictured herself grabbing the old casserole dish her mother had lent her and she hadn't got around to giving back. Aiming it at her husband's head. Had she hoped to kill him? To knock him unconscious, at least? She wasn't sure. All she'd known was that he was hurting her. Causing her terrible pain and not for the first time. All she wanted was for it to stop. For her son not to hear her cries. Not to wake up and hear his mother wailing as his father attacked her.

She'd been desperate, so she'd hit him back.

And now she had no doubt that he would punish her.

'I'm sorry.' Her voice was barely a whisper.

Drew took the tea towel away from his forehead and examined it, as if looking at the evidence of what his wife had done to him. He raised an eyebrow. '*Sorry?* That word doesn't seem quite adequate enough, does it? I mean, it's not much of an apology, when I'm standing here with blood pouring down my face, is it?' He looked at her. 'You *will* be sorry though. Sorry you ever set eyes on me, one of these days.'

Sarah felt faint. She slid down to the floor, her back against the kitchen cupboard. Maybe it was the shock. The consequence of attacking her husband after he'd attacked her. What had she been thinking, fighting back? She'd known. Known that was the worst thing she could possibly have done during one of Drew's *episodes*. Every other time he'd hurt her, she'd been passive, accepting the blows, trying not to show her distress at what was happening. But this time, something inside her had snapped. Her son was asleep down the hallway, grizzly and unwell, needing her attention. And all her husband could think to do was pull her hair and raise his fists. She wasn't sure she could take this anymore.

She took a breath as she looked up at him. 'I'm sorry I hurt you. I shouldn't have. But it was the first time. It wasn't the first time *you've* hurt *me*.'

Drew stared at her for a few seconds. He curled his lip into a sneer. 'Is my wife finally standing up for herself?' He chuckled. 'No, of course you're not. You're on the floor where you should be. *Beneath* me.' He stopped talking and glanced towards the hallway as he heard a sudden noise outside.

Loud sirens, not unusual in their area.

Sarah stiffened. Had someone heard her scream and called the police? Old Frank from a few flats along maybe, she thought, remembering how he'd called an ambulance the year before when he'd found her wandering dazed along the walkway. She looked at the blood beginning to thicken on her husband's forehead. She herself appeared to be fine. It was Drew who was injured. What if the police were on their way up to the flat right now? What would he tell them had happened?

She heard the sound of muffled voices, seeming to be coming from the walkway. She jumped as a fist banged on the door.

Drew pointed a finger at her. 'Stay here.' He sounded as if he were talking to a dog, his tone the same as the one she used to use when she confined Boswell to the kitchen when someone came to visit.

Sarah tried to focus, blinking rapidly to clear her vision. Putting her hands to the floor, she pushed herself up. Part of her felt as if she were in a dream. As if all this – the violence, the abuse – was happening to someone else. Not to her. Never would she have imagined that this would be her life.

She crossed the room, the pain in her scalp now radiating across her head and down her face, as if it were an electric current. As she stood at the small gap between the kitchen door and the frame, she tried to be as quiet as possible, so her husband wouldn't know she was watching him.

Drew stood at the front door, his back to her. Facing him, a young police officer, who looked as though he should still be at school, was looking at her husband with concern. Another officer stood silently behind him, as if there only as an observer.

The first officer spoke. 'Mr Allison? What happened? Do you need an ambulance?'

Sarah watched as Drew shook his head. She could only just hear what he was saying, his words muffled by the distance between them and the tea towel he was still holding to his face.

'I know you, don't I? Don't you come to my gym? A good squat technique, if I remember rightly.'

The young police officer's cheeks coloured, as if he were a student being complimented by a teacher. 'I do. Not *that* good, I'm still . . .' He shook his head. 'Anyway, Mr Allison, I'm afraid I'm here because one of your neighbours reported a disturbance? He says he heard a scream?'

'Ah, yes.' Drew bowed his head, as if embarrassed. 'That was me, I'm afraid. Bit of a big girl when it comes to pain.'

Sarah felt a rush of anger. It hadn't been Drew who'd screamed; it was her. She'd screamed when he'd grabbed her hair, pulled her backwards with all his might.

'Can you tell me what happened?'

Drew leant closer to the young officer. 'Look, this is a bit embarrassing. My wife, she's not that long had a baby – our little boy is only eight months old – and she's been suffering from postnatal depression. You know how it is, all those hormones running wild . . .'

The police officer glanced at his female colleague behind him before he nodded. He looked as if he had no clue.

'We had a little tiff. Sarah burnt the dinner, and well she just *lost* it. Blamed me for the whole thing even though I'd only just got in from work.' Drew shrugged. 'Next thing I knew there was a heavy casserole dish flying towards me. I tried to duck but I guess I just wasn't quick enough. I must be getting old.'

Sarah listened to her husband's words. How he blamed her for what had happened, despite being the one who had attacked first. Despite being angry because she'd been out for a cup of tea and then had to look after their sick son. Was that what people would think if she tried to tell someone what she was going through? That she was hormonal? Simply suffering from the *baby blues* as she'd tried to claim to Dan she was?

The police officer moved from one foot to the other, appearing to be thinking. Eventually, he seemed to make a decision. 'Would it be okay if I check on your wife? To make sure she's all right?'

'Sure. No problem at all.' Drew lowered his voice, as if he were inviting his new friend to be part of some conspiracy. 'Just take it easy on her, though, would you? She's very delicate at the minute. The doctor says it shouldn't last too long.'

Sarah moved away from the door, standing with her back to the kitchen window as they approached. Her husband had insisted on her going to see the doctor not long before, claiming she was depressed and becoming difficult to live with. As they'd both sat in the consulting room, she'd listened to him tell the GP how her moods were erratic, how demanding she was, how distant from both him and her child. It was Drew who had suggested she might need the antidepressants she'd been taking for a few days now. She'd considered not taking them, pretending she had and flushing them down the loo, but Drew had stood over her every morning and checked her mouth in the same way a nurse might in a psychiatric facility.

She could hear the officer talking as he and her husband walked through the flat, his tone friendly.

'They still talk about your dad at the station all the time, you know. All the old-school coppers have got a story about him.'

'That's good to know. Sorry, what was your name again. Officer . . .?'

'Just call me Paul.'

Sarah had heard Drew talk to people in the same tone many times, even her own parents when they first met. Her husband had a way about him. A way of making every single person he spoke to feel as if they were more important than anyone else in the world. Except her, of course. Except his own wife. She braced herself as they came into the room, Drew leading the way.

'Sweetheart, this nice young man here would just like to check you're okay. Apparently, someone heard me scream and thought it was you. I feel a bit silly, to be honest. What must the neighbours think of us?'

The police officer looked at her. 'Mrs Allison? Are you okay? Are you hurt at all?'

Sarah didn't answer. She looked at the floor, trying to imagine the next few moments of her life, what would happen if she went down one path instead of another. How would Drew react if she suddenly said that, yes, she was hurt? That her husband, the very man who the police officer seemed to be treating like some kind of local hero, had attacked her and had done it before, many times? That, beneath her clothes – the leggings, the long-sleeved shirt – she was covered in bruises from head to foot? She looked back up, seeing the blood on her husband's head, the wound she herself had caused.

The look in Drew's eyes.

'I'm fine,' she said quietly. 'Thank you.'

Drew's tone was jolly. 'Paul, I'd really appreciate it if you don't take this any further. It was just a silly misunderstanding. No long-term damage done. I expect I'll just have a headache for a little while.'

Sarah thought about all the times *she'd* had a headache, or a backache, or a stomach ache, after Drew's fist had connected with her soft tissue with the speed of a juggernaut.

The police officer looked doubtful for a few seconds. When he spoke, his words were directed at Sarah. 'Well, you're very lucky, Mrs Allison, that your husband doesn't want us to take any action. You might want to talk to your doctor about getting some help with your mood swings.'

'Oh, we're already on that, Paul. Don't worry. I'm ensuring Sarah gets all the help she needs. She's well looked after.' Drew gestured towards the door. 'I'll see you out. Thanks so much for coming. I guess you never know, do you, if it's going to be something serious rather than just a silly tiff?' His voice faded as he led the way through the hall.

Sarah felt the room spin around her as she waited for him to come back. So many times, she'd imagined herself telling someone what was happening to her. Yet, now, here she was, standing here, covered in bruises, having said nothing while her husband blamed *her* for what had happened. Because she fought back *one time*. Was this how her life was going to be, forever, until she died? Drew making her bleed, day after day, while she felt completely at a loss to do anything about it? Failed to say a word against him? If someone had told her when she was younger that she'd be tolerating someone, *anyone*, treating her the way Drew did, she'd never have believed it.

She braced herself as he walked back into the room, part of her expecting another blow. A punishment for attracting the attention of the neighbours, the police. She felt a thud of fear as she heard her son begin to cry. *Please not now, sweetheart. Please stay quiet for just a little longer.*

Drew puffed out air. 'Well, I hope you've learnt your lesson from that little episode, babe, because if it weren't for me, you'd now be on your way to the nearest police station looking at being charged with assault. Think yourself lucky you have a husband who is as understanding and generous as I am.' He glanced over his shoulder, wincing at the noise coming from the baby's room. 'I think that's my cue to go back to the gym for an hour. Maybe I can get a decent meal there, seeing as I can't get one in my own home. You'd better make sure the brat is quiet before I get back or I'm afraid I won't be responsible for my actions.'

He walked into the hallway and grabbed his keys before slamming the front door behind him. In the bedroom, at the back of the flat, Dylan started to wail loudly.

Sarah stood for a few seconds, her husband's words reverberating in her mind like an echo: *make sure the brat is quiet. I won't be responsible for my actions.* She listened to her baby crying. Dylan was the only good thing that had come out of her marriage. Her son was her life and she'd do anything for him. When she was younger, like every teenager, she'd sometimes taken her own parents for granted. Not given a thought to how they worried about her when she was out with friends, or when she first started going to bars and clubs. Now, she knew exactly what they'd gone through. How having a child could make you sick with worry.

Her legs not feeling quite strong enough to hold her up, she went into the hallway, the walls around seeming to be closing in before moving away again. She checked the pot that sat on the table by the door. Drew had left in a hurry; he hadn't taken *her* keys with him this time, only his own set. An oversight on his part, she thought, as he stormed off in anger.

As quickly as she could, Sarah went into the baby's bedroom and scooped him from his cot. Dylan was crying furiously now, his cheeks red and wet with tears. She shushed him as she unfolded his pram, jiggling it as she tried to settle him inside. Pushing her hand beneath the thin mattress her son was lying on, she rooted around until she found what she was looking for.

Find another way, Dan had said to her, when he'd scribbled his number on a scrap of paper, that day outside the coffee shop six months before.

She couldn't use her mobile – Drew would know exactly who she was calling – and there was no landline in the flat. Why would they need one? her husband had always said. Landlines were for old people.

Old people indeed, Sarah thought now. She clutched the crumpled piece of paper in her hand and pushed the pram out of the front door, heading down the walkway with her precious son towards old Frank's flat.

Chapter 21

Claire now

When I get back to the house, more journalists are gathered on the pavement. They move towards me as one as I climb out of the car. Like a gang of vultures, flocking towards their prey.

'Mrs Wallace, just a few words . . .'

'Mrs Wallace, how do you feel about . . .?'

I ignore them and walk up the path as quickly as I can, hoping that the same thing isn't happening at Guy's place. That they'll at least have enough respect to leave my ex-husband and my grandson alone. I glance over my shoulder at the street, wondering if I'll see the same red Citroën I saw at the hospital, if it really was a reporter trying to get some information on Dan's condition. Thank goodness Drew's brother has a police officer to protect him. I wouldn't put it past these members of the press to pretend they were innocent hospital visitors. The patrol car drives by once again. At least I know someone is nearby if the press intrusion intensifies.

I go inside and slam the door behind me before locking it. Boswell stares up at me and wags his tail hesitantly. No doubt he's been barking while I haven't been here. I stand in the hallway for a few seconds and try to get my breath. The events of the last twenty-four hours, not to mention the lack of sleep, are catching up with me and I feel as if I could drop to the floor and stay there for a week. Unfortunately, I don't have time. Tonight is probably going to be our busiest of the year on the helpline. The weekend when most bosses treat their staff to a night out is bad enough without the complication of a dangerous escaped prisoner. Despite what's going on, despite my own personal involvement in the situation, I can't let my team down. I have to try and carry on as normal. Even if Drew Allison and the journalists outside are attempting to ensure that I don't.

I move from room to room and draw the curtains. Outside, the snow is beginning to fall thicker and faster and it's getting dark. The journalists pull up their hoods as I cover the front window. With any luck, the cold will drive them away before too long, especially when they realise I have no intention of speaking to them. As I head into the kitchen and flick on first the heating and then the kettle, I think about Dan. I can't help but feel guilty at how much he's suffered. How broken he is. All because he chose to intervene. To try and help my daughter, my family.

He confronted his brother, the very night Sarah disappeared.

Furious at the way Drew had been treating his wife, Dan had called that afternoon and asked if the two men could meet up later. With Sarah at Keeley's wedding and Guy and I looking after Dylan, the two of them had decided to take a late-night stroll to a quiet spot along the pathway that ran next to the canal, where they could talk things through, where Dan had hoped to get Drew to see sense. The discussion had ended with them almost coming to blows, each of them losing their temper. In the end, Dan had given up and walked away. He told his brother he never wanted to see him again.

Drew was arrested just a few hours later.

Now, Dan is lying in a hospital bed, his spirit and his bones as crushed as each other. So many lives ruined by one man.

I feed the dog and let him out, opening the door only as much as he needs to slip through the gap. Looking up at the velvet sky, I hear the sound of a helicopter hovering somewhere nearby, a thin light illuminating the trees below as the police look for their escapee. I let Boswell back in and secure the door before heading into the living room to have a little tidy-up before I boot up the laptop. Calls are likely to start coming in early tonight. The weather will no doubt heighten the nerves of the women who are out alone, as well as what they've seen on the news. I need to be ready.

I pick up the remote control and switch the TV on again, listening to the headlines as I fold washing and pick up Dylan's toys. Part of me doesn't want to know what's happening, see any updates, but a larger part of me knows I have to try and keep ahead of Drew Allison's actions. The headlines are not too different to what they were yesterday: the little girl in Scotland has been taken into care; parliament is still in chaos. There's only one piece of news that's slightly different, Dan's name standing out like a neon light as it scrolls across the screen. I glance up at the panic alarm, installed late last night, wondering if I might have to use it at some point. The thought makes me shiver.

My mobile rings and I grab it from the top of the sideboard as I stuff my grandson's things inside, piling them on top of a stack of old board games we haven't played for a long time. I've never been one for keeping a pristine house. Guy often tells me off for being a hoarder, but, since Dylan moved in, it's become even harder to keep the place tidy. 'Hello?'

'Claire? It's Jane Fellows.'

Never once has our FLO referred to herself simply as *Jane*, her surname always following her first.

'Hi, Jane.'

'Everything okay?'

'We're fine. Dylan is with Guy.'

'I take it you heard about Dan Allison.'

I move things around before trying to close the sideboard door again, the corner of a box stopping it from closing completely. My heart flutters. I know exactly what's in the box; I put it in the cupboard myself just under three years ago. 'I did.'

'I just wanted to let you know that we're about to head into a press conference. The press is demanding more information since the story about Dan broke. It's going to be on the news channel in literally two or three minutes.'

I look up at the TV again and see the presenter holding a hand to his earpiece as if he's hearing something unexpected. 'Okay, thank you for letting me know.'

'It may be a little stressful for you, hearing some of the things we talk about. That's why I wanted to give you a heads-up.'

'I appreciate it.'

'I also wanted to let you know that if Allison isn't caught by tonight, it's likely we're going to go with the safe house option for you all. Tomorrow morning at the latest. I'm sorry, Claire. I know it's not ideal, but we don't have much choice.'

I sigh. 'Okay.'

I end the call and keep my eyes on the TV screen as I kneel beside the sideboard and pull out the box that was preventing the door from closing. I put it on the carpet next to me. The last time I looked inside was almost exactly a year ago, on the second anniversary of the night my daughter disappeared. As I take the lid off, I remember what Guy said yesterday about each passing year being just as difficult as the one before. Will it ever get any easier? I ask myself. Somehow, I doubt it.

Despite the throb of the radiator, I feel cold as I examine the few mementoes of Sarah's life, that I put away for safekeeping after the police investigation, almost the same time that I began to wear the letter S necklace. Some of the things in the box are what Sarah left behind after she moved in with Drew: drawings from when she was younger; a small pot she made at school;

her degree certificate. Others came from the flat, given back to us after the crime scene was cleared.

Lifting out a parcel of pale pink tissue paper, I open the delicate leaves. Inside, Sarah's wedding ring sits almost untarnished. Its pink gold seems as bright as the day I first saw it when we collected her from the airport, when she told us about the wedding we'd known nothing about. It's a horrible piece of jewellery, I've always thought, clunky and old-fashioned, as if it came out of the Eighties. It was found in the same bin bag as Sarah's clothing, returned to us once the police had done forensics tests. I'd thought about throwing it away at the time, not wanting to be reminded of my daughter's marriage, the decision that had set her on the path that led to me sitting here now, the blood on her belongings. In the end, I'd put it away with her other things. It's part of Sarah's life, I guess.

I look up at the TV as I hear the newsreader talk about a development in the case of the escaped prisoner, the press conference Jane just told me about. After crawling to the remote control, I turn the sound up a notch so I can hear what's going on. I sit back on my heels, the cardboard box still in front of me.

On the screen, the picture flits to a different location. A grey-carpeted room suddenly appears, an audience sitting in rows of chairs. As the newsreader, out of shot now, explains what's happening, I can hear an underlying rumble of voices, see the flashes of cameras.

I watch as three members of the police force walk in from a side door, each of them taking a seat behind a long table facing the crowd. A row of spongy microphones points in their direction. The person in the middle of the three is a man I recognise: Assistant Chief Constable Stuart Boyne, who Guy and I spoke to numerous times during the investigation. Boyne is dressed smartly, in full uniform, the epaulettes on his shoulders polished to perfection. The person to his left, in plain clothes, is someone I haven't seen before. On his right is Jane Fellows.

Boyne clears his throat and waits for the room to quieten. He puts on a pair of spectacles and speaks into the microphone directly in front of him, introducing first Jane and then the other person as a Detective Superintendent Riley. The cameras in the room continue to click and flash. I wonder if any of the reporters present belong to the group that have been hanging around my house, following me.

I listen as he begins to talk, his words focusing on the safety of the public and what his team are currently doing to catch up with the man earlier identified as Drew Allison. His voice is monotonous, as it always seemed to be when he was talking about my daughter, as if he's reciting something he's learnt by heart. The police need the residents of the town to cooperate with them in catching up with the perpetrator, he says, and to report anything they think remotely suspicious.

I inhale as he begins to talk about Sarah. What Drew did to her, how he's consistently refused to reveal the whereabouts of her body. Hearing the details again, having to relive what happened, now, three years later, feels like someone is putting a knife into my heart. No wonder Jane felt she had to warn me this was happening.

I try to distract myself, to shut out the words Boyne is saying. The dog sniffs around me as I go back to the box that houses my daughter's things. Delving to the bottom, I find an envelope. Inside it are the scan pictures of my grandson, taken at the hospital during one of the appointments Drew never wanted Guy and me to attend. With it is the tiny wristband that Dylan wore when he was born. We didn't see him until he was three or four days old. Sarah needed to rest, her husband kept telling us, when we called to try and make arrangements. I take a few seconds to look at them before slipping them back inside, then I look back up at the television to see that Boyne has now handed over to Jane Fellows.

Jane speaks clearly and slowly. 'The family of Allison's victim are being kept informed during every step of our search for him.

148

Their safety, as well as that of the public, is at the forefront of this operation, and should the threat against them increase, we will take the next steps in ensuring they are protected.'

I dig into the box again, my hand touching something smooth at the bottom, something that feels like a glossy photograph. As I pull it out, I feel the hairs on my arms stand up. It's a picture of Drew, smirking as he always seemed to be. How it got in the box of Sarah's things, I'll never know. I thought I'd got rid of all the pictures of my son-in-law, but somehow this one must have got past me. Perhaps it had stuck to the back of one of the photos of Sarah I'd put in there.

I put it on the floor in front of me and look up at the TV again, Boyne now telling the numerous reporters at the conference that he's prepared to answer just a few questions. The members of the press all speak at once until he forces them to wait and picks someone out.

I stare down at the picture of Drew as I listen to the answers to the usual generic questions: can the police really ensure the public's safety? Do they think the prisoner in question is still in the area? Will someone be held accountable for what has happened? Lose their job? Be forced to resign? I look up as one reporter asks about the rumour that Drew had help in his escape. *Was it a guard?* she asks. *Someone on the inside?*

The detective superintendent to Boyne's left speaks for the first time. 'For a number of reasons, we're not releasing any details about that specific subject at the minute. Yes, we do believe that Drew Allison had help to escape and that someone is now helping him evade capture, but we are not going to talk about that at the moment other than to encourage that person to do the right thing and come forward.'

She points to another reporter who seems to be falling over himself to ask his question.

'And what can you say about the rumours of someone else having gone missing? An ex-girlfriend of the prisoner?'

I look up sharply, gasping at the reporter's words. Sensing my upset, Boswell clambers over my lap in order to lick my face. This is something I've heard nothing about.

I listen carefully as Boyne, the most senior of the three, chooses to answer. 'We've also seen the rumours circulating on social media and all we can say at this stage is that we're currently communicating with the family of the woman concerned. Other than that, we can't comment at this stage.'

I feel a tear roll down my cheek. Drew Allison, still getting away with the same things he got away with before. *Please let them be wrong*, I think. *Let the rumours be completely untrue.*

Gritting my teeth together, I lift up the picture of Drew and tear it into tiny pieces before snatching up Sarah's wedding ring and throwing it to the other side of the room.

Chapter 22

Sarah before

Sarah sat at the kitchen table in her childhood home. She felt safe there, the smell of the house the same as it was when she was growing up. Boswell lay at her feet, as he had since she'd arrived back, a little short of a month before. On the far side of the room, her mother stood at the stove, making hot chocolate in a pan, as she'd always done during times of crisis. It was what Mum did best: feeding people, looking after them. When Peter next door had once had a heart attack, Mum had taken home-cooked meals round to him and June every day for a month.

Drew's brother sat opposite her, his brow creased with concern. He'd visited almost every day, to the point he now felt like a member of the family. 'I can't believe they're letting him off, just like that. As though he's never put a foot wrong.'

Sarah shifted her position on the wooden chair. Some of her injuries had taken a long time to heal and still made her uncomfortable. It was strange. After she'd hidden her bruises, the cuts and the scratches, for so long, it now felt weird for her parents and Dan to know about them. To know exactly how her husband had treated her, how his actions had led to her losing her first baby, which she now realised was completely Drew's fault. He'd tripped her up on purpose. He'd cut her with his razor on purpose. Never once had he not been in control of what he was doing, despite his claims of *accidents*. She raised an eyebrow. 'Can't you? This is *Drew Allison* we're talking about. Everyone loves your brother, don't they? Not to mention the fact that your mother has kicked up an almighty stink about the whole thing.'

Drew had been arrested just days after she'd called Dan from old Frank's place. After she'd walked out of the flat with nothing more than her baby and his pram, the crumpled piece of paper with the telephone number on it in her hand. Sarah had left all her stuff behind: her dresses and jeans, underwear, her shoes and books, not to mention all of Dylan's clothes and toys. Part of her had known all along that the police wouldn't charge her husband. *Apparently, there's not enough evidence*, their family solicitor had told her parents, *to take him through to a prosecution*. This was despite her having made a statement, shown the police what he'd done to her. Was it any wonder women were reluctant to come forward?

Dan's cheeks flushed. 'Mum's baby can do no wrong in her eyes. She's always been the same. She adored her second husband, Drew's dad. That's why she's always treated the two of us differently. Donald gave her the status she'd always craved.'

Sarah's mum approached the table, a large mug of hot chocolate in each hand. She put them on coasters and sat down. 'You have different dads?'

Dan nodded. 'My dad was pretty nondescript from what little I know of him. He died when I was very young. Mum married Donald when I was about two or so and Drew was born shortly afterwards. She couldn't believe she'd landed herself such a great catch, bragged constantly to her friends about how her new husband was an outstanding citizen and had been awarded an MBE for his services to charity. Not to mention the fact that he was a policeman.' He looked into his mug for a second.

'Unfortunately, it was a classic case of charity definitely *not* beginning at home.'

Sarah felt a shiver run the length of her spine. 'He was abusive?' When she'd married Drew, she'd thought she'd known him so well. Yet he'd never mentioned anything like this. In fact, despite his father's reputation in the town, her husband had barely talked about Donald.

Another nod. 'Mum ran around after him as if she were a servant. And as Drew grew older, of course, he began to copy the behaviour he was seeing. His father was his hero, and it wasn't long before he was treating Mum the same way Donald did. I couldn't bear it sometimes. I felt so guilty for not sticking up for her more often. I was older than Drew, I could have stopped it, but every time I tried, I'd just get the shit beaten out of me. As I grew up, the only thing that kept me sane was the thought that I'd get out of there one day. That I could go to uni and get a job and then I'd never have to go back to that house ever again.'

The few times Drew had spoken to Sarah about his brother, it had been to belittle Dan for choosing to work as a teacher. *Long hours and crap pay*, he'd said. *He should've known better*.

Her mum spoke again. 'Did no one suspect? That this was going on? Teachers? Neighbours?'

Dan shook his head. 'If they did, they never did anything about it.' He took a sip of his drink. 'You both must have heard how everyone talks about Donald Allison. You probably heard it at Dylan's christening. All his old cronies still sucking up to him, even now he's six feet under. He was everyone's favourite local councillor, a man of the people. No one would dare cross him. If they did, they'd probably have lost their business, or suddenly found their reputation in tatters, some rumour about child pornography or cocaine addiction seeming to come from nowhere.'

'He'd have done that?' Sarah was shocked, although part of her knew she shouldn't be. 'Lied about them to protect himself?'

'He would and he did. Believe me, some of the stories I heard would shock you. He and Mum tried to hide it, but I knew what was going on. Donald Allison was as feared as he was respected.'

Like Drew, Sarah thought.

Her mum got up again to collect her own drink. 'No wonder he's been let off so easily.' She came back to the table with a mug and a plate of biscuits. 'I just wish you'd told us sooner, sweetheart. Not put up with it for so long. Your dad and I suspected that something wasn't right, but we had no idea that things had gone so far. How much you were really suffering. I feel so awful. We should have done something to help you long before it got to this stage. What I wouldn't do if I got my hands on that . . .'

'Don't get upset, Mum.'

When Sarah had first told her parents exactly what had been going on, she'd felt guilty. As if their pained expressions were her fault. As if she'd chosen for this to happen. She wished she could turn back the clock. Make her time with her husband disappear. But then she wouldn't have Dylan. Her complicated feelings about her marriage exhausted her.

She looked back at Dan. 'When I saw you in the café, you told me Drew had done this before. Was it an ex-girlfriend? Was he as bad with her as he's been with me?'

Dan nodded slowly, as if thinking about how much to reveal. 'It was pretty bad. I knew he wasn't treating Hannah right and I tried to persuade him to end the relationship, to get him to see what he was doing, but of course he didn't listen. She tried to leave a few times, but in the end, she always went back to him. I think she was scared of what would happen to her if she didn't.'

'What happened?'

'Well . . .'

Sarah looked up as her dad came into the room.

'Hi, Dad, did Dylan go down for his nap okay?' Ever since she'd come home, Dylan had followed his grandfather around in the same way that Boswell followed her. She wondered if he missed having his father around, despite the fact that Drew had shown little affection towards his son in the nine months since his birth.

Her dad nodded. 'Fine. No problem.' He turned as he heard a loud knock at the door. 'I'll get that.'

Sarah felt her skin bristle. Every time someone came to the door – the postman, a delivery driver, one of Mum's friends – she felt as if she were waiting with bated breath to see who it was on the other side. She never dared answer it herself, not unless she was completely sure who was knocking. She was convinced that one day she'd open it and that her husband would be standing on the step, smirking at her. Had Drew actually got the message that their relationship was over? That he should stay away? Or was he simply biding his time before he made his next move?

Her dad came back into the kitchen. 'It's Keeley.'

'Oh . . .' Sarah stood. 'Is she coming in?'

'She seemed reluctant to. Said she just wanted to see you for a minute.'

'Okay.'

Sarah went through the hallway, feeling a little guilty that she hadn't seen or spoken to Keeley since her friend had last called at the flat. With everything going on – trying, and failing, to bring charges against Drew, attempting to make a start in rebuilding her life – she hadn't even had chance to let Keeley know she was back at her parents' house. She presumed someone else must have seen her in the area and passed the news on.

She pulled the door open wider. 'Hi, come on in.' It would be so much easier to chat now that Drew wasn't lurking in the background. Watching her. Judging her. Was there a chance that she could actually get back to having a normal life from now on?

Keeley shook her head. 'I'm not staying, thanks. I heard you were back here and I just wanted to check you were okay. Is it true? Have you actually split up with Drew? You seemed so happy.'

Sarah sighed. 'It's a long story.'

'I couldn't believe it when I heard. Last time I saw you, you said everything was fine. Never better.'

'I know. It's just . . . it's been *a lot* to take in. Sorry that you had to find out from someone else.'

Keeley hesitated. 'It was Drew himself who told me, actually. I saw him, in town, a week or so ago.'

'You spoke to him?' Sarah straightened.

'Only briefly. He was in the frozen food shop, buying a ready meal for one. That's when I suspected something might not be right. I know how much you loved cooking for him. I asked him if everything was okay, if you and Dylan were okay, as I hadn't seen you for a while, and he said you'd left. Moved out. He seemed awfully sad.'

Sarah tried to quell her anger. Trust Drew to be making out that *he* was the victim. Again. Exhausted from all the discussions she'd had to have about her marriage over the past few weeks – with her parents, Dan, the police and family solicitor – she didn't want to go through it all again now. She could explain the details to Keeley later. When she was feeling stronger, when she finally got to spend some quality time with her friend, like they used to. She changed the subject. 'How's the wedding plans going? Sorry I haven't been around much to help. I feel dreadful that I've let you down.'

Keeley shrugged. 'Don't worry. We're getting there. Just a few things to finalise.'

'I could help if you like. I'm sure Mum and Dad would look after Dylan.'

Keeley's expression seemed to brighten. Obviously, she'd missed Sarah as much as Sarah had missed her. 'That would be great.' She seemed to relax, suddenly looking like the best friend she'd always been, no longer awkward or uncomfortable. 'Listen, while I'm here, Alice and I have organised a bit of a night out with the girls, in a couple of weeks. I wasn't going to mention it because, well . . . Anyway, would you like to come?'

Sarah hesitated. Her first thought, still, was that Drew wouldn't approve. That he wouldn't like her dressing up, putting on heels, doing her hair, for anyone other than him. That he'd presume she had an ulterior motive for wanting to be out on the town on her own, was a terrible mother, abandoning her child, just so she could have a good time. Even now, she couldn't get away from worrying about what he would say and think. What he would do to her if she did something he saw as wrong. Would she ever feel any differently? She tried to smile. 'Sure, I'd love to.' She could always cancel, if she felt uncomfortable, she thought. Say Dylan needed her. Keeley would understand.

'Great, I'll text you the details.'

'Oh, ring Mum's landline.' Sarah didn't have her phone. As soon as she'd left the flat, she'd smashed it up and thrown it into a skip, so her husband was no longer able to track her every move. She *hoped*. Her parents had said they'd get her a new one. She felt bad at having to rely on them, now she was a mother herself, supposedly responsible for her child, but she had little choice. She had no money of her own.

Keeley frowned. 'Okay, no problem. I'll speak to you soon.'

Sarah looked up and down the street before closing the door. As she stood with her back against it, she pictured her husband, in town, pondering over microwave meals, as if his world had come to an end. Feeling sorry for himself. Did he still not see how he'd brought this whole situation on himself? That things could have been very different?

She grimaced as Dan came out of the kitchen. 'I feel like I'm walking on eggshells, wondering when he's going to appear.'

He nodded. 'That's understandable.'

'Do you think it's over? That he's out of my life?'

Dan bobbed his head from side to side. 'Maybe, but . . .'

'But what?' Sarah stood straighter, anxiety making her stomach fizz. 'What was it you were going to say, in the kitchen, before Dad came in? About Drew's ex-girlfriend? The one you said he abused before me?'

Dan hesitated. He looked at the floor before looking back at Sarah. When he eventually spoke again, he seemed sad. 'I think maybe we need to arrange for you to meet her.'

Chapter 23

Claire now

I sit with my laptop on my knee and try to focus on what I'm doing. It's difficult to concentrate but I need to send out messages to check that my team are all where they're supposed to be, that they're all fed and watered and prepared for the busy night ahead. I glance up at the clock on the mantel: almost nine. On the TV, the news is still showing clips of the press conference. I should turn it off – that's what Guy would tell me to do if he were here – but I know already it's not something I'm going to do. I can't. At least I've muted the sound again, so I don't have to hear my daughter's name over and over.

The green icon flashes up on my screen as my first call comes in within minutes, the queue that's beginning to build already no doubt a sign of what's to come. I slip my headset over my ears.

'Hello, you're through to Claire at *Walk Me Home*. How can I help?'

'Hi, Claire, it's Beth.'

Beth is one of our most regular callers, her voice almost as familiar to me now as someone from my own family. The last time I spoke to her was maybe a fortnight ago, when she was walking home at close to three a.m. She's much earlier tonight.

'Hi, Beth. On your way home already? I thought your night would only just be starting.'

She sounds a little out of breath. 'Yeah, usually it would be, but something told me I should just cancel the rest of my jobs tonight and head home to relieve the babysitter. I don't fancy staying out. You know, with the weather being so bad and everything that's going on. There's just . . . an atmosphere that doesn't feel quite right.'

I clear my throat. Beth knows full well how connected I am to *everything that's going on*. She's read the interviews, the press releases. She knows exactly why I set up the helpline. 'I don't blame you. Do you need me to send out a pair of walkers?' I scan the laptop screen to see who's free.

'No, no. Don't worry. It's early yet so there's plenty of people around. I was just feeling a little unnerved, but I'm fine just talking on the phone, if you don't mind?'

'Of course I don't mind. That's what we're here for.'

'But there might be other women calling who need you more . . .'

'Beth,' I interrupt her. 'I'm here for you, and I'm happy to stay on the phone with you until you get home.'

She sighs. 'Thank you.'

'You're welcome. Now, tell me about that little boy of yours. Is he still doing well at school?' Over the past couple of years, I've got to know Beth quite well. Her pride in her son is obvious when she tells me how much Jasper has thrived since he started at one of the local primaries. In many ways, she reminds me of Sarah. My daughter would have been a great mum to Dylan. If only she'd had the chance.

'Oh, he's doing great. He's getting so tall now, Claire. He'll be bigger than me soon.' She pauses. 'I miss him, you know, when I'm out working. I feel so guilty at leaving him with someone else, even when all he's doing is watching some TV and then going to bed. Since his dad died, he gets left with sitters so much.'

160

The dilemma of working single mothers the world over. Even though my circumstances were very different – Guy able to work flexibly and my mother helping out – I remember having similar feelings when I went back to work after Sarah was born. Every minute away from her made me feel like more of a failure. And then, of course, later, I felt as if I'd failed her completely. As if, as her mother, I should've sensed much sooner than I did what was happening to her. 'You'll have to give him an extra big hug when you get home tonight.'

'I'll do that.'

'You're a great mother, Beth. Don't let anyone tell you any different.'

She chuckles. 'You've never even met me.'

'No, but I have a good instinct for people.' One that should have sounded a very loud alarm when I first met my daughter's future husband, I try not to think.

'I sleep with men for money, Claire. I'm no saint.'

Don't judge yourself too harshly, I think. *None of us are saints.* I remember an interview I did with one of the more popular women's magazines, a few months after I founded the helpline. When the article came out, the headline had described me as *inspirational*. I'd been embarrassed by it at the time. If only they knew. 'You're doing your best, Beth. That's all you can do. All any of us can do. We're all just winging it really.'

'I suppose.' Beth hesitates again. 'Can I ask, Claire? Are you okay? I've seen the news and I was worried. About you and your grandson. Are you safe?'

I glance at the TV again. On the screen now, an outdoor reporter is standing in front of a wooded area not too far away, a thick yellow scarf wrapped around her neck. She's talking quickly, gesturing to the dark, tree-lined park behind her. The snow that's gathering on her hair is making it damp and frizzy. She holds out her microphone before talking to someone who seems to be a passer-by, a witness to something maybe. According to the subtitles, white words in a black box, there's been another sighting. A suspicious figure, dressed in dark clothing, has been seen lurking in the area. I look back at the laptop.

'I'm okay, Beth; don't worry.'

'It's just that you run this helpline, do so much for us women who are walking home by ourselves, but you're there, in your house, on your own, I presume.'

I look at the screen again. The studio presenter is now opening and closing his mouth before the image of a large weather map appears. Sheaths of white cover the whole country. 'Honestly, I'm fine. It's all in hand. Nothing to worry about.'

I wait as Beth approaches her house and lets herself in, saying goodnight once I know she's safely inside. On my screen, I can see that a queue of calls is waiting, despite it still being early. The news of Drew having been spotted near to town will be unwelcome.

I take three more calls: one from a girl who's been out since lunchtime and has decided to head home after being sick and the other two from women who have changed their minds about going out after seeing stories flash up on their social media channels about the escaped prisoner and, particularly, the reason behind his imprisonment. *In the meantime, my male colleagues get to enjoy themselves as usual,* one of them complains. *They don't need to worry too much about how they're going to get home.* I can't help thinking she's right.

Taking advantage of a gap between calls, I pull off my headset and pick up my mobile. I click on Guy's name.

He answers quickly. 'Hey.'

'All okay?'

'Yep, all fine. I've just read Dylan a story and put him down. Out like a light.'

'Did you see the press conference?'

'I did.' He hesitates. 'Not an easy watch.'

'No. Do you think there's anything in the rumours? About the other girlfriend?'

'I honestly have no idea.'

'Jane said they'll be moving us to a safe house if this doesn't end soon. Tomorrow morning at the latest.'

He sighs. 'I'll pack up some things.'

'Might be best. Have you locked the door? The windows?' I feel suddenly panicky. On the TV, the report has moved outdoors again. The same young woman in the yellow scarf is now talking to what appears to be another passer-by, an older woman who's talking about how *this type of thing* is rare in the area, how she's been reluctant to walk her dog since she heard the news.

'Yep. All done. You?'

'Uh-huh. You'll use the panic button, if you see anything?'

'You know I will. How was Dan?'

I remember how I'd stood in the hospital corridor and told Guy I was at Gilbert House. I didn't want him to know that I was potentially putting myself in danger. He always could tell when I was lying. 'He's in a pretty bad way.'

'I knew you wouldn't be able to resist going to see him. You do know Drew could have been there somewhere, watching you. Knowing damn well you'd go to the hospital to visit his brother.'

I think about the red Citroën and wonder again who might have been behind the wheel. 'Amy said the same thing. I couldn't just ignore him though. Hide away while he suffers. I feel so bad at how he was dragged into everything.'

'It's not your fault, Claire.'

'No, but as I said to him, it's not his either. It's none of ours.'

'Did you take Amy her hat?'

'I did.' I rub at my arms. It seems so cold tonight, even with the heating on. Even Boswell has now migrated to his fluffy bed near the radiator. 'With any luck, Drew Allison will freeze to death out there and we'll wake up to the news his frozen corpse has been found somewhere.'

'We should be so lucky.'

My turn to sigh. Guy's right. 'Maybe sleep right next to Dyl tonight?'

'Already on it. Grandad is camping out on the put-up bed about two inches from his.'

Despite the fact that Guy and I are now divorced, that we couldn't make our marriage work, I trust him implicitly. I know he'd fight anyone to the death to protect his grandson. Even Drew Allison. *Especially* Drew Allison. I look at the picture of my daughter again, studying her relaxed expression. I miss seeing her smile. Miss seeing her come down the stairs, dressed up to the nines, hair and nails done, like she always did when she was still at home. 'We're doing okay, aren't we? As grandparents? I mean, we're the only ones he has – Audrey has shown no interest, despite us offering to discuss access – but we're enough, aren't we?'

'I think we're doing brilliantly, Claire. And it's Audrey's loss. Stay safe.'

'You too.'

I end the call and glance at the clock again. Not far off tenthirty. The office parties and staff nights out will be well under way, the helpline probably clogged between now and the early hours. I put my headset back on and click on the green icon on my screen to accept another call. My stomach flips as I notice the number has been blocked, but I answer as normal.

'Hello, you're through to . . .'

'Claire! I'm so glad it's you who answered. I wouldn't want to have got through to any of those other *boring* phone operators of yours again.'

My heart thuds. I can barely hear her, but I know immediately that it's the same strange caller as last night. With so many things going on, I'd hoped not to hear from her anytime soon. 'What do you want?'

'Don't be like that, Claire. All I want is to talk to you about your favourite son-in-law. What if I were to tell you that he isn't very far away? And that he'd very much like to talk to you? How would you feel about that, eh?'

Her voice seems even more muffled than it was last night, her unusual accent even more pronounced.

'If you want me to listen to anything you have to say, I need you to speak more clearly.'

'Ah, Claire—' still muffled '—I'm sure when you speak to Drew himself, he'll speak as clearly as you want him to.'

My mouth is dry. The thought of speaking to Drew Allison again, either face to face or even over the phone, fills me with horror. It's as if he's the bogeyman, hiding under the bed, that Sarah used to sometimes talk about when she was a child. So evil, he's almost inhuman. Who is this person who's calling me? And what does she have to do with Drew? With *any* of this? 'Look, I don't know who you are or what you're trying to achieve, but I'm telling you now, I *do not* want anything to do with that man.'

My caller goes quiet for a few seconds. Outside, the sound of the helicopter seems to be closer than it was before, as if it's hovering directly over my house. I glance at the panic alarm again.

'Hmm, I must say, I'm surprised. I really thought you'd want to hear what he has to say about where your precious daughter is.'

I fight back tears. My *precious daughter*. How dare this woman refer to her that way.

I'm about to speak again when something catches my eye on the muted television screen. As I look up, I see three or four police cars silently come to a stop, their blue lights flashing as officers pile out of them and run into the darkness.

Chapter 24

Sarah before

Sarah almost felt as if she were looking in a mirror. *Obviously my husband has a type*, she thought, as she stared at the woman sitting across from her, Hannah's features so similar to her own they could have been sisters. They both wore their long, chestnut hair loose in waves. Like Sarah's, Hannah's eyes were brown. The only difference between them was that this woman wore little make-up and her clothes were drab. Her nails were bitten down to the quick and unpainted. Sarah wondered if she was looking at a potential future version of herself. What she might have looked like after Drew Allison had worn her completely into the ground. Made her someone she wasn't.

She watched as Hannah made herself comfortable on the wooden chair, hanging her bag behind her and propping up the walking stick she used against the table. That was another difference between them. When Sarah saw the woman she and Dan had come to meet walk through the door of the coffee shop, the same one that Drew had found out Sarah had been visiting when she was supposed to be at the park with Dylan, she'd noticed immediately that Drew's ex-girlfriend was struggling with a profound limp.

She tried to smile. 'Thanks for coming.'

Hannah shrugged. She glanced around the room, her eyes flitting from one customer to another, seated at the tables around them, as if she were vetting them. 'Could I get some water, please?'

'Sure.' Dan stood. 'Coffee, Sarah?'

'Hot chocolate, please.' It was a luxury she'd never allowed herself when she was living with Drew – too much sugar, he'd always said – but now she craved it. Perhaps because it reminded her of her childhood, of the days before her life had turned into a nightmare. She and Keeley had used to make it after nights out or during the Christmas holidays, adding marshmallows and squirty cream.

She watched her brother-in-law move towards the counter before looking back at Hannah. 'I know it was a lot to ask, you coming to meet with us. I'm aware this can't be easy for you.'

Another shrug. Hannah glanced over her shoulder at the door. She was obviously very nervous. 'Dan and I used to get on quite well. In the beginning anyway. It's nice to see him again.'

'Did he explain to you why we asked you to come?'

Hannah nodded. 'He said that you're Drew's *wife . . .*' the word seemed to stick in her throat and she hesitated '. . . and that you recently decided to leave him.'

Sarah smiled as Dan came back with their drinks. The warmth of the mug, as she wrapped her hands around it, was comforting. 'I was just saying to Hannah how much we appreciate her coming.'

Dan nodded, looking across the table. 'I know this isn't the easiest subject for you to talk about, Hann.'

'Being in an abusive relationship isn't something you get over easily.' Hannah touched the glass in front of her but didn't drink.

Sarah swallowed. The word *abusive* still sounded strange to her. The idea that she herself had been in such a relationship was difficult enough to comprehend, but hearing someone else say they'd also been abused by the same man made her feel as if she'd been hit by a freight train. What had she expected? That

Drew's ex was going to say she'd been perfectly happy with him? None of them would be here if that were the case. 'How long were you together?'

'Almost a couple of years. We met at work. I was part of the admin team at his gym. He sent a bouquet of flowers to my desk every day for a month until I agreed to go out with him. Apparently, he'd done the same to the girlfriend before me. She'd left without giving notice before I started.'

Sarah thought about all the gifts her husband had sent to her when they first met. She'd thought she was so special. That Drew was treating her the way he was because she was *the one*. Just one of many, it seemed now. 'And how was it when you did eventually agree to go out with him?'

'Oh, it was great.' Hannah chuckled softly. 'At first. Drew was the perfect gentleman. He couldn't have been more charming. He paid for everything, picked me up at the doorstep and took me home, whenever we went out. Opened doors for me, the lot. It was like going out with the central character of a rom-com.'

Sarah sighed. 'He was the same with me.'

Dan leant forward in his seat. 'I seem to remember sensing that things had changed between you maybe about six months in? Am I right?'

Hannah nodded. 'It could have been around then when he started treating me differently, but I think there were red flags from day one, to be honest. I just chose not to see them, mainly because I was enjoying his attention. My fault, I guess.'

Sarah tried not to show her anger. Even now, Hannah seemed to be blaming herself for Drew's behaviour. It wasn't her fault. That was what men like him did to women. Made them question their own judgement. 'What kind of red flags?'

'Well . . .' Hannah looked behind her at the door again. She put her hand on her walking stick, resting it on top, as if she were preparing herself to flee. 'For example, on our first date, he chose what I ate under the guise of recommending a dish he'd had before, saying I'd love it and that he didn't want me to miss out. He also said it had fewer calories than the rest of the menu. That was a big thing for him, getting me to eat the foods he thought I should. I just thought he was being considerate. I'd never had a man take much interest in what I ate before.'

Sarah nodded. Like herself, Hannah was slightly built. She wondered if, also like herself, she'd been fuller-figured before she met Drew. Had he demanded she follow the same strict regime? No snacks? No treats?

'Also, after we'd been seeing each other for a few weeks, I noticed that, whenever he complimented me on my clothes, it was only on certain outfits. When I wore other things, he wouldn't say anything. Not a word. So, of course, I then began to automatically wear the outfits he'd complimented, even if I didn't feel comfortable in them. Which I didn't always.'

Dan's tone was gentle. 'And after that? What happened?'

'Oh, it got much worse after that, believe me.' Hannah shifted in her seat. She picked up her stick before turning to scrabble behind her for her bag. 'Look, I've said too much already. I'm really not sure I should be here, to be honest. If Drew ever found out I'd spoken to you . . .'

'Wait.' Sarah put a hand across the table but stopped short of touching Hannah's arm. The woman was nervous enough as it was. 'Don't go, not yet. I know how hard this is for you. I know what you've been through.'

Hannah raised an eyebrow. 'Do you?'

Sarah looked her in the eye. 'I do. I know.'

'Then you have some idea of what he'll do to me if he were to find out I was talking about him. Stirring up trouble, especially with *his wife*.'

Sarah glanced at Dan. Hannah seemed to be terrified, on edge from the minute she'd walked in. It was understandable that she'd be worried about Drew finding out she'd interfered – Sarah would probably feel the same herself – but it seemed strange for her husband's ex to be quite so scared. Surely her own relationship with him was behind her now? Hannah had moved on. Hadn't she? She looked back across the table. 'I can see that you keep looking at the door. You aren't still worried about Drew coming in, are you? After all this time? Because I haven't seen him since . . .'

Hannah's eyes widened. 'Are you kidding me?' She looked at Dan. 'You didn't tell her?'

Dan's face reddened. 'I didn't want to scare her. She's been through enough already.'

'And *I* haven't, I take it?'

'That's not what I said, Hann.'

Sarah looked from one to the other. She could sense that the few other customers in the café were watching them now, noting the sharp tone in Hannah's voice. She was glad she'd left Dylan with her parents, instead of bringing him with her, sure her son would have picked up on the tension. 'Tell me what?'

Hannah looked at her. 'What Dan hasn't told you is that I *tried* to leave Drew Allison many times, but I always ended up going back. Mostly because I was scared of what he'd do to me if I didn't.' She pushed her glass away, her water untouched. 'But when I left for the final time, everything went quiet. He didn't come to see me. Didn't pester me, didn't ask me to go back. I thought it really was over, that I'd escaped.'

'But that's good . . .'

'I haven't finished.' Hannah held up a hand. 'After about two months, just when I thought I finally really was safe, that I could get on with my life, Drew suddenly turned up at the friend's house where I was staying. When I opened the door, no longer on guard and not expecting it to be him, he forced his way in and beat the shit out of me, to the point that I ended up in hospital. My leg was broken so badly, it still doesn't work now.' She touched the stick beside her again, as if to make sure it was still there. 'I'm really not so keen on the thought of that happening again, Sarah. And it will if he finds out I've got myself involved with his wife's *problems*.'

Sarah couldn't speak. She'd presumed Hannah had some kind of disability. Arthritis or something similar. She tried to gather herself. '*Drew* did that to you? Your leg?'

'Yes.' Hannah nodded. '*Your husband* did that to me.'

'I'm so sorry.'

'You may think I got away from Drew Allison, but I'm telling you now . . .' Hannah shook her head '. . . I didn't get away at all. That man destroyed my life. Even now, I'm in constant pain because of what he did to me. I can't walk far. I can only work part-time. I'm probably going to lose my job because I keep having to have time off. I don't sleep or eat. I barely go out anywhere. That's why I'm *still worried*, as you so aptly put it.'

Sarah didn't know what to say.

'And you know what? Even now, it isn't over. Every so often, when I think I might just be beginning to get some normality back, Drew turns up again.'

Sarah frowned. 'What do you mean?'

'I mean, I'll arrive home and he'll be there, watching me from across the street.'

'He's *stalking* you?'

'Call it what you like. No matter how many times I move, he always finds me. Or I'll go into a supermarket and he'll just happen to be shopping there, or having a coffee near where I work. And you wonder why I'm constantly looking over my shoulder.' Hannah took a breath. She looked exhausted.

Dan shook his head. 'I'm so sorry, Hann. I didn't realise it was still happening. Can't you speak to the police?'

'And have him say I'm hysterical, like he always used to? That I'm the one following *him*?' Hannah's lip curled. 'Oh, your brother doesn't make it obvious of course. He's far too clever to make his sporadic appearances in my life look like anything but a coincidence, but he's always there. He probably always will be. Even if I moved to another town, another *country*, I have no doubt he'd still turn up at some point.'

Sarah remembered how he'd told the police officer who came to the flat door about *her hormones*. She had a sudden thought. 'What about the other girl, the one you mentioned had gone out with Drew before you? Who left the gym? Couldn't she back you up? If Drew was the same with her, then she could be able to help both of us. Surely the more evidence . . .?'

Hannah reached behind her for her bag again, this time bringing it forward and putting her weight on her stick with her other hand. She pulled herself up slightly awkwardly, waving Dan away as he stood to help. 'I really do have to go.'

Sarah stood as well. 'Did I say something wrong?'

Hannah looked at her for a few seconds. Suddenly, her expression softened. 'Look, I know why you married Drew. I probably would have as well if he'd asked me when we first got together. I don't blame you in the slightest for falling for him and now finding yourself where you are. But, even now, when you know enough about him to want him out of your life, when you feel like you might have got away, I really don't think you have the slightest idea what you've let yourself in for.'

Sarah braced herself. She had a feeling she didn't want to hear what Hannah was going to say next.

'That girl you're asking about? The one before me? From what I've heard, she had a lot of issues. She had no family, not many friends, no one who really cared what happened to her. And when Drew Allison had had enough of her . . .' she hesitated '. . . it seemed that no one missed her when she disappeared off the face of the earth.'

Sarah felt her hot chocolate threatening to come back up as she watched Drew's ex hobble to the door and leave.

Chapter 25

Claire now

I listen to the wind-tunnel-like sound over my headphones, wondering where my caller is. If she's outside, in the snow. Perhaps feeling cold and miserable, a scarf muffling her voice as she tries desperately to please the person who has instructed her to make this phone call and torment me by claiming she has information about my daughter.

I stare at the screen in front of me. The words that tell me she's blocked her number, as she always does.

I know who she is now; I've worked it out.

This woman, on the other end of the line, is the *female* prison guard who helped Drew Allison escape.

I think about what Guy told me, about his mother hearing, in one of her Facebook groups, that Drew had had some help on the inside. That someone had thought him reformed, worthy of another chance. Innocent, even. *Some bloke*, my ex-husband had said. It seems clear to me now, that person would most likely be a woman, rather than a man. Another victim of my son-in-law's persuasive charm. Another person who failed to see him as he really is.

I have another sudden thought.

'Was it you? Outside my house last night? Across the road?' I think about the figure I saw, slimmer than my son-in-law, less broad. I'd thought it could be a reporter, a woman, but never since had I thought it could be *this* woman. 'And in the garden?' The shadow, flitting back and forth, making the dog growl.

'Of course it was. I've been watching you, Claire. No point in calling the helpline if you weren't on duty. Although, I should have known. You don't seem to have had much of a life for a while now. No husband, no friends. No socialising. It wasn't only your daughter you lost that night, was it?'

I ignore the question. 'And in the red car? At the park yesterday? Was that you as well?' I'd been so sure that this time it really was a journalist, watching me and my grandson.

'Yep, me again.' Her voice fades as it has done every time, the connection seeming worse than ever. 'Guilty as charged. Drew wanted a picture of his son. He wanted to know if you were looking after Dylan properly. I managed to get a quick snap before you whisked him away.'

'And at the hospital? Today?'

'He wanted me to check if his brother was still alive. To find out if the press was concealing how bad he was. The police officer at the door of his room put paid to me seeing for myself. We passed each other, you know, me and you. Me coming out as you were going in. You were absorbed in conversation on your phone. The ex-hubby, was it?'

I feel a surge of pure rage, knowing I was close to this woman without being aware that she was there. 'Why are you doing Drew's dirty work? He could have just called me himself if he wanted to talk to me.'

'Because he knew that as soon as you heard his voice, you would've hung up. And more than likely, you would've then called the police.'

She's right. If I'd accepted a helpline call and heard a man's voice, that would have been reason enough for me to be suspicious. If I'd then recognised the voice as belonging to the man who's my worst enemy, I'd have ended the call immediately, without listening to a single word more than I had to. 'Drew doesn't deserve so much as a second of my time.'

'He wants to talk to you, Claire.'

I take a breath and try to calm myself. I need to think about the best way to handle this situation. 'Wait. I don't want to talk about Drew, not yet. I want to talk about *you*. Seriously, why are you doing this? Why are you helping him?'

She sounds confused, uncertain for the first time since she began calling me. Her strange accent slips but only slightly, her voice still muted and distant. 'What do you mean?'

'Do you think he loves you?'

The line goes quiet again. Outside, the helicopter is still hovering, the whir of its blades seeming to be so close they're making the house vibrate. On the TV, the reporter with the yellow scarf has been replaced by a man in a raincoat, with a shirt and tie beneath it. He looks cold, his cheeks pink, his lips tinged blue, as he keeps his head low against the almost horizontal snow. Behind him, the lights on top of the police cars I saw earlier cast an eerie glow through the dark night. The blue flashes make the reporter's complexion even more pallid than it already is. Next to the cars, a large blue-and-yellow-checked van is parked at an angle.

The subtitles on the screen try to keep up with the reporter's words. An anonymous caller has reported spotting Drew Allison a short time ago, in the wooded area that's less than a mile from my house. Police and sniffer dogs are on his tail.

I try again. 'You know they're going to catch him, don't you? He's been spotted. There's a helicopter overhead. And if you're with him, that means they're soon going to catch up with you too.'

She laughs, the sound strange and tinny. 'And you think we're stupid enough to let that happen, Claire? That the so-called anonymous caller, who has just claimed to have spotted Drew, might *not* have been some innocent bystander? That it might be someone much, much more involved with what's happening?'

'You mean you . . .?'

'Nothing like a good old-fashioned tip-off to make the police go in completely the wrong direction, is there?'

I shake my head. Nothing has changed in the last three years. Drew still knows how to stay one step ahead. Changing the subject, I attempt again to make a connection with this woman. 'What's your name? You haven't told me.'

There's no reply, but I know she's listening.

'Look, I know you only rang the helpline because Drew wanted you to contact me. That it was the only way you could get hold of me.' I've changed my mobile number more times than I can remember. It's the only way to keep the press at bay. 'But *Walk Me Home* is here to help *all* vulnerable women, no matter what their circumstances. Women like *you*. Let me give you my mobile number and we can talk properly . . .'

I recite the number through the microphone.

The woman laughs again. '*Vulnerable*? Me? Don't think I don't know what you're doing, Claire, trying to get me on side. To make me feel as if you're offering me a *safe space*, as they like to say these days. Believe me, I am completely in control here. I know exactly what I'm doing.'

'Do you? Or is Drew just pulling your strings, like he has with so many other women before you?' I wonder if I'm pushing her too far. If she'll just hang up.

'It's not like that.'

'Isn't it? Why? Because you think you're *different*? Because you think he feels the same way about you as you do about him? Drew Allison doesn't love anyone apart from himself – you know that, don't you? Once he's used and abused you, he'll drop you like a dirty tissue.'

'You have no idea what you're . . .'

'I know exactly what I'm talking about!' The dog jumps as

176

I raise my voice. 'I saw what my daughter went through. How he changed her, destroyed her. He'll do exactly the same to you. You're a fool if you think otherwise.'

I almost end the call myself, not wanting to hear her answer. I'm no longer interested in how she'll insist on defending that man. I'm angry. Angry with this woman for letting herself be duped in the same way the others were before her. Angry with myself for not being able to warn Sarah before she was drawn too far in. Most of all, I'm angry with Drew Allison for what he did and what he continues to do.

Instead, I take deep breaths as I wait for her to speak again.

She clears her throat. Her words, when she speaks, are no clearer than they were before. 'Look, Claire, as I've tried to tell you, Drew wants to talk to you about where Sarah is. He's not after causing trouble. He says he's prepared to discuss the situation calmly and reasonably. To come to an arrangement. And once you've negotiated, once he's got what he wants, he's prepared to let you and your ex-husband get on with your lives. Forever. He'll leave the area and never come back. That's a promise.'

'What *does* he want?'

She hesitates. 'That's for him to tell you. Not me. But he does have one condition. You don't involve the police. You don't even tell them we've contacted you. He's adamant there'll be no involvement from the authorities at all. You sort this out between the two of you or not at all.'

I look at the picture of my daughter on the mantelpiece, at the TV screen, at the panic alarm that I could press at any time and have the police here within minutes. I listen to the sound of the helicopter overhead as I look back at my laptop screen. I have no idea where this woman is, where she's calling from. Would a tech team be able to locate her if they were here? I don't know.

Eventually, I speak into the microphone, gritting my teeth.

'Tell Drew Allison to go fuck himself.'

I end the call and rip my headset off.

Chapter 26

Sarah before

It had been a long time since Sarah had been anywhere socially. When she was with Drew, they only ever went out as a couple, for a meal, or to the cinema on the odd occasion. Since Dylan was born, they hadn't been anywhere at all. Drew had simply stopped suggesting it, despite the fact they had numerous family members and friends who'd have been more than happy to babysit. Once, when the baby was just three or four days old, her husband had left her alone and gone to a work event. Sarah hadn't minded at the time, not really, but he hadn't come home until the morning. He'd refused to tell her where he'd been or what had kept him out all night. Perhaps he'd been stalking Hannah. Or some other woman. Who knew?

Sometimes, she'd wondered if Drew had been faithful to her. In the early days of her marriage, Sarah had been sure there was no one else, but later, after Drew had shown his true nature, after he'd started hurting her, her husband had become secretive. Sometimes, his phone would ring and he'd pause before he answered it. Or he'd make the caller wait until he'd gone into the small office at the far end of the flat and shut the door. She'd tried to tell herself the calls were simply work-related, that he needed privacy, away from Dylan's cries, to talk properly. Deep down, though, Sarah knew. She knew that her husband was talking to other women, no doubt more than one. And now, after what his ex-girlfriend had told her in the coffee shop, about him turning up outside her house, her workplace, she knew it was unlikely her husband had stuck to his wedding vows, even before he became abusive.

Now, she attempted to relax as she looked around the club she was in. She was certainly out of her comfort zone. The main room was modern and bright, the pink neon lights that decorated the walls almost blinding her, and it was packed. There were people everywhere: filling the dance floor; spilling from its edges; crowding around the bar. A large part of Sarah just wanted to be back at her parents' house with Dylan. To watch her son and make sure he was safe. But it had been so long since she'd spent any time with her friends. Now that she wasn't with Drew, she needed to try and make more of an effort. To try and be herself again. Or as close to that person as she could get.

Her parents had encouraged her to come on the night out Keeley had invited her to.

'Go, sweetheart, enjoy yourself,' her mum had said. 'Show that husband of yours that you're moving on. Dylan will be perfectly all right with us, and you can just call Dad when you want picking up.'

In the end, she'd given in. A night out was probably what she needed and she was sure her mum was right that Dylan would be fine. Despite what Hannah had said about Drew's insistent nature, since Sarah had left the flat, he hadn't shown any interest in seeing his son. Or in asking her to reconsider her decision. He'd stayed away from them both.

Keeley leant towards her and spoke into her ear. She had to talk loudly to make herself heard above the music. 'Are you enjoying yourself?'

Sarah nodded. She was trying to, anyway. The two of them were standing with their backs to the bar, drinks in hand. She hadn't drunk alcohol since the baby was born and her head was spinning a little; the cocktail her friend had ordered for her was a bit stronger than she would have liked. Drew hadn't approved of drinking in excess, only ever having a glass of wine with dinner or an expensive whisky on the odd occasion. He thought women who went out binge-drinking with their friends were the lowest of the low. Cheap. Asking for trouble. 'Thanks for inviting me.'

Keeley smiled. 'I'm so glad you came. It's been ages since we had any fun together.'

A long time since Sarah had had any fun at all. 'Me too.'

'See that guy over there?' Keeley gestured towards a group of men near the dance floor. 'The one with the beard? I think he has his eye on you.'

Sarah looked over. The thought of anyone watching her suddenly made her feel panicky. She was officially still married, and even though she'd walked out on her husband, would hopefully be able to divorce him eventually, she had no desire to meet anyone else. Not yet. She'd been through too much. She needed to spend some time healing. Building her confidence back up so she could properly go out into the world again. She shook her head. 'I'm not interested.'

'Are you sure?' Keeley nudged her with her elbow. 'He's cute.'

'I'm sure.' All she wanted was to live a quiet life with her son.

'Okay.' Her friend changed the subject. 'So, how about me and you go shopping this week? You can help me pick out my dress for the wedding. Alice has already got hers, but I need some serious help. You know I can't do it on my own.'

Sarah smiled. 'I'd love to.' She was looking forward to Keeley and Alice's big day. She was sure she'd be feeling stronger by then, more settled. Perhaps she would finally be able to do something normal, enjoy herself instead of feeling anxious all the time. Worried she was doing something wrong. She straightened and put her drink on the bar. 'Just popping to the loo. Could you watch my bag?'

'Sure.'

She pushed her way through the crowd, feeling a little claustrophobic. No one seemed to care where their elbows hit as she passed. Sarah took a deep breath as she tried not to think about a time when a sharp dig into her ribs was part of her normal life. Her injuries had mostly healed now, the bruises gone, but she'd never forget the feeling of having another person cause her the physical hurt her husband had. She was trying her best, *really* trying to be Sarah again, but deep down, she knew she'd never be quite the same.

As she went down a narrow set of stairs, the lighting inadequate and the toilets seeming to be very far away, she wondered what Hannah had been like in her previous life, prior to getting involved with Drew. Her husband's ex had been on her mind a lot lately. She and Dan had got on when they first met, Hannah had said in the coffee shop. Had she been more friendly then? More sociable and outgoing, before her experience of being abused, controlled, beaten, had caused her to become bitter and resentful? Sarah suspected that was the case. She hoped she didn't end up the same. Isolated and withdrawn.

She reached the corridor at the bottom of the stairs, relieved to see there wasn't a queue leading to the bathroom door. She'd decided that, once she got back upstairs, she was going to down her drink and make more of an effort to get into the spirit of the night. The DJ had already played some of her favourite songs and she didn't want to waste the time she'd spent getting ready – topping up her tan, choosing an outfit – standing around at the edge of the crowd. She was going to have a dance. Maybe she would even flirt a little with the guy that Keeley said was eyeing her up. That wouldn't do any harm, would it? She didn't want to take things any further but just getting used to chatting to people again would be nice.

As she rounded a dark corner, heading towards the ladies' room, Sarah smiled to herself at the thought of the nice time to come.

Then she jumped as a tall figure suddenly stepped out of the shadows and loomed over her.

'Babe! Fancy seeing you here. Didn't take you long to completely forget about me and come out on the lash with your slutty friends, did it? Hoping some hot guy will chat you up, are you? Don't think I haven't been watching you, checking out all the available talent.'

Sarah gasped. Her hands shook as she immediately scrabbled at her right and left side for her bag, tears threatening as she remembered she'd left it upstairs with Keeley. Her new phone, the one her parents had bought her after she'd told them Drew had used her old one to track her movements, was inside it, tucked securely in the zip pocket. How could she have been so stupid? She should have known that Drew being quiet, staying away from her and Dylan, was all some kind of ploy. That he would turn up eventually, that he would in no way put up with her trying to have a life without him. She should have listened to Hannah. Should have seen it coming. *What an idiot.*

She stuck out her chin, trying to hide her fear. 'Leave me alone, Drew. We're over.'

He put a hand to his chest in mock offence. 'Oh, Sarah, I'm hurt. That's not very nice now, is it? After everything I did for you. All those pressies I gave you when we first met, all those fancy restaurants I took you to, the meals I paid for . . .'

Sarah nodded. 'The slaps you gave me, the jabs in the stomach, the punches, the hairs you pulled from my head . . .' She shouldn't be goading him; she knew that. She would just end up making the situation worse. She was terrified, her whole body shivering, but part of her was also so angry with him for what he'd done, how he still made her feel. With herself for what she'd allowed to happen. Why did she ever let this man into her life?

'Ah, you're exaggerating.' Drew waved her away. 'You're a big girl, Sarah, you can take it. Too spoilt by Mummy and Daddy, that's your problem. Just like that brat of ours is going to be, if he stays with his *devoted* grandparents for much longer.'

Sarah didn't know what to do. She desperately needed the loo now but there was no way she was going to push past Drew to get to the bathroom. She was sure he'd make her sorry if she tried. 'Leave Dylan out of this. He's just a little boy. He's your *son*.'

He scoffed. 'Except you wouldn't think that at the minute, would you? Not one attempt to get in contact? To offer me some time with him? Anyone would think I was a bad influence.'

Sarah began to turn away, thinking about the way Hannah hobbled out of the café after they met up; her bad leg; the stick Drew's ex would probably have to use for the rest of her life. She needed to get out of here. Get away. Find another toilet, or wait until she could get home. There was no point in standing here and trying to reason with Drew. She needed to forget the night out and go upstairs to find her phone. To call her dad and get him to come for her as quickly as he could.

'I'll take him off you, you know.'

She stopped, barely able to breathe. Despite pretending to herself, all these weeks, that she was safe, part of her had known all along that this was coming. That this was what he'd threaten her with, sooner or later. When he was ready.

'I'll apply for full custody, and I'll get it. You know I will. I'll do everything in my power to ruin your and your family's reputation, just like my father did to his enemies. I'll make you look as if you're not fit to take care of a child. As if you never should've been allowed to conceive in the first place. I'll win, and I'll take Dylan and, who knows? Maybe our son will turn out to be just as clumsy as his mother. Maybe it'll be his turn to have a few little *accidents*.'

Sarah stood for a few seconds, her back to her husband. As she'd done so many times before, she pictured herself going down one path or another. Turning back to Drew and telling him she'd fight him with every breath in her body, that he'd never take her son away from her.

Or giving in.

Eventually, she turned around. She was suddenly very tired. 'What do I have to do?'

Drew folded his arms and leant against the wall. 'That's the easy bit.'

Sarah waited; she knew what was coming.

'All you have to do, *darling*, is come back to where you're supposed to be. Be the wife I expected you to be when I first suggested we get married. When I took you on that rather expensive holiday to Las Vegas. Not that difficult, is it? But if you don't, if you insist on choosing your parents over your husband, prefer partying with your waste-of-space pals, then I'll have no choice. I'll have to take Dylan instead. And who knows if he'll be as strong as his mother? If he'll ever grow from the boy he is into a strong and healthy young man?' He shrugged.

Sarah swallowed down bile. She stared at this man in front of her. The one she once thought she'd loved. Who she thought was perfect for her. How could she have been so blind? So stupid as to think their marriage would work. That she could ever get away from him now. She stood for a moment, trying not to think about what lay ahead. What she'd be committing herself to if she did what Drew wanted. This was no empty threat. If she didn't go back to him, he would make her suffer unbearably. And he'd do it by hurting Dylan. Did she really have any choice?

She turned as she heard a voice behind her.

'Everything okay down here? Thought I was going to have to send a search party.' Keeley frowned as she looked from Sarah to Drew.

Drew waved her away. His voice was overly loud in the small space. 'Oh, Sarah and I were just catching up. She was just telling me how she's not really enjoying herself tonight. This isn't really her thing, you know. My wife is much more of a quiet-night-in kind of girl.'

'I thought you were having a nice time.'

Sarah looked back at her friend. 'I was.' She turned to face her husband again, her voice barely a whisper this time. 'You win. I'll be home first thing in the morning.'

Not wanting to see the look of satisfaction on his face, she quickly moved away, heading past Keeley and towards the stairs.

Chapter 27

Claire now

I pace the living room, back and forth, Boswell watching me, curious as to why I'm not on the sofa, answering calls as I usually am at this time on a Saturday. The mug of fresh coffee I've made is warm in my hands. I need the caffeine to wake me up. To help me think.

I walk to the front window and move the curtain to one side, creating a gap just big enough for me to look out. It's snowing heavily now and, as I predicted, the journalists who were hanging around earlier seem to have been driven away by the conditions. The front garden is covered by a cushiony layer of white. The leaves of the few small trees and bushes Guy planted when we moved in droop under the weight of the flakes. Glancing across the road, I half-expect to see a figure standing there again, like I did last night. Not Drew or a journalist, as I thought before, but my son-in-law's accomplice. The latest in a long line of women who have fallen for his false promises. She wasn't just at the front of the house, but in the back as well, at the park, at the hospital, watching me. I let the curtain drop as I see the police patrol car come past again, sleet splashing up from its wheels.

I could just go out, I think. Flag them down and let them know what's happened. Or contact Jane Fellows and tell her about the calls I've been receiving. She'd be able to advise me. She'd know exactly how to handle this crazy situation and contacting her would be the right thing to do. It's exactly what I *should* do.

But I know already that it isn't what I'm going to do.

Instead, I head back towards the middle of the room and take a large gulp of coffee, thinking. The woman who is helping Drew told me that my son-in-law wants to talk to me, *calmly and reasonably*, she said, about where Sarah is. I think again about all the weeks that the police spent searching for my daughter, three years ago. All the places they dug and rooted through, the brambles and debris and trash they trawled through to try and find her. They found her clothes and wedding ring, they found her blood, they found the hacksaw they thought Drew had used on her. Yet, try as they might, they couldn't find her body. And now, it seems, Drew wants to talk to me about where she might be.

But he doesn't want the police involved. *He does have one condition*, the girl on the line said. And if I don't go along with his plan, I may never know what he has to say to me. Do I really want to? I wonder. Is it really a good idea to get involved in Drew's games again, after we've tried so hard to move on? No matter what my caller said, I'm certain that my son-in-law has no idea how to be *calm* and *reasonable*. He'll have no intention of treating us fairly; I simply don't believe it.

I look at the TV. The news headlines are still scrolling across the bottom of the screen, the sound still muted. The outdoor reporter looks freezing, as if he'd give anything to be at home with his family, where it's warm. Behind him, the police and their dogs are still out, searching the woodland that now looks like a scene from a Christmas card. According to my caller, they're searching in entirely the wrong place, the helicopter above simply wasting fuel as it hovers, directing its light to the ground to aid the search. I should have known Drew would find it easy enough to evade the law. That he'd have thought of every eventuality, known how best to avoid capture. How long did he plan it? I wonder. This escape. Months? Years? From the minute he stepped down from the dock as he was taken away to prison?

Telling my caller that Drew could go fuck himself was probably the worst mistake I could have made. Whenever anyone turns against him, stands up to him, my son-in-law immediately goes into defence mode. Now, as he did with my daughter so many times, he'll want to punish me. How he'll achieve that is something I don't yet know, but the idea frightens me. I have no idea what to do.

I jump as I hear my mobile ring and I suddenly remember how I'd given the woman on the phone my number. How I'd recited it, like a child doing times tables, while she didn't seem to take any notice. I was sure she hadn't even heard. Perhaps it's just Guy, I think, checking up on me again. Or Jane Fellows, wanting to give me an update. I sit on the sofa and look at the phone screen. My first instinct was right. The words *Private Number* fill the screen.

I don't give her a chance to speak. 'I'm sorry. I didn't mean what I said. I was angry.' I hate myself for apologising. Why should I?

'You may be too late, Claire. Drew isn't sure he wants to talk to you anymore.'

I squeeze my eyes closed. I'm almost doubling over with anxiety, my head to my knees as I try and hold the phone to my ear. Drew is playing with me again and I don't know how to deal with it. I make a decision. I won't be able to rest until I hear what he has to say. 'Tell me what I have to do.' As much I don't want to speak to my son-in-law, never want to set eyes on him again, I know now that I have to. I don't have a choice. 'I won't tell the police. I promise.'

The line goes quiet. Straightening, I stare at the television screen, at the out-of-studio report that now seems to have moved somewhere else. The same reporter is now standing in front of a row of houses that I recognise, not very far from my own in

Penketh. I know them because Guy and I have often talked about wanting to buy one when we retire. Once, when we were feeling spontaneous, we booked an appointment and went and looked around the show home, the two of us acting like newlyweds and pretending we had much more money than we had, that we could afford to live in such luxury. It was the kind of thing we used to do, my husband and I. In the days when we had fun. When our lives weren't ruled by grief and trauma.

The houses are now decorated for Christmas, a tree that's at least seven feet tall towering behind the news crew, its lights making the camera foggy. At its base, an illuminated reindeer appears to be grazing on the lawn. According to the subtitles, Drew has been spotted again, lurking in this street where the reporter is now, another anonymous phone call apparently sending the police from one site to another. If only they knew it was just another ploy. Another way of throwing them off the scent. Another game.

I speak into the phone. 'Are you still there?'

'I'm here, Claire. I'll have to speak to Drew, see what he says. I can't promise anything.' For a second, although still indistinct and talking strangely, she sounds almost human.

'You do know he's playing with us, don't you? *Both* of us.' I picture my son-in-law, smirking, like he was in the picture I tore apart. It was a feature of his face I came to hate very quickly. I suddenly have a thought. 'Is he there with you now? Let me speak to him.'

'I . . . I can't do that. He'll only speak face to face.'

I don't answer. So much for just one condition.

'I'll call you back soon. Make sure you answer. Your helpline might have to do without you for a little while.'

I'm left sitting with the phone to my ear, listening to silence. I put it down and am still for a few moments, feeling exhausted, bereft. After Drew went to prison, did I ever imagine that he'd come back into our lives like this? That I'd have to deal with him all over again? Was I naive to think, when he was led away from the courtroom, that was the last we'd see of him? Quite probably. I glance at the window, the curtain hanging slightly cock-eyed from where I looked out earlier. Perhaps the patrol car is due to pass by again soon. I could still do the exact opposite of what I've promised, I think. Could still contact the police, play Drew at his own game by being dishonest.

I pick up my phone again, a sudden urge overshadowing all others. It's not the police I'm going to call. Right now, I need familiarity, comfort. Family.

There's only one person I want to talk to.

Chapter 28

Sarah before

Sarah stirred. She'd tried her best not to fall asleep. In the few months she'd been back at the flat, she hadn't dared close her eyes for very long. She spent her nights in Dylan's room, curled up on a mattress on the floor near his cot, and her days feeling overtired and anxious. When she'd first come back, Drew had insisted she sleep in the same bed as him, that they were still man and wife and should behave as such, but Sarah had been determined. She'd agreed to come back for the sake of their son. Just because she was here, under the same roof as Drew, that didn't mean she had to pretend it was what she wanted.

She shifted her position, her back hurting from where her husband had pushed her against the kitchen counter that morning. He'd already been in a dreadful mood as soon as he got out of bed and the fact that she'd failed to prepare a high-protein lunch for him to take to work had only made him worse.

'You expect me to work all day without food?' he'd shouted at her.

Sarah didn't always play along these days. She wasn't as passive as she was before. Sometimes, she'd simply stick out her chin and admit that she hadn't done what Drew expected of her. That she hadn't cooked or cleaned or been the wife he wanted her to be. What more could he do to her? There was only one path she could take that was worse than the one she was on now, and she didn't want to think about that. Not while she had her son to protect.

She was so scared for Dylan. Scared, now he was getting older, that he'd see what his father was doing to her and presume, like Drew had when he'd seen his own father's behaviour, that that was how a marriage should work. What if her son continued the cycle? Took the lessons he was learning and applied them to his own relationships in the future? Sarah felt as if she couldn't win. She was here, back in her marriage, to save her son. Yet, leaving would be the best thing for him in many ways. How was she supposed to deal with that?

Her parents had done everything they could to persuade her not to come back. They'd make sure Drew was prosecuted, they'd said. Do everything they could to make the authorities listen, see what their son-in-law was doing to their daughter.

'Guy, stop her,' her mum had wailed, as Sarah had packed the few belongings she'd collected when she'd had to start afresh in her childhood home. 'Make her see sense.'

Her dad had looked lost, his eyes brimming with tears as he'd held Dylan in his arms, the grandson he'd only recently had a chance to get to know. 'Love, you don't have to do this. We can sort it. We're going to see our solicitor again. He'll advise us. You can divorce Drew and . . .'

'Please don't go,' her mum had interrupted. 'Think of Dylan.'

Sarah had winced at those words, at how much they'd hurt. She hadn't told her parents exactly what Drew had said to her when he'd turned up at the club the night before. Her son was *exactly* who she was thinking of.

She knew her parents meant well, that their distress was genuine, but talk of solicitors and legal help was a waste of time. She was sure of it. It was as if her husband had some kind of superpower. A way of hypnotising people into thinking he was something he wasn't. Something very drastic would have to happen for the authorities to take notice, for anyone to finally see the heroic Drew Allison as he really was. Something they couldn't turn a blind eye to. Couldn't turn away from and simply pretend it wasn't happening.

Dan had also asked her, *begged* her, to reconsider. She pictured his face as he tried to get her to think about the future she was creating for herself and Dylan if she went back.

'He'll never let you go – you know that, don't you? Not if you give in now. If you do this, he'll think he has power over you forever. There'll be no going back.'

Going against the wishes of everyone who loved her, who'd fought for her, had been the most difficult thing Sarah had ever done.

She felt her eyelids flutter as she fell into a dream, only vaguely aware of the soft snores of her son not too far away from her. She usually tried to sleep only in small bursts. A couple of hours, at the most, snatched when Drew was at work and Dylan was napping. During the night, she needed to be alert, just in case. She never knew what her husband might do next. She remembered what Keeley had said to her once, the night of the dinner party they'd hosted to celebrate the wedding: *He's a man who likes to surprise you, I'll give him that.*

Keeley didn't know how right she'd been. Her husband certainly was full of surprises. Even if most of them were unpleasant ones.

She began to dream, horrific images playing out before her eyes, as if on a reel. Images of things that had happened in real life since she'd come back, that haunted her as soon as she closed her eyes. Her husband standing over Dylan, pointing a finger and screaming: *I'm going to send you away and you'll never see your mum again. You are such a naughty boy.* Dylan hadn't understood the words, but he'd known the tone. Her son had cried until he was hoarse. When she'd first met Drew, Sarah had thought he was

193

the love of her life. Now look at her, sleeping in fits and starts on an uncomfortable mattress, falling into nightmares of what her son's father had said to him. Not trusting her husband enough to leave him alone with their child for even a second.

She turned to her other side, suddenly feeling uncomfortable. It was the dream, she told herself, in her half-asleep, half-awake state. Scaring her so much, filling her with so much horror, she had no choice but to quickly come back to consciousness. She tried to take a breath. The room she was in suddenly felt claustrophobic, as if there wasn't enough air. She was hot. What felt like pins and needles were travelling up her calves and into her thighs.

Sarah opened her eyes.

The mattress she was lying on was on fire.

She screamed, batting at the orange flames with her hands. Smoke licked at her throat, drying it instantly and making her feel as if she couldn't get enough oxygen. Looking up, she could see her husband standing over her, a smile on his face. In one hand, he held what looked like the bottle of white spirit they'd kept under the sink since they'd decorated Dylan's room. In the other, he had a box of matches.

'Drew, help me!' The words seemed reluctant to leave her mouth, coming out as little more than a croak.

Drew threw back his head and laughed.

Sarah tried to roll over, as she'd learnt to do at school during a health and safety lesson, hoping to smother the flames. She was panicking. Was this it? The moment when Drew took his abuse one step further? Were her parents and Dan right? Had she made a massive mistake in coming back? Had she made Dylan even more vulnerable?

Suddenly she gasped, feeling as if she were no longer burning, but drowning. Cold liquid filled her mouth and entered her lungs, making her cough. Sarah looked up at her husband.

Drew had thrown a bucket of water over her.

He stood and looked down at the mess, his lip curling as it

often did when he was in her presence. As if he was disgusted by what he saw. He sneered as he spoke. 'Guess you don't have any choice but to come and sleep with me now, do you?'

Sarah tried to get her breath. 'But, why? *Why?*'

Drew shook his head, as if he were disappointed in her. 'Do you really have to ask that question?' He picked up the bucket and the bottle of white spirit. 'Don't forget I can easily do the same to the brat if you don't do exactly what I ask of you.'

He left the room.

Sarah could barely move. Her legs felt numb and she was so cold she'd begun to shiver. The oversized T-shirt and leggings she wore at night – clothes that made her feel as unattractive as she could possibly make herself – were soaked through. She looked at the blackened room around her, wafts of steam rising from the ruined mattress, hot spots sizzling as they cooled. Through the open door, she could just see the smoke alarm, on the hallway ceiling, wires hanging from it, the battery missing. Drew had dismantled it.

Trying to rouse herself from her shocked state, she crawled across the floor towards her son's cot, terrified at what she might find. She didn't know how badly she was burnt, but what Sarah did know was that her body didn't seem to be quite working properly. She forced herself to keep moving, to pull herself up the wooden bars just high enough so she could see her baby.

Dylan was still asleep, just a slight rasp to his breathing, a small cough, telling her that the smoke from the fire had reached him before the water doused the flames. Sarah panted heavily as she looked at her son, as she examined him for any signs of damage. Drew had set fire to the bedroom *his own child* was sleeping in. How much lower could her husband actually sink? What more could he do to her, to Dylan, in order to prove the total control he had over his family?

She sank to the floor and closed her eyes. She'd thought that by coming back she'd appeased Drew. Made him see that she was willing to go along with what he wanted. Willing to play out the scenario he wanted her to: be his wife to the outside world; have no life of her own. But now she could see that was never going to be enough. *Nothing* would ever be enough. Drew was never going to be satisfied, no matter what anyone did to try and please him. He was always going to feel the need to punish the women in his life. To hurt them. It was ingrained in him.

Something needed to change.

Sarah looked at her baby in the cot. She looked at the dismantled smoke alarm, her blistered legs and arms, the burnt mattress behind her. She didn't know what yet, but she was certain she now had to do *something* to get away from her husband.

Chapter 29

Claire now

I bring my phone screen to life and click on a name. As I wait for the line to connect, I'm breathing heavily, feeling as if everything around me is, once again, spiralling out of control. Boswell stares at me from the hearth rug. He knows something isn't right. He can sense my distress. Above him, my daughter is also watching me, from her wedding picture, the Christmas lights reflected in the glass like stars. A tear springs to my eye as I remember how much her father loved her in that image. His gorgeous girl. He was so proud of her.

'Everything okay?'

I take a breath, suddenly scared to speak. 'Not really. He's been in touch. *Drew*. He wants to talk to me, face to face. He says he wants to discuss what happened. Talk about the fact that the police couldn't find the body.'

'You've spoken to him?'

'Not directly. Not yet. Through someone else . . .'

Silence for a few seconds. 'I'm on my way.'

I feel panic swell inside me. 'No, you mustn't. You have to stay safe. He could be waiting for you outside. Or he could be here.

Anywhere . . .' Risking my own life is one thing. Risking the lives of my family is altogether different.

'Don't argue. You can't deal with this on your own. We have to face it together.'

I end the call and sit for a moment, my limbs twitching. I don't know how to keep still. For years, Guy said he could always tell when I was worrying about something by the constant movement of my hands and feet. Now he'd be able to see that I'm in complete panic mode.

I pull the laptop onto my knee and quickly type out a message to the rest of the team, telling them they'll have to finish tonight's shift without me. That I'm suddenly not so well. I feel dreadful for letting them down on what is a massively busy night – I can see on my screen that the calls are coming in now as thick and fast as the snow is falling outside, all of our volunteer walkers assigned to jobs – but I know they'll understand. They, more than anyone, get what my family has been through. They know how I'll have been affected by the weekend's events. I send the message and shut the computer down. I'll make it up to the team later. If I'm able to.

I look at the clock. Almost eleven-thirty. The time when some people will be thinking about heading home from their nights out, booking taxis and arranging lifts, not wanting to face the bad weather unless they have no choice. The night Sarah walked home from Keeley's wedding, it had been cold then too. Her husband hadn't wanted her to go – of course he hadn't – but she'd persuaded him somehow. Told him, when she'd gone back to him, that it was the one condition she herself was going to insist on. That she'd missed her best friend's engagement party and other preparations, but that she wanted to go to her special day. That Guy and I would look after Dylan while Drew was at work, and that he wasn't to interfere or object.

I remember again the phone call she'd made to me, the last words we'd spoken, as mother and daughter, before the call was cut short and I'd had to telephone the police.

'Have you been okay?' I'd asked her. 'Since the fire? I still don't get how that happened, sweetheart. How you said you were cleaning with white spirit, and it just burst into flames. It doesn't make sense.'

'It was just an accident, Mum. I told you, I'm fine. All healed now.'

Of course I'd known she wasn't telling me the truth. That she hadn't been burnt *by accident*. That Drew had done something, caused her to be hurt. I'd wanted to kill him, there and then. Dash around to the flat before Sarah reached it and smash my fist into her husband's face. Make him feel the same pain he'd made her feel.

'He's killed her,' I'd screamed, later, after the police told me what had happened, in the mobile unit. What they *thought* had happened. What they'd found. 'He's done it. He's finally killed her.'

I rub a hand over my face and pick up my phone again. No doubt before long, Drew's accomplice is going to call me and tell me what I have to do. Give me the instructions I need to follow in order to speak to him. Part of me feels as if I'm in a dream. As if, any moment now, I'm going to wake up and find that Drew Allison is still behind bars. That none of the events of the past twenty-four hours have happened. That he can't reach us.

Boswell lets out a sharp bark as he hears a sudden noise at the back of the house, the slight shift of the back gate, the soft clunk of the bolt. I jump up, anxiety shooting through me like an electric current as I remember the shadows I saw yesterday, how Drew's accomplice told me she'd been watching me.

But this time, I know that the person sneaking through the dark alley and into my garden, the person hiding from any potential prying eyes – the police, the reporters, my mysterious caller – is someone I want to see. Someone who is on my side.

I go into the kitchen and keep the light off while I open the back door. Despite the circumstances, my heart sings when I see who is in the shadows on the other side.

'Amy, come in, quickly.' I look around the garden nervously, hoping all the neighbours are tucked up in bed, that there's no one watching, as I usher her in.

She steps over the threshold and hugs me briefly. As she pulls away, she touches the letter S at the base of my throat and smiles sadly.

'You don't have to call me *Amy* anymore, Mum. I think it's about time you went back to calling me Sarah again.'

Chapter 30

Sarah before

Sarah made her way up the dim concrete stairwell that led up to the flat, her high-heeled boots chafing her a little. They'd rubbed at her ankles, through the thick stockings she'd worn to the wedding to hide the scars on her legs. The scars from when her husband had caused her to be burnt. She'd mostly healed now, on the outside anyway. She'd had to tend to the burns herself, Drew having forbidden her from going to A&E again, or seeing a doctor. Instead, she'd applied calamine lotion every night and had inspected her wounds carefully in the hope they wouldn't become infected. On the inside, she knew she'd never quite get over what Drew had done the night he'd set fire to the mattress she was sleeping on. With her son so close by. That moment was the beginning of the end for her.

She smiled at the young man who was sheltering in the stairwell. She'd seen him at Gilbert House once or twice. His clothes were bedraggled and the guitar he took everywhere with him, that he sometimes used to entertain the other visitors, was usually slung over his back. Now, he held the instrument on his lap, strumming it quietly in respect of the late hour. Sarah bent and put some money in the black case that lay open on the step, in front of him. He nodded his thanks.

Her stomach churned as she reached the first-floor walkway, still holding her phone to her ear. Her mother was at the other end of the line, talking about Dylan, about how her dad would have picked her up if he hadn't been ill, how her husband should be making more of an effort. Sarah thought back to the party she'd just left. Keeley had looked beautiful, radiant in the dress Sarah had said she'd help her choose but then hadn't after she'd gone back to Drew. After the wedding, her friend had tried to persuade her not to walk home on her own. She'd be happy to pay for a taxi, she'd said, if Sarah didn't have enough money. Keeley was worried that the area around the flat wasn't well lit and that there were no security cameras. *What if Drew isn't home when you get there?* she'd asked.

Sarah had thanked her but had insisted she'd be fine. It wasn't far, she'd said. She was glad she'd got to go to the wedding. It would have been so easy to say she couldn't make it. To have given in to her husband's reluctance about her going anywhere without him. But she'd persisted and she was happy she'd made the effort to see her best friend.

One more time.

Before things changed.

She stopped for a few seconds, a couple of flats along from her own, number twenty-three. She could see that there was a light coming from the little window by the front door, a yellow puddle spilling onto the walkway. Someone was inside. She swallowed heavily. So many times, since she'd married Drew, she'd suffered inside that flat, both mentally and physically. Been beaten, strangled, burnt. Shouted at and goaded and mocked. Been frightened for both herself and her son. It had never felt like home, not once. Instead, it had become the place of her worst nightmares.

She tried to focus as her mum spoke to her at the other end of the line.

'Have you got your keys ready?'

Sarah began to slowly move forward, her legs feeling as if they had weights at the end of them. She felt her burns begin to tingle. 'Yep. At the door now.'

She stood and faced the flat. She didn't want to go in, knowing that once she stepped over that threshold, her life could change in ways she could never have imagined. She tried to picture her future. What might happen if she stayed with her husband until Dylan grew up, until she was an old lady, even less able to defend herself than she was now. She couldn't even begin to get an idea of what kind of life she might have. What kind of upbringing her son would experience. How he might blame her for his own trauma, for not doing something about her situation, for going back, for not leaving. For believing that everyone loved Drew Allison and that, no matter how hard she seemed to try, she couldn't get the help she needed.

She held the phone away from her, knowing her mother was still at the end of the line, and put her key in the door. She turned it slowly.

As the door to the flat opened in front of her, Sarah couldn't help but smile. She looked along the narrow hallway, all her doubts melting away. She was doing the right thing; she knew that now. This was her only way out.

Her father moved to one side and let her in.

Chapter 31

Dan before

Dan walked slightly ahead of his brother. The towpath that ran alongside the canal was quiet after dark. The dog walkers of the area mostly avoided it once the sun had gone down. The air was chilly, clear sky above perhaps threatening a frost in the morning. As he reached a small clearing, he adjusted the wool hat he was wearing, so it sat lower over his face, and pulled the collar of his jacket up before turning to look at his brother.

Drew rubbed his hands together and stamped his feet. 'Jeez, I have no idea why you've dragged me out here. It's fucking freezing. We could have just talked in the flat.'

Dan shrugged. 'I didn't want Sarah and Dylan to hear us.'

'They're not there.' Drew lowered himself to a small stone wall and sat. He pulled a pack of cigarettes from his pocket and waved it at Dan. 'Want one?'

Dan shook his head. He didn't even know his brother smoked. Drew certainly never did when he was around the girlfriends he wanted to impress so much, when he first started dating them. Most likely, he hadn't around Sarah. He'd always liked to appear to be someone he wasn't. At first, anyway. 'I thought you didn't like her going out without you.'

'I don't.' Drew lit a cigarette and shook out the match. He took a long drag. 'She should be at home where a woman belongs. But I figured it would do no harm just this once. It is her best friend's wedding, after all. As long as she doesn't get pissed and start falling all over the men there, as women always do.' He chuckled. 'I told her I was working so her parents would have to look after the brat. Didn't fancy spending the night listening to him whining for his *mummy*. Where I've *actually* been is in the pub, lining up the beers. Until you called, that is, and told me you wanted to meet me here at this godforsaken place. What's going on?'

Dan paced up and down the path. It was all he could to restrain himself. He'd never been a violent person, never been in a fight, not even when he was at school, but listening to his brother talk about women, about *Sarah*, the way he did was almost more than he could bear. He shoved his hands into his pockets. 'I need to talk to you, about the way you treat Sarah. Everything you've done to her. It needs to stop, Drew. You need to let her go.'

Drew scoffed. 'What? So you can have a go yourself? Don't think I haven't seen the way you look at her. At that ridiculous dinner party she insisted on throwing. At the even more ridiculous christening Mum wanted to have to celebrate the *brat's* arrival. Go for it, mate. I don't mind sharing. Can't see how anyone would want her though, now she's got all those scars. Ugly bitch.'

Dan turned towards his brother and yelled. 'Why did you marry her in the first place?' He lowered his voice; he didn't want to attract any attention. 'Why not walk away? If you didn't love her, why not just let her get on with her life?'

Drew shrugged. He put the cigarette to his mouth and inhaled before speaking again. 'Because I could. Simple as that. Everything I've done is because I could. Isn't that reason enough?'

'But she loved you! Does it not occur to you that you could have been happy with her? That you could have had a normal relationship, if you'd just made the effort?' He pointed a finger. 'You are *not* Donald, Drew. You didn't have to do what he did.'

'So I could have turned out like you? A drip who chooses to work with brats like mine all day?' Drew stood up and flicked his cigarette away. 'You know what, big brother, you and Sarah would suit each other. Go on, have a go at her. See if she'll let you get your leg over. I give you my permission. After all . . .' he spread his hands '. . . she's my property . . .'

Dan felt a rush of rage travel through his body. He ran towards his brother. Pulling his hands out of his pockets, he dug his nails into the side of Drew's face. He dragged his fingers back towards himself, leaving sharp gouges in his brother's cheek.

Drew's eyes widened. He put his hand to his cheek before looking at the blood on his own fingers. He laughed. 'Has anyone ever told you, you fight like a girl? What are you going to do next, tough guy? Hit me with your handbag?'

Dan waved him away. 'I give up. Do what you like, Drew, but don't be surprised if all this comes back to haunt you sooner than you think. You'll only have yourself to blame; remember that.' He shoved his hands in his pockets again and began to walk away, desperate to wash his brother's, his enemy's, skin from under his nails. 'I, for one, am done with you. Go home. Your wife will be back any minute now, probably ready for you to punish her for going out in the first place. I never want to see you again.'

He could hear Drew still chuckling as he walked along the path and back towards his car.

Chapter 32

Sarah before

She looked around the flat. Everything was ready, she hoped. Everything in place, so that they could go through with their plan. Would it go wrong? Perhaps it would, but at least she'd know she'd tried. Tried everything to put an end to her situation. To destroy the life that was destroying her.

It had taken a while for her idea to take shape. Sarah had thought long and hard about it after the incident with the fire. About what the eventual outcome might be; the pros and cons. In the end, she couldn't see what else she could do. She couldn't leave it to fate to decide what happened to her and Dylan. She had to take action, even if it led to disaster. Which it feasibly could.

The first person she'd told was Dan. She couldn't do this alone; she knew that. She'd called her brother-in-law when Drew was at work, asking him to meet her at the café where they'd first bumped into each other and later met with Hannah. She knew it was a risk. Drew could be watching her, tracking her again. He could even have paid someone to follow her – she wouldn't put anything past him – but it was a chance she was prepared to take.

Dan hadn't been too sure.

He'd looked at Dylan in his pushchair before leaning across the table towards her. 'Sarah, you do realise what the consequences could be if this goes wrong? I mean, we're talking serious stuff here.'

She'd nodded. 'I know that, but if I don't do *something*, then I have no doubt that your brother is going to kill me. Possibly Dylan too. I can't just sit around and wait for that to happen. You heard what Hannah said he did to her, how that other girl seemed to disappear off the face of the earth. Has it occurred to you that Drew could have got rid of her? Hannah said the other girl had no family, no one who'd miss her. Drew would have known that, wouldn't he? Don't you think he could do the same to me and somehow get away with it? Look how much he's got away with so far.' She'd pulled up her sleeves and showed him the scars on her wrists, from when she tried to put out the flames. 'Nothing sticks to him; we know that.'

Dan had grimaced, the sight of her injuries obviously upsetting him. In the end, he could see she had no choice and had agreed to help. Sarah knew how much he was risking himself, that they'd both be in serious trouble if they got caught. The next thing she wanted his help with was convincing her parents.

Her mum and dad were actually less shocked by the idea than she'd imagined. Her mum's eyes had widened when Sarah and Dan told her what they were thinking, as if she were going to object, but when they'd finished, she'd simply nodded.

'If you want the truth, sweetheart, I don't see what choice we have. We have to do *something*. I don't care what the consequences are for us, as long as this stops.'

Even meeting up with her parents could have caused the plan to go wrong. Sarah had made an excuse, telling Drew she had to arrange for her mum and dad to babysit Dylan on the night of Keeley's wedding. That she needed to familiarise them with her son's routine, so he wouldn't fret about being there without her. As soon as she'd agreed to go back to live in the flat with Drew, she'd told him she wasn't missing the chance to celebrate her friend's union with Alice. It was the only thing she'd ask, she'd told him. And then she'd do exactly what he said.

Now, she stood in the flat's hallway, Drew's laptop open on the console table in front of her, and watched her father sprinkle blood on the floor, as if Dad were creating a piece of abstract art. The blood was her own, the cut she'd made along the inside of her thigh making her eyes water. When he'd finished, he rubbed some more of the blood along the blade of the hacksaw he'd taken from Drew's meagre collection of tools and put it in the bin bag he held. The bag also held the clothes Sarah had taken off as soon as she arrived: her dress and underwear, one of her shoes. Her wedding ring.

She closed the lid of the laptop. It had taken her some time to work out what Drew's password was, her husband always having guarded his privacy in the same way a vicious dog might guard his territory. But taking him a cup of coffee one day, perfectly made now she'd finally mastered his machine, she'd looked over his shoulder and followed his fingers as he typed. She'd been so quiet he hadn't even noticed she was there until he'd turned around.

'Search of *how to dispose of a body* complete, alongside a clumsy attempt to delete it.' She stood up and walked over to her father, noticing how pale he looked. Her dad had genuinely had a nasty bout of the flu and should have been in bed, never mind becoming involved in criminal activities, framing his son-in-law. 'I'm sorry I had to ask you to do this.'

He shook his head. 'You're my daughter. I'll do anything to get you and my grandson away from that bastard. Did you make sure you left evidence of the cleaning materials your husband supposedly purchased? The bleach and cloths?'

She nodded. 'All ordered online a couple of days ago and delivered while he was at work. He must have missed those few spots you've left, when he was in a hurry to get rid of me.' She pointed at the floor.

Her dad nodded grimly.

Sarah hugged him briefly before taking the other one of the boots she'd worn to the wedding and dropping it onto the hall floor. Then she put her hand to her throat. She was sad to lose her necklace, but it was an important part of the plan. She ripped at the chain, breaking it in two, and dropping it near her shoe. The letter S was already in the trunk of Drew's car, planted the day before when they'd gone grocery shopping together along with some small fibres, ripped from the inside hem of the dress she'd worn tonight. She'd also deliberately scratched her finger then, making out to Drew she'd caught it as she'd loaded in the carrier bags while he stood and did nothing. She'd rubbed the blood on the lip of the trunk when her husband wasn't looking. What difference did one more scar make? Drew hadn't even noticed the pendant that usually sat at the base of her neck was missing – he barely even looked at her these days – but if he had, she'd have just told him she'd lost it. He wouldn't have cared if he hadn't gifted it to her himself.

She checked the time on her phone and looked at her dad again. 'We need to get going. Drew will be on his way back by now. Dan won't be able to delay him much longer.'

She and Dan had checked their phones were synchronised and he'd timed his meeting with his brother almost to the second. He knew exactly when to scratch Drew's face, when to walk away and tell Drew to go home to his wife. He also knew that, when the time came to speak to the police, his role was to deny all knowledge of even having seen his brother. He would already have deleted the details of any communication between the two of them from his phone, in the same way Sarah had quickly deleted the conversation from her husband's phone and emptied its recycle bin when he'd conveniently left it in the bedroom just before she left for the wedding, and Dan would be adamant that he couldn't provide anyone with an alibi, no matter what claims Drew would likely make following his potential arrest.

Sarah would never be able to thank Dan enough for what he'd done, what he was *doing*, for her. It was a lot to ask.

Her dad gathered together what they needed to take with them. The evidence they would now dump in various places, a few miles from the flat, to create a trail leading right back to her husband. 'We need to get down the stairs and get out of here quickly if we want to avoid crossing paths with him. Thank goodness for the broken security cameras; Drew couldn't have picked a better place to live. As soon as we leave and we know he's back, we can give your mother the go-ahead to call the police.'

Sarah began to get herself ready, pulling a dark wool hat onto her head and tucking her long hair beneath it. When everything was done, when they'd planted all the evidence, there was a pair of sharp scissors and a box of bleach waiting for her at her parents' house, along with a cheap pair of the ugliest reading glasses her mum had been able to find, a pair of blue-coloured contact lenses to disguise her brown eyes, and a shabby charity shop outfit. Sarah had recently stopped tanning and painting her nails and she most certainly wouldn't need her make-up or her eyelash curlers anymore. Through her work, Mum had secured her a place in a hostel. Like the homeless person she was supposed to be, the person whose only life before now had been on the streets, Sarah would turn up there tonight with few belongings and no paperwork. The person she was about to become – she'd already chosen the name *Amy* – did not exist. Not officially.

As she pulled on a dark jacket, she thought about the young guy she'd passed in the stairwell on the way up, the money she'd put in his guitar case: hundreds of pounds more than he usually received when he busked, she imagined. Her parents had given it to her. The guy was a regular at Gilbert House, someone her mum had known for years, someone she trusted. When they'd explained the situation to him, he'd been more than happy to help. To claim he'd seen Sarah in a scuffle with her husband in the doorway of the flat. She just hoped that, when it came to it, the police, the courts, if they ever got that far, believed him.

She took a last look around the flat, a place she hoped she'd never have to come back to, no matter what lay in store for her in her very uncertain future. She knew full well that getting away from Drew didn't suddenly mean she would have a perfect life. Far from it. The woman she'd always been – Sarah Wallace – would have vanished into thin air. She'd have no money and no job, no home to call her own. And worst of all, she would have to hand her son over to her parents, only able to see him when she was sure it was safe; a few minutes in the park or in a café here and there, or when her mum brought him into Gilbert, would be the only moments she'd have with her beloved boy. But it was better than never seeing him at all. And Dylan would be safe; that was the main thing. She looked at her dad.

He raised an eyebrow. 'Ready?'

She nodded. She was ready.

Sarah took a deep breath and screamed as loudly as she could.

Chapter 33

Claire now

Having Sarah in the house again seems so strange I can barely get my head around it. This was her home for such a long time, over two decades before she moved in with the man who ruined her life. Now, she's here, for the first time in three years. I stand in front of the fireplace and watch Boswell jump around her feet as she sits down on the sofa. The dog recognised her immediately, despite the short, lightened hair and glasses, the clothes that are so different from what Sarah used to wear, the lack of make-up. Amy couldn't be any more different from my daughter, but Boswell still knows his favourite person.

It took me a long time to get used to calling her by another name. At first, when I went to visit her at the hostel, taking her the few meagre things I'd collected together for her, I sometimes got muddled and started to address her by her real name, before stopping myself. We'd be in big trouble, we both knew, if anyone in Sarah's – Amy's – new life realised we were mother and daughter. The first time she came back to Gilbert to volunteer, I was terrified someone would recognise her, my fear reaching its peak once when Keeley stopped by to say hello to me. But, with our high turnover of staff and volunteers, not to mention the way our visitors come and go, and the way Sarah isolated herself from everyone else there, no one ever did realise it was her. The only people there who knew who she was were myself and the young man who'd agreed to act as a witness. I've always trusted him not to say anything. There's a code of honour among Gilbert regulars; they protect their own.

I go into the kitchen and make her a hot chocolate, aware she's walked from the hostel to here through the thick snow with only worn plimsolls on her feet. While I'm there, I double-check I've locked the back door. Whenever I'm with Sarah, I feel terrified that someone will realise what we've done. That's she's still alive. We are up against so many people: Drew, his accomplice, the police. Now she's here, in the house, that feeling of anxiety is multiplied. I take the drink into the living room, along with a treat for the dog to distract him.

Sarah takes the mug from me, a desperate expression on her face. 'Please tell me Dan's okay.'

I sit down next to her and nod. 'He's badly hurt, but he'll come out the other side. Eventually. There's a police officer outside his room.'

'I was right in what I said though.' She looks at me. 'Drew could easily have been lying in wait for you there. He knew exactly what he was doing when he beat Dan up just enough to put him in hospital and no more.'

I nod again and put a hand to her arm. That gesture, as well as the hug she gave me when she arrived, is the most contact I've had with her for a long time. I rub my thumb along the scars at her wrists, the burn marks her husband left her with. My beautiful child. 'I'm sorry Dan got caught up in this. I know you think a lot of him.'

She looks at her feet. Her demeanour is so different from how it used to be, it's as if she's adopted the persona of Amy permanently. As if she'll never be anyone else now. The whole time she's been in her new role, my daughter and I have made every effort to speak to each other as *Amy* and *Claire*, both of us determined not to waver, and Guy and I have never referred to her by her real name, even when it's just been the two of us, no one else around. All three of us have done our absolute best to remain in character for three years. Until tonight. 'We were supposed to be meeting up this afternoon. Just to go for a walk. But then Drew interfered, of course.'

I nod. I'm aware of how close she and Dan have become recently. The two of them have spent a lot of time together, as friends, since Sarah became Amy. Drew's brother has done so much for us, kept our secrets, that he's almost a member of the family now. When Sarah heard the radio announcement this morning, that Drew had got to Dan, injured him, it must have been so painful for her to hear. I'd hoped Dan might become someone my daughter could build a life with eventually, someone who could teach her that being in a partnership doesn't have to be painful, but now, who knows what will happen?

She looks up at me. 'I should've known this might happen. I always knew the plan could go wrong, even after all this time. Drew will never forgive us for what we did to him. He'll never accept that it was him who drove me to it, that he gave me no choice.'

'I know.' I look at the television, at the reporter still standing in the falling snow. He has an umbrella up now; perhaps he insisted on it, threatened to walk out if someone didn't provide him with at least a small amount of shelter. I look back at Sarah. 'The woman who's been calling me, she's the prison guard who helped Drew get out. I'm sure of it. She says she called because if I knew it was him trying to get in touch, I wouldn't have even entertained the idea of speaking to him. She was right.'

'Has she called again tonight?'

I nod. 'Like I told you on the phone, she said he wants to talk, about what we did.' Not about where we could find Sarah's body – of course, I always knew the police would never find her, no matter how far and wide they looked – but about how we'd framed him for murder. Me, Sarah, Guy and his own brother; we'd done it together. We'd tricked him. 'She says, once he's got what he wants, some kind of compensation, I imagine, he'll leave us alone. Let us get on with our lives.'

Sarah takes a sip of her hot chocolate, wrapping her hands around the mug. Her ragged sleeves are now pulled low over her scars. 'What do you think he wants?'

I shake my head. 'I don't know. Money? Your dad seems to think he might want to get far enough away so that the police will never catch up with him. Maybe go abroad somewhere. I could give him enough to do that. It wouldn't be easy, but . . .'

It's Sarah's turn to shake her head. 'No. It can't be that simple. Drew is too fond of mind games to want something as simple as money. Believe me, I got to know his ways better than anyone during the time I was living with him. It's more than that. He wants revenge. He wants . . .' She looks at me, her eyes suddenly brimming with tears.

'What? What is it?'

'He wants *Dylan*.'

I almost scream as my mobile rings again. Picking it up, I press my thumb to the screen before holding it to my ear.

I speak through gritted teeth. 'Tell that monster he is never, *ever*, getting his hands on my grandchild.'

I feel sick as the most terrifying words I think I've ever heard come down the line, each one hitting my heart like a bullet. The voice I hear isn't that of Drew's accomplice, as I was expecting, but my son-in-law himself, talking so clearly, he could be in the same room as me.

'Too late, Claire.'

216

Chapter 34

Sarah now

Sarah pulls her hood low over her face as she hurries after her mother, trying not to slip on the snowy drive. As they both climb into the car, she's trying her best not to cry. What her mum has just told her is worse than any of the abuse she suffered at the hands of her husband. Worse than when he'd called her ugly, or slow, or stupid. When he'd put his hands to her throat. Told her she wasn't the first woman he'd been violent with. She tries to quell her panic. She needs to be strong for her son.

Drew has Dylan.

She turns in her seat as her mum looks around her to make sure no one is watching them and then starts the engine. 'Tell me again what he said.'

Her mum shakes her head. 'I've told you. He's somehow managed to find out where your dad's living, no doubt through that accomplice of his, and he's gone there.'

'But Dad has a panic button, doesn't he?'

Mum nods. She backs the car off the drive and turns it away from the house. 'If he'd had a chance to press it, I think we'd have known by now.'

'We could call the police.'

'No.' Her mum shakes her head firmly.

'Why?'

'Just trust me.'

Sarah grunts in frustration. Her mum had tried to persuade her to stay behind, hide in the house while she went to see what had happened at her dad's place, but Sarah had insisted. She'd got her parents into this mess by marrying Drew. They'd be living a perfectly normal life if it hadn't been for the decisions she herself had made. She needs to see it through.

'Is Dad okay?'

'I don't know, Sarah. I really don't know. Drew hung up before I could ask.'

'Why can't we call the police? If it's me you're worried about, them finding out . . .'

'Of course I'm worried about you, Sarah.' Her mum takes her eyes off the road for just a second. 'But it's not just that.'

'Then what?'

Mum sighs as she turns off the main road. 'Drew said he'll hurt Dylan if we make any contact with the police at all.' She speaks more quickly. 'He may be bluffing. This may be another one of your husband's games and he may not even have been anywhere near your dad's place when we get there, but we can't take any chances. Not where Dylan's concerned.'

Sarah puts her fist to her mouth and bites down on it. She feels as if the car just isn't going fast enough. As she stares through the passenger window, at the snow-covered streets, she hopes and prays that her mum is right, that this is just another of Drew's childish tricks. That they'll get to her dad's bedsit and both Dad and Dylan will be surprised to see them. *Everything's fine*, her dad will say. *Nothing to worry about. Drew's just winding you up again.*

Her mum brings the car to a stop in front of the old terraced house, looking up at the first-floor window that fronts the room Sarah's dad has been living in since he left the family home. Sarah had been heartbroken when she'd found out her parents were splitting up. Growing up, she'd always hoped her own marriage would be like theirs, the two of them like the best of friends, always laughing and having fun together. Before things went so wrong.

She looks at her mum. 'Do you have a key?'

Mum nods. 'He gave me one so I could water his plants that weekend he went to Bristol to see his cousin. Your grandmother did nothing but complain about it. Said I had no right to still have access to his stuff. I think she thought I was going to clear him out while he wasn't there.'

They climb out and head for the front door, her mum unlocking it and pushing it open quietly, aware that there are other people living in the downstairs rooms. They head up the narrow stairwell, Sarah's heart beating so fast, she feels as if it might explode. Is she about to come face to face with her husband for the first time in three years? Drew could still be here, waiting for them in the shadows, ready to leap out and attack at the first opportunity. Throw both her and her mum off balance and send them hurtling back down the stairs, their bones snapping as they fall, neither of them in any fit state to help Dylan or her father.

As they round the corner at the top of the stairs, Sarah puts a hand to her mouth. The door to her dad's studio flat is open.

Her mum goes ahead of her and hesitantly opens the door more widely, both of them anticipating an attack. Inside, the flat is dark. Only a dim, eerie glow enters through the thin curtains.

'Guy?' Mum's shaky voice is answered only by the hum of the small fridge, the throb of the heating system.

Sarah flicks on the light switch by the door. She gasps.

Her father is lying in the middle of the floor, face down. One arm is twisted beneath him, the other sticking out at an odd angle. There's blood on the back of his head. The thick red liquid seems to be clotting, sticky on her dad's greying hair. He looks like the murder victim in a cheesy whodunnit, as if he should be outlined in chalk.

Her mum kneels down on the carpet and puts her fingers to her ex-husband's neck. 'He's alive. Call an ambulance.'

Sarah feels a swell of panic. She looks around the room, empty apart from the shabby second-hand furniture her dad has made do with since he moved in, a grey toy rabbit that used to be her own lying abandoned on the bed. The door to the small bathroom stands open; the space on the other side seems to be dark and empty. 'Where's Dylan?'

Her mum looks up at her. 'First things first. Your father needs an ambulance and he needs it now.' She points to the coffee table. 'Use your dad's phone. Do *not* give them your name. *Sarah*, are you listening to me?'

Sarah nods. She feels as if all the blood has drained from her body and she's beginning to shiver. She moves towards the coffee table, her legs wobbly, and, picking up her dad's phone, types in the emergency number. She recites the address and tells the operator that someone is badly hurt. When the woman at the other end asks for her details, she ends the call and drops the phone back on the table. There have been times, over the last three years, many, many times, when she's wondered if framing Drew, faking her own death, was the worst thing she could have done – when a week has gone by and she hasn't seen her son; when she hasn't been able to be with him on his birthday or at Christmas – despite knowing there was no alternative. Now though, she feels like she must be the worst mother in the world. Her only wish was to keep him safe, and he's gone.

She turns back to her mum. 'What now?'

Her mum pulls a blanket from the bed and drapes it over her dad. 'As soon as we see the ambulance pull up and we know your dad is in safe hands, we leave. The police will be on the scene before we know it, once the paramedics become aware a violent crime has been committed. We can't risk having them ask us lots of questions, wanting to know what's going on, who you are, where Dylan is, not after Drew threatened to hurt him on the phone if we involve anyone else. We have to play along with him for now. We can sneak out the back door and come back round to the car. Hopefully without being seen.'

Sarah clenches her fists and lets out a sob. She's trying so hard not to break down, but she's not sure she can do it. She just wants to know her son is okay. She stands straight. 'You said yourself Drew might be bluffing. Making empty threats. I know you think it could make things worse, but what if we just tell the police everything when they get here? I don't care anymore if they know I'm still alive. I know you're worried about me, but I'll face the consequences. We can tell them about what we did, how we framed Drew and that he's taken Dylan to get back at us. They'd know how to find him. They have search teams and dogs . . .'

Her mum stands up and comes towards her. She puts her hands on Sarah's arms. 'And they haven't found him yet even though he's been out since yesterday. Sarah, every single move he's made has been to throw them off the scent. Not to mention the fact that he wouldn't think twice about hurting your little boy if he thinks for one second we've done exactly what he said not to. No, we need to wait for him to contact us again. Which he will. That way, we'll have a much better chance of him leading us to Dylan. And of us making a deal with him and getting our boy back.'

Sarah gives in to her sobs.

'I'm sorry to be harsh, but this is Drew Allison we're dealing with. I know it seems easier just to give in, to ask someone to help us, but think how many times we tried to get help when he was abusing you. How many times the police believed him and not you. How they insisted they didn't have enough evidence to prosecute, despite what was under their noses, how they thought *you* had hurt *him*. It took extreme measures, turning ourselves into criminals, to finally get you away from him. Even though he's been to prison, hurt Dan and your dad, would they still consider taking his side against yours once they know you set him up? See him as a desperate victim, acting in self-defence against us, the *villains*? Would he hurt Dylan, worse, and somehow manipulate the situation, as he always does, to make it look like it was your fault? We know what he's capable of, Sarah. We have to sort this out ourselves.'

'So, what do we do? What do we do now?' Sarah felt as if she were a child again, looking to her mum to tell her what to do.

'We get out of here and we wait for our next instructions.'

They both turn as they see a blue glow coming through the curtains. The room around them lights up as it blinks, on and off.

'Come on.' Her mum takes her arm. 'We need to get down the stairs before they come up. The doors are open; they'll be with your dad within a minute or two.'

She grabs the toy rabbit and they head down the stairs, rounding the hallway corner and walking quickly to the back of the house just as the front door opens behind them. Sarah hears someone call out – *Hello?* – before footsteps hit the stairs above them.

They go outside, the cold air stinging the skin of Sarah's face as they enter the back alley and head around towards the road. They climb into the car as quickly as they can and her mum pulls away from the house before Sarah even has her seatbelt on. She sees one of her dad's neighbours come out of the next house along, obviously curious as to who needs medical help. She has no doubt that, as soon as word gets out about her dad's visit from his son-in-law, the street will be lined with journalists.

Her mum drives half a mile or so before the phone she dumped into the well between the seats begins to vibrate and buzz. She pulls into a quiet industrial area and parks up before answering. The inside of the car is dark, only the bright moonlight coming through the windscreen, but Sarah can tell from the look on her mother's face that it's Drew again.

She puts the phone on speaker. 'You hurt my husband, you bastard.'

'Ah, Claire, don't you mean *ex*-husband? Well, you'll be pleased to know he put up a good fight. For someone of his age anyway.'

Sarah leans towards the phone. 'Where's Dylan? What have you done with my son?'

'Sarah! How nice to hear your voice!' Drew sounds as if he's speaking to a long-lost relative. 'I'm afraid you've also got your terms mixed up. You mean *our* son, don't you? Well, if you sit tight and listen, very, very carefully, I'll tell you exactly where our son is and what you have to do next if you ever want to see him alive again.'

'You . . .' Sarah spits out the word.

'Don't interrupt me, lovely wife. Or else I'll do exactly what I promised your mother and I'll not only hurt but I'll *kill* our precious little boy within seconds. And I can't promise it won't be painful for the little angel. Now, are you both listening?'

Sarah grips the side of her seat as her mum speaks through gritted teeth.

'We're listening.'

Chapter 35

Claire now

As I wait for my son-in-law to speak again, I'm suddenly not in the car anymore. I'm in a different time and a different place: in the airport, in Manchester, waiting for my daughter to arrive back from her holiday in Las Vegas. With the boyfriend Guy and I didn't think she was all that serious about. Who had bombarded her with gifts and romantic gestures but who we thought she might eventually get bored of and move on. When Sarah had come into the arrivals hall, I'd greeted her with a hug, tired and eager to get home through the traffic, but glad to see her all the same. During those few moments, before she surprised us with her news, Sarah was still my daughter. Not a victim of abuse, someone ground down by constant domestic violence. Not a homeless person, with just a few shabby clothes and an old radio and two-bar heater to her name. She was my child, home safe where she belonged. It was only when she held up her left hand and showed us the ugly wedding band he'd bought her, that our lives, both hers and ours, had changed forever.

Changed because of *this* man, now on the other end of the phone.

'I must say, Sarah, it's very nice to hear your voice again. Aren't I supposed to have killed you? Chopped your body up into hundreds of pieces and hidden them somewhere where no one will ever find them? Yet, here you are, alive and well and talking to me, alongside your dear mother, as if nothing ever happened. It's like a miracle. The *tragic* Sarah Wallace rising from the ashes. Wait until the press finds out.'

I try not to grip the phone too hard. We're going to need it. 'You wouldn't dare.'

'Wouldn't I, Claire? It would make a great story, don't you think? I can just see the headline now. *Mother of murder victim convicted of fraud. Daughter found alive, as the world discovers the inspirational Claire Wallace, founder of the famous Walk Me Home helpline, isn't all she seems.*'

Sarah's voice suddenly makes me jump.

'Stop it! Just stop it!'

'What is it, lovely wife? Don't you think I'd get paid handsomely for such juicy information about your mother, who everyone seems to think is some kind of saint? Is that how you saw yourself, Claire? When you founded that amazing project you're so proud of? That you'd managed to save your daughter from her awful fate, so now you wanted to do the same for other women? *Saint Claire* . . . It has a nice ring to it.'

'Just tell us where Dylan is!' Sarah is shouting now.

I hold up my other hand. Although the area we're in seems quiet, we don't want to draw attention to ourselves. The police will be on the lookout for anything that seems suspicious, especially after what's happened to Guy. Just because we can't hear the helicopter now, that doesn't mean it might not fly overhead any second. 'Look, Drew, if it's money you want, we can come to some kind of . . .'

Next to me, Sarah shakes her head. No doubt, she's wondering how I can be talking about money, when all she wants to know is if her son is safe. She doesn't realise I have to stay calm, talk to my son-in-law on his level, in language he understands. As frantic as we are, there's no point in appealing to his emotions.

'Of course I don't want money, Claire! As if I'd be so crude, so *basic*. You really should know me better than that by now.'

'Then what *do* you want? Tell me what we have to do to get my grandson back.' I try not to picture Dylan: frightened, wondering where his granny and grandad are, why they've disappeared, just like his mother seemed to do when he was very little. 'At least tell us he's safe. That you haven't hurt him.'

Drew sounds indignant. 'I told you, I'll hurt him if you don't do exactly as I say. I'll have you know that my precious boy is currently sleeping peacefully, right here by his old dad. Exhausted from all the excitement, I imagine.' He pauses. 'Oh wait, that could be the sedative I gave him.'

Next to me, Sarah covers her face with her hands.

My phone buzzes as a text comes through. Jane Fellows' name flicks onto the screen before quickly disappearing. No doubt she's been trying to call me while Drew is occupying the line. She'll want to know that I'm safe. To ask if Dylan is with me, now that the police are aware his grandfather has been attacked, to offer us shelter in the safe house she talked about earlier. She'll probably be starting to panic, thinking the worst when I don't answer. Thinking there'll be hell to pay if Drew has got to all of us.

He speaks again. 'Don't you two be worrying about our little Dylan. We're taking very good care of him.'

Sarah looks up, leaning towards the phone again. 'We?'

'Your mother must have told you about the *friend* who's been kind enough to help me.' His voice becomes an exaggerated whisper. 'She'll do practically anything for me, you know. Head over heels.'

'Ah, yes, the prison guard who you charmed, *fooled* into helping you.' I try to focus on what is more important. 'Just tell us exactly what we have to do to get Dylan back.'

'Well . . .' Drew hesitates. He actually sounds as if he's stretching and yawning. 'If you insist. There are three things I'm going to ask of you . . .'

My daughter speaks again. Her frustration with Drew's seemingly casual attitude is getting the better of her. 'Just tell us.'

'Patience, Sarah. You always were a bit of a hothead. Your mother's daughter for sure. So, firstly, and very importantly, like I said to you before, *do not speak to the police*. I can't stress this point enough, ladies. If you involve the police, try to contact them at any time before all this is over, you'll never see your gorgeous little son and grandson again.' Another pause. 'Not alive anyway.'

Sarah shakes her head. *He's goading you,* I want to say. *Don't fall for it. Dylan needs you to stay strong.*

Instead, I speak into the phone. 'We understand. No police.'

I glance at Sarah again and see her nod, albeit a little reluctantly.

'Good. Secondly, I want to *see* you both, my two favourite ladies, in real life, face to face. Talking on the phone is too risky. You never know who might be listening.'

I swallow. *You would be the one to know about that,* I think, *checking on my daughter wherever she went.* 'Just tell us where and when.'

'The marina. In an hour. Head for the canal and I'll call you again, to tell you where to go from there. Wouldn't want to give you too much information at once now, would I?'

I seethe as I picture his smirk. 'And you'll have Dylan with you?'

'That's for you to find out when you get here, Claire. I'm not sure you're in any position to demand any promises from me at the minute.'

I roll my eyes.

Sarah leans over and speaks again, more calmly this time. 'You said there were three things you wanted to specify. What's the third?'

'Well, Sarah.' Drew chuckles softly. 'That's the bit I'm saving for when I see you. I want to see your reaction, look at your faces. If you want to know, be at the marina. One hour. Don't be late, or you never know what might happen. A lot of deep water around there and I'm pretty sure our darling son hasn't learnt to swim yet . . .'

I look at my daughter. Drew is enjoying this. Even after all these years, his time behind bars, he's still enjoying playing with us. I take a deep breath. 'We'll be there.'

Chapter 36

Sarah now

As her mum drives, she spots the helicopter, hovering over a copse of tall trees in the distance, its long beam of light turning the snow below yellow. It's not the first time she's seen it. When she made her way to Gilbert House earlier in the day, she'd seen it in the snow-laden sky above town. Again, when she'd rushed around to sneak into the back of her childhood home after her mum called her, Sarah feeling like a fugitive herself as she'd tried to hide in the shadows of the houses she passed, avoiding the glow of streetlamps. If only the people up there knew that the two innocent-looking women in the nearby car were heading straight towards the person they're searching for, she thinks. All it would take would be one phone call from her mother and the police would know where Drew is.

Do not speak to the police, her husband had specified. *You'll never see your . . . son . . . again.*

As much as she hates Drew, would love to turn him in, she believes what her mum has said. That he'd hurt Dylan if he felt it would help him. That he's capable of manipulating any situation to his advantage. Of making others look wrong and himself right, no matter what has gone before.

Her mum's phone buzzes again but they both ignore it. It won't be Drew, not yet. He'll know they won't have reached where he wants them to go.

Sarah looks at her mum. 'What do you think he's going to tell us when we get there? What does he want?'

Her mum shakes her head. 'I have no idea. Knowing Drew, it could be anything. All I want to hear is that we're going to get Dylan back. Whatever your husband wants – money, my life savings, my house – I'll give to him, as long as my grandson comes back to us.'

Sarah stares through the windscreen, the snow hitting the glass before quickly disappearing. She shakes her head. 'I told you before. That's too easy. Drew is much more complicated.' She looks back at her mum. 'Do you think he wants us to clear his name? Do it his way, on his terms? Go to the police with him, and help him surrender without a scene, without the risk of him getting hurt or just being dragged back to prison without having his say? Tell them how we set him up so he can then have a life with this woman he's with? The guard?'

'Maybe. I'd be lying if I said the thought hasn't crossed my mind.' Her mum looks thoughtful. 'Although he'll still be facing the fact that he's hurt Dan and your dad. Let's just wait and see what happens when we get there.'

They continue the journey in silence. The roads are quiet, anyone not on a Christmas night out no doubt staying indoors due to the bad weather and the dangerous situation they've seen on the news. As they turn around a corner, Sarah notices a news crew further along the residential street. The reporter she last saw on her mum's TV screen is standing on a corner, stamping his feet and blowing into his hands to keep himself warm. If her husband is telling them the truth about where he is, then this guy is way off course. Nowhere near where he should be to get the scoop he wants.

She wonders about the relationship between Drew and the

woman who's helping him: his accomplice, who her mum says worked at the prison and helped him escape. How did he manage to convince her to risk her job, her reputation, her freedom? Did he slowly woo her, in the same way he has so many women before, in the same way he did Hannah and the girl before her and Sarah herself when she first met him? Did he use all his powers of persuasion to show her that he's likeable, trustworthy, as so many people in his life have thought he is? So he could eventually use her to get away?

They enter the narrow lane that leads down to the canal and Mum parks the car next to a hedge. The area around them is dark, the snow that's still falling from the sky, the blue-white ground, giving the whole place a surreal feel.

Her mum turns to her. 'Stay in the car. I can deal with this on my own.'

Sarah shakes her head. 'I'm coming with you. This is *my* mess. *My* husband and son.'

Her mum sighs as she picks up her phone and checks its screen. 'You always were stubborn.'

They climb out, Sarah hugging herself against the cold, still shaking. She pulls the old winter coat she grabbed from her mum's hallway, before they rushed out, more tightly around her and holds on to Dylan's grey rabbit. As if it's the only thing connecting her to her old life. Sometimes, she feels as if she were never Sarah at all. As if she's a completely different person now. She thinks about when she and her dad arrived back at the house, after planting all the evidence that would lead the police to Drew. Tears had poured down her cheeks as she stood in the same bathroom where her parents had bathed her when she was just a little girl and her mum had taken a pair of scissors to the long hair she'd always loved. Afterwards, Mum had bleached it. A rushed and messy job that they hadn't done well enough. Sarah couldn't risk staying in the house for too long, in case someone suspected she was there.

She'd still been upstairs when two police officers came to the door, to break the news to her parents about what they'd found at the flat. Mum had thrown on an old dressing gown she'd always hated, the nearest thing she had to hand to hide the bleach stains she'd managed to get on her clothes and fingers. All Sarah had been able to think, as she hid behind the bathroom door and listened to the conversation going on below, was: *please don't insist on coming in. Please don't ask to use the toilet or to check around, for whatever reason.*

She hadn't even been able to say goodbye to her son, not properly, even though she wasn't sure when she'd be able to see him again, speak to him. Her parents had hurriedly taken their sleepy grandson next door to Peter and June's and had then gone with the police to the crime scene, all of them terrified that whoever was in charge would immediately see through their lies. After they'd left, Sarah had sneaked out of the house through the back door and along the alley and had made her way to the hostel on her own. When she arrived, she'd told them she'd come from another town, where she'd been on the streets for years, that someone she'd spoken to at Gilbert House had told her she could have a place there. She had nowhere else to go. They'd given her a room and food and she'd been there ever since.

They look right and left before crossing the railway line, Sarah trying not to slip as she finds her footing between the wet slats. The line is as quiet as the road they've just come down. The trains have stopped for the night and the only sounds she can hear are her mum's quick breaths and the gentle squawks of the ducks and the geese as they settle on the canal that runs parallel to the river's estuary. After going through the gate, they stand on the stone bridge for a few seconds and look across the water. Drew has said for them to come to the marina. Now they're here, neither of them has any idea what they're supposed to do next.

She brushes flakes of snow from her eyes. The area feels so different in the dark, a far cry from the sunny, busy place she and Keeley used to walk to so often in the summer holidays. She wonders if Drew is watching them somewhere. Laughing. It wouldn't surprise her.

She watches her mum check her phone. 'Anything?'

Mum shakes her head. 'Only Jane Fellows.'

'The FLO?'

A nod. 'She'll be worrying.'

'I hope Dad's okay.'

'We can't think about that now.' Despite her words, her mum's voice wavers a little as she gestures towards the path ahead. 'Come on. Let's walk a bit further.'

They walk next to the water, the surface of the canal dark and uninviting as the snow hits it and disappears. On the other side, a series of boats bob up and down. Some look run-down and unused, others as if they might be used to regular visits. Sarah tries not to imagine eyes staring out at her from tiny portholes. What if Drew has tricked them? she wonders. Lured them here while he runs away with Dylan? Takes his son somewhere they'll never find him? She looks briefly to the blue-black sky. Sarah has never been religious, but she feels the need to pray now. *Please let my son be safe.* She can almost see her thoughts disappear into the oblivion above her.

They reach a series of boatyards, their tall wire gates secured with huge padlocks. Behind them, billowy tarpaulins partly cover the boats the yard owners are working on. A broken mast lies sideways across a deck. The bottom of a huge hull shows a dark and gaping hole. Metal chains rattle. In the distance, in a small clearing, a red Citroën seems to be the only car parked in the shadows. She wonders if it belongs to Drew's companion. If she's been driving him around, helping him stay on the run, in her nondescript vehicle.

Her mum's phone suddenly lights up: a call coming through. Sarah can see the words *Private Number* on the screen. Drew. She watches as her mum answers, putting it on loudspeaker again so Sarah can hear both sides of the conversation.

'We're here. Just like you asked. We haven't contacted the police or anyone else. Now, tell us where Dylan is and what you want from us so we can get him back.'

'Ah, Claire, you think I'm going to make it so easy? And here's me thinking you knew me.'

'Don't mess with me, Drew. We've done what you asked. Sarah and I are both here, together. Now we need to bring this to a close.'

'You and Sarah were always a team, weren't you? I often told my wife she shouldn't be going running to Mummy and Daddy every time she thought she needed to. Being married to me should have been enough for her, don't you think?'

'You mean, getting the shit beaten out of her every day? You're right, she had no idea how lucky she was.'

'You know, Claire, I sometimes wonder if it was your idea, to frame me. Surely my not-so-bright wife didn't come up with that plan all on her own? Or was it your husband who thought of it? Nah, not steady old Guy. Too dull. Maybe my loving brother was the mastermind behind it all? Dan was desperate to take my place, you know. I really should have seen it coming, shouldn't I? That night when he attacked me, like a big girl's blouse? Very unlike him to resort to violence. I should have guessed there was something else going on. Not my finest moment.'

Sarah feels her cheeks flush, despite the cold. Nothing had gone on between her and Dan, not then.

'If you want us to go to the police with you, to clear your name then that's what we'll do. We'll confess everything. Unlike you, we're prepared to face the consequences of our actions.'

That annoying laugh again. 'Is that what you think I want? My, my, Claire, I never had you down as the naive type. Let's meet, shall we? And bring this to a *close*, as you say. Cross the canal and keep walking. You'll eventually see a barge, long and blue, named the *Lady Sarah*. Can you believe that? What a name, eh? I'll be waiting for you there.'

Her mum ends the call and gestures across the canal. 'Come on.'

'He didn't say anything about Dylan.'

'No, he didn't.'

'What the hell does he want?'

'I don't know, Sarah, but I'm beginning to have a bad feeling . . .'

She follows her mother across the narrow bridge and onto the far path, the grey rabbit still in her hands. The ground beneath her feet is treacherous, Sarah's thin shoes not adequate for the wet conditions. They're the only pair she has these days. Nothing like a few years ago, when she worked in her marketing job. What she wore on her feet seemed important then, her collection of designer heels something she took great pride in. She thought they made her look more attractive. Funny how someone's priorities can change so drastically.

Her thoughts turn to Dan, now lying in a hospital bed. Sarah's heart hurts at the idea of what he's been through. Her mum had said he was going to pull through, that she thought he'd be okay, but Sarah can't help but feel guilty at how she dragged him into her messy life. She should have just left him alone.

It's true that nothing happened when she was still with Drew. It hadn't even occurred to her to see her brother-in-law like that. It was only later, after the trial, that she and Dan had grown closer, but even then, they'd mostly only been friends. Not so long ago, he'd taken her on an actual date for the first time. She'd worn a dress and smart shoes she'd borrowed from one of the other girls in the hostel and they'd gone to a cheap restaurant. Somewhere she might have felt out of place before, when she was Drew's wife, because it wasn't expensive enough, but where she felt uncomfortable now because it was way beyond her means. Dan had been kind and chatty, as he always is. They'd had fun. Got along, as they always do. *Did.*

Now, after everything that's happened, Dan might never want to see her again. She doesn't blame him – why would he want to? – but without him in her life, she might never know now what it would be like to have a real loving relationship. To be respected, treated as she deserves to be. All she would know about grown-up relationships would be lies and deceit and violence. She tries to push the thoughts away. Now is not the time to be worrying about herself and her future.

Still, Dan would have made a much better father than his brother ever did.

She slips in the snow and rights herself quickly. She's so cold now. She hopes Drew at least has the sense, the compassion, to be keeping his son warm on a night like this. If not him, then maybe his companion. Surely this woman must have some idea of how Sarah is feeling? Or is she as narcissistic as the man she's helping?

She stops as her mum suddenly comes to a halt in front of her. Sarah can hardly see anything, despite the white snow all around them. The area they are in now is poorly lit and isolated, not another soul around, it seems. She waits for her eyes to adjust. 'What? Are we here?'

Her mum points ahead of them.

Sarah's blood starts to run cold.

Standing in front of her, coming out of the shadows like a demon emerging from hell itself, is her husband.

Chapter 37

Drew is standing at the edge of the narrow path, dressed all in black: scruffy black jeans and a matching sweatshirt, dirty trainers on his feet that, much like the shoes my daughter is wearing, look like they once belonged to someone else. On the water next to him, a long narrowboat sways gently. The words *Lady Sarah* are painted on its hull in swirly white, faded letters. I wonder if it's just coincidence that he found an abandoned boat with such an apt name.

My son-in-law takes a step towards us and spreads his hands, as if he's back at the dinner party he and Sarah had. The one and only time he willingly invited us into his home. 'Well, well, well, isn't this nice? All three of us, back together again. Like the family we were always meant to be.'

In the corner of my eye, I see Sarah instinctively take a step back. Even now, she's frightened of him. Frightened he'll suddenly hurt her, like he used to. The memory of the pain he caused her is likely still sharp.

I put a hand towards her, in the same way I used to when my daughter was young and we crossed the road together. No matter how old she is now, I'm still her mother and it's still my job to look out for her. 'You can drop the act now, Drew. Just take us to Dylan and tell us what we have to do to get him away from you.'

'Ah, Claire, you're such a spoilsport. You could at least pretend you're glad to see me.' He pulls a sad face.

'I'm really not that good an actor.' I know my sarcastic tone is unlikely to help the situation, but it makes me feel better. I refuse to show Drew how scared I really am.

'Well, if you're going to be mean, maybe I should just keep the brat all to myself. I am his father, after all, and it can't have been easy for you, Claire, looking after him, at your age, while my wife and I were – how shall I put it? – *indisposed*.'

Next to me, Sarah moves forward again.

'You're no father. You never were. You're just a sperm donor, nothing more. Dylan spent his early life terrified of you. Not able to play, or make a noise, in case he disturbed you.'

Drew's eyes widen. 'My wife has suddenly found a bit of backbone, I see. I didn't think you had it in you. When did that happen, Sarah? When you were pretending to be someone else? I must say, you're looking a bit rough these days. So pale and *drab*. And your new persona obviously doesn't have the same taste in clothes as the *real* you did.' He curls his lip. 'Your new look really doesn't suit you.'

I look him up and down. He's lost weight since I last saw him, his cheeks hollow, his build less bulky. Patchy stubble covers the lower areas of his sallow face. I'm guessing prison life didn't suit him. 'You don't look so hot yourself, Drew.' I'm aware I'm goading him as much as he's goading us.

'Oh, that hurts, Claire.' He holds a hand to his chest. 'Really it does. Especially as it's you and your daughter here who are completely responsible for the unfortunate circumstances in which I currently find myself.'

I roll my eyes. I've had enough. 'Look, we've stuck to our end of the deal. Now you have to stick to yours. Otherwise, we're turning around and leaving.'

238

Drew raises an eyebrow. 'I'm sure you're not going to do that, Claire, but, as I'm in a good mood, I won't keep either of you from your precious boy for even a second longer than I have to.' He looks at Sarah. 'Although I'm sure he'll have no idea who you are, *Mummy*, you not having been around for him all this time.'

I jump in before Sarah reacts. 'Ignore him.' I speak to Drew again. 'Are you going to bring him out to us?'

He shakes his head. 'Oh no, Claire, that would mean waking the poor little thing up. What kind of father would do that to his son? No, you'll have to come to him, I'm afraid.' He gestures to the boat next to him. The deck is covered in wet snow. 'Mind you don't slip as you board now. I wouldn't want either of you plunging into the murky depths of the freezing-cold canal.'

I look at Sarah and see she's thinking the same as I am. As soon as we board that boat, both of us are vulnerable. Drew could attack us and neither of us would be seen again. No one knows we're here. Guy would never know what had happened to his family. But what choice do we have? We need to see Dylan. To know for definite that he's here and what Drew wants in exchange.

I put out my hand and take Sarah's. Her fingers are cold as she grips mine tightly.

Together, my daughter and I step over the gap between the towpath and the boat. The deck is slippery beneath our feet, the thick snow likely hiding numerous hazards. Behind us, I can hear Drew following. His breathing is slightly laboured. As I suspected when I first saw him, it seems that he isn't as fit, as healthy, as he was before he went to prison.

We wait as he moves in front of us and opens a small wooden door. The top of a series of narrow ladder-style steps is just visible inside. They disappear into the dark interior.

Drew holds out a hand. 'Ladies first.'

I go in front of Sarah. If there's anything nasty waiting, I want to be the first to experience it. To give her warning, a slim chance of getting away. The steps aren't easy to negotiate and I put one foot below the other carefully and slowly. A strong odour of grease and oil, of wet algae, invades my nostrils as I descend.

I take Sarah's hand again as she comes down behind me, the two of us clutching at each other in the dark and claustrophobic space. I'd hoped to feel braver, to be bold, but not being able to see so much as a few inches in front of me is disconcerting and I feel flutters of fear low in my stomach. What if Dylan isn't even here? What if Drew has already got bored of having his son around?

My son-in-law comes into the cabin and shuffles around in the dark for a few seconds before a yellow glow slowly comes to life and lights up our surroundings. He's lit an oil lamp.

He shakes out the match and holds the lamp up in front of his face, watching us.

I grip Sarah's hand tightly as I look around, wondering if someone might be curious about the light inside the old boat, realising at the same time how unlikely it is that anyone will be near enough to see at this time on a very cold night, especially under the current circumstances. They'd have more sense. I wonder if the police will search the marina at some point. Even without a tip-off, they may get to it eventually. Perhaps the helicopter will fly over.

The interior of the boat is long and thin, a small table and chairs taking up most of the room in the shabby galley kitchen we're now standing in, barely enough space for the three of us. Beyond the kitchen, a living area of sorts is home to a sagging sofa on one side and a scuffed black stove with a pipe chimney on the other. A closed door on the left leads to what is probably a toilet, a glint of metal to one side maybe a box housing essential tools. Another door, at the very end of the living quarters, is just visible. The bitter, musty smell seems to be getting stronger.

Drew gestures towards the far door with the lamp he's holding, the yellow light moving back and forth across the low ceiling. 'Walk down to the end. Both of you. And don't even think about making any sudden moves. My trusty accomplice is in the bedroom with the brat. If she gets so much as a hint that anything has happened to me, she knows exactly what she has to do.'

I don't dare ask what that is. I look at the door at the other end of the cabin. My hope that my grandson is in there, that his mother and I will soon be reunited with him, is suddenly overwhelming. If Drew is lying, if we get to that room and Dylan isn't inside it, I don't know what we'll do.

We do as he says, Sarah and I moving in sync towards the door. The floor, even inside the boat, is slippery, wet footprints running the length of it. I suddenly lose my footing. My left hand goes to the floor as I fall sideways.

I right myself as Sarah reaches out to me. 'I'm fine, don't worry.' I keep going, more carefully this time. When we reach the end of the cabin, I turn to my son-in-law. 'This woman who's been helping you. Obviously, she thinks she's in love with you, and you with her, otherwise she wouldn't have risked herself to help you escape. Please don't hurt her, once all this is over. Whichever way you decide to live your life, with her or without her, she doesn't deserve . . .'

Drew waves me away. 'Shut up, *Saint* Claire. Not everyone's welfare is your business.'

He steps in front of us and, holding the lamp up, pushes the door open. The room is mostly dark. The weak light doesn't quite reach the far side.

I follow Drew inside, again making a meagre attempt to protect my daughter from anything unexpected inside the bedroom: a blow that may come from behind the door; an attack from someone who may rush at us.

As Drew moves to one side, the light reaching further now, I put my hand to my mouth. I feel as if I've been punched in the gut, as if all the air has been forced out of my body.

In front of me, I can see my grandson, his arms around some-one's neck, his face buried in the nook of her shoulder. Dylan looks as if he's in a deep sleep, no doubt still suffering the effects of whatever sedative his father has given him, but at least he's alive. At least he appears to have been cared for, looked after.

What I can't quite take in, what I can't quite believe, is *who* is holding him.

Standing in front of me, my grandson in her arms, a determined look on her face, is Sarah's best friend.

Keeley.

Chapter 38

Sarah now

Sarah moves in front of her mum, feeling as if she's under water. She stares at Keeley, her best friend since they were tiny. They'd met on their first day at primary school, their coat pegs next to each other. From that first moment, they'd spent all their time together: making up games in the playground during their lunch break, hosting fashion shows in their bedrooms, eating tea at each other's houses. They'd talked about boys, and girls, they liked, about travel, about how they'd always be friends, no matter which direction life took them in. Even when Sarah went to university, they'd kept in constant touch and Keeley had come to visit her on more than one occasion.

Now, Keeley is standing in front of her, holding her son. Her son who was *snatched*.

She looks at her mum. She can hardly speak, the words sticking in her throat. 'You said the woman who was helping him was a guard, from the prison.'

Her mum stares at her; she doesn't answer.

'Well, actually . . .'

Sarah turns towards her husband as he speaks.

Drew is smiling. He's obviously proud of himself that he's well and truly pulled the wool over their eyes this time.

'Your mother made a pretty big assumption there, Sarah, which surprised me, I have to say, when she mentioned it over the phone. I never said that it was a screw who was helping me on the *outside*. The guard who did help me escape . . .' he puts the oil lamp on an old dresser and paces back and forth, like a professor giving a lecture '. . . was in reality a burly, six-foot, bald bloke, who I bribed with a substantial amount of money, provided by my very generous mother. For some reason, Claire presumed it was the woman who was calling her who'd got me out of there.'

Sarah's mum stutters. 'So, it was *you*? On the phone? Keeley?'

Keeley speaks for the first time. 'Yes, Claire. It was me who called you. Who told you that Drew wanted to talk to you. Who's been helping him all along, since he got out. I did wonder if you'd recognise my voice, but the scarf wrapped around my face, my horrendous fake accent, obviously worked as I hoped they would. It was me who was waiting outside the prison for Drew, when he escaped. I hid my car a little way out and drove him straight back here.'

Her mum looks completely thrown. 'So, it was you, in the little red Citroën, taking pictures of Dylan? And in my garden, standing across the road from my house? At the hospital, watching me?'

'Of course it was me. As I told you on the phone, Drew wanted me to keep an eye on you, follow your movements so we could carry out our plan. It was true what I said. I even passed you, when you were waiting for the lift, to go and visit Dan, but you were so wrapped up in yourself, you didn't even notice me.'

'But you called me, you yourself, over the helpline, to say you thought Drew was following you.'

'Because I wanted to frighten you. To be the first to let you know he was out, that the time was coming for you to finally face up to what you'd done to him. It was easy just to send your walkers on their way once they'd reached me. They looked a bit

244

confused, but they didn't mind in the end. It gave them a chance to skive off for a ciggie.'

The room becomes blurry as Sarah's tears begin to flow. 'But, Keeley, *why*? Why would you do this?'

Keeley turns and gently lays Dylan on the narrow cabin bed behind her. Sarah's son is big for his age; he must be getting heavy. She turns back. 'Do you really need to ask me that, Sarah? You completely betrayed me. You know that, don't you? Ruined my wedding day by pretending to be murdered. I felt so guilty that I'd let you walk home on your own, that I hadn't insisted you get a lift or a taxi. Alice and I never got over it. It was all we could think about afterwards, how we'd never be able to celebrate our anniversary because it was the day you died. We split up just a few months after we got married. Why the fuck didn't you think to include me in your plans? You brought Drew's brother into your secret little club but left *me* on the outside. I was your best friend and you let me think you were dead. Have you any idea what that feels like?' She looks at Sarah's mum. 'And you, Claire, you never even came to see me. Not once. Never even called to ask how I was coping. What was it you said to me on the phone? *I'll always be here for you?* When were you *ever* there for me? You weren't. You've barely spoken to me for three years.'

Sarah's mum shakes her head. 'I'm sorry.'

'Don't be. Your daughter was no better. All those times I went round to the flat to try and help you, Sarah. To see how you were. Offer to look after Dylan. And every single time, you sent me away. I wasn't there just for you. I was getting *married*. I needed my friend.'

Sarah doesn't think she's ever felt so shocked. She twists Dylan's bunny around in her hands. 'How did you find out? How did you know I was still alive?'

'Drew told me. Just over a year ago, after thinking about it for a long time, I went to visit him. To confront him, about what he'd done to you. How he'd taken my best friend away from me.

But when I was there, he told me the truth about what had happened. What you'd all done. Of course, I didn't believe him at first. Didn't believe it was possible, but when he told me he suspected that your mum was hiding you somewhere in plain sight, so you could still have access to Dylan, I began to see that what he was saying could be true. So I came to Gilbert House one day, under the pretence of calling in on Claire, and that's when I saw you. *Amy.* I knew that's where she'd be hiding you. You looked so different, as far away from Sarah as you could possibly be, but once I looked closely, I knew it was you. I've known you forever. That's when I knew Drew was telling me the truth. You'd betrayed both of us.'

Sarah's mum steps forward. She points at Drew. 'This man is a monster, Keeley. He beat Sarah until she bled. He made her miscarry her first child.'

Sarah glances at Drew and sees his eyes widen, just briefly, before he resumes his arrogant stance. He didn't know.

'Sarah couldn't get anyone to believe her. We had *no choice* but to do what we did. He would have killed her otherwise. How can you be *helping* him?'

'How could I not?' Keeley shakes her head. 'Sarah exaggerated. I've got to know Drew a lot since I first went to visit him. I know he didn't do the things Sarah accused him of. He couldn't have. She made it up, to get attention. Because she knew she wasn't a good enough wife to him.'

Sarah takes another step forward. 'No, Keeley, that's not true. I never lied about what Drew did, not once, apart from to cover for him. I had so many bruises, cuts, scratches.'

'I never saw the bruises. How many times did I come to see you and you told me you were fine? That you were cooking or baking? There wasn't one sign that you were injured.'

'Only because I hid it all from you! I didn't want anyone to know what was happening to me. I was ashamed.'

'But you went back to him! After you left and went to your

246

parents' house, you went back. In the club that night, after you'd gone, Drew told me how you'd begged him to give you another chance. How you said you'd made a big mistake in leaving.'

'No. It was the opposite. He told me he'd take Dylan away from me if I didn't go back.' Sarah pulls up the sleeve of her coat. 'And when I did, he *burned* me. He set fire to my bed.'

'Everyone knows that was an accident. You said it yourself.'

'Because I was terrified of what Drew would do if I told anyone the truth. To me *and* to Dylan . . .'

Drew steps between them, smiling again. He's delighted to see the chaos he's caused, the fractures in the relationships between those around him.

'Now, ladies, let's not fight.' He puts his hands out to both of them, as if he's refereeing a boxing match. 'It isn't very dignified, is it? You two hollering at each other? Aren't you forgetting why we're here?' He gestures towards Dylan. 'To negotiate the future of that precious little boy there?'

Sarah looks at her son. Dylan is still in a deep sleep on the bed, his mouth slightly open as he breathes through it. Her heart feels as if it's been torn in two. She can't believe the person she thought was her best friend would do this to her. Would side with her abuser. Take her son away from the safety of his grandfather's care. That she'd stand back while Drew hurt her father, beat him to a pulp. What was Keeley thinking?

She takes hold of her mum's hand again. Mum has gone quiet, as if seeing Keeley here, the girl she's fed, tucked into bed, given lifts to, on numerous occasions, has taken away her power of speech.

Sarah looks back at Drew. Like her mother said earlier, she's beginning to get a bad feeling. 'Tell us what you want.'

It's Keeley who answers. 'He wants you to clear his name. Come clean and admit you framed him. Then he and I can start a new life. He's aware he might be facing further charges, for hurting Dan and your dad, but they should be minimal, under the circumstances . . .'

'But we asked you that.' Sarah gasps and looks at Drew. 'Mum told you we would . . .'

Drew clears his throat loudly. He begins to pace again.

Keeley looks at him and frowns. 'What?'

'Well, actually, dear Keeley, that's just what I told *you*.'

'What? What do you mean?'

Drew looks from her to Sarah and back again. 'What I said. The whole *clearing my name, starting a new life* thing. That's just what I told you. So you'd agree to help me keep one step ahead of the police and get Sarah and Claire to come here. I've been using you, right from the beginning. I knew as soon as you came to visit me, you'd come in handy. Although, I'm afraid I don't really have much use for you now. Not anymore.' He shakes his head sadly. 'You and me. You didn't really think that was ever going to work, did you?'

'But . . .' Keeley swallows. She looks as if she's about to burst into tears. 'Then what . . .?'

Sarah lifts her chin. 'Just stop, Drew. Stop messing us all about and tell us what you really want.'

Drew is quiet for a few seconds. He puts a hand to his chin before looking back at Sarah. 'What I want, my dear wife, is *you*. A straight swap. Dylan goes back to your mum and you come with me, so you and I can begin a new life together on our own, not me and this blithering idiot here or with our wailing brat. The police never need to know what happened. You can stay dead. I'm never going to clear my name, not after everything I've done. Even if you and your loving mother come forward and confess all, I'll still be in deep. So, best we run away into the sunset together, eh?' He shrugs.

Next to her, Sarah hears her mother sob.

Drew looks into her eyes. 'You're the one that got away, Sarah. And I'm afraid I really have to put that right.'

Sarah gasps as Drew moves towards her and grabs her arm, but before she can even think about fighting back, all hell breaks loose.

Chapter 39

Claire now

Drew and Sarah think I've been rendered speechless by everything going on around me – the shock of seeing Keeley, the thought of going ahead with what my son-in-law wants, the idea of losing my daughter all over again – but what they don't know is that I've been taking it all in. Listening to and absorbing every single word.

And I'm *damned* if I'm going to let that bastard take my little girl.

I raise the spanner I picked up from the toolbox in the main cabin of the boat. The one I quickly grabbed when I pretended to lose my footing on the wet floor. I've been holding it down by my side the whole time we've been in the bedroom, in the hand that's furthest away from Drew and Keeley. It's heavy and my arm has been aching for the last few minutes. At one point, I almost dropped it, the tool greasy, probably from years of use. It takes all my strength to lift it above my head.

I run at Drew, taking him by surprise. He seems to think he's finally got his way, won the game, given us no choice but to agree to his ridiculous plan if we want Dylan to grow up in safety, and he's not expecting me to come at him so quickly. Looking after a young child the past three years has kept me fit. I'm not as old and weak as my son-in-law thinks I am. I catch him off-guard.

I bring the spanner down heavily against the side of his head, thinking, as I see bright red blood immediately appear, of my ex-husband. Of how Drew did something similar to him, hit him hard, when he wasn't expecting it. I channel all my anger into the blow I deliver. Guy is a good man. The best. Drew made a big mistake when he hurt him.

He drops to the floor, the boat moving slightly as his weight hits. A strange sound leaves his lips – a cross between a scream and a gurgle – as if something isn't quite right inside him. Despite what he's just told her, how he called her an *idiot*, Keeley rushes towards him. Her face is suddenly pale as she too falls to the floor beside the man she's convinced herself she loves. Even now, Drew always seems to have someone at his beck and call.

Tears stream down Keeley's face as she puts her arms around him and cradles his head in her lap. She rocks back and forth, wailing. 'Drew, no . . .'

I turn to look at Sarah. Taking advantage of Keeley having moved away from the bed, my daughter hurries to where Dylan is asleep and bundles her son into her arms, his grey bunny squashed between them, before turning back towards the door. As she passes Keeley, she pauses, just briefly, and looks down at the girl who was once her friend. Although she should carry on going, shouldn't stop, Sarah can't seem to help it, her feet stalling as she struggles to take in what she's just found out about someone she once trusted.

Keeley looks up at Sarah, her face streaked with tears, mascara on her cheeks. As I watch them, I see that the connection between the two girls is still there. The Keeley I'm looking at now is the one I welcomed into my home. Who I treated like she was my own daughter. Who laughed and sang and cried and danced in my presence. She's still there, that sweet girl, beneath the steely appearance she's been projecting since we arrived at the boat.

Perhaps she hasn't been completely brainwashed by Drew Allison after all.

Except I'm wrong.

From her position on the floor, Keeley suddenly lets Drew's head flop from her lap and lunges for Sarah, grabbing hold of my daughter's coat and pulling herself up, as if her life depends on it. As she straightens, she grabs hold of Dylan, trying to wrestle him from Sarah's arms. 'You're not taking him. You don't deserve a family, not after what you did. You don't deserve to just walk away and live your life as if nothing's happened.' Her eyes look wild, as if she's lost all sense of reason, all sense of who she is. Who she *was*.

Sarah screams at her. 'Let go of him, Keeley.'

'I won't. Drew meant what he said. He loves me. He just panicked, that's all. Once he wakes up, I'll persuade him that the best plan now is for us to keep Dylan and we can be a family together, the three of us . . .' She breathes heavily, one hand holding tightly on to Dylan's dinosaur pyjamas.

I scoff. 'And you really believe that would work? That he wouldn't treat you exactly the same way he treated Sarah? That he wouldn't abuse you, hurt you? Even after you know what he did to Dan and Guy? Are you blind? His ex-girlfriend has just gone *missing*, according to the news. Did you not hear that? Do you know anything about it?'

Keeley hesitates. For the first time, she seems unsure. Then she looks behind her at Drew and shakes her head. 'He's not what you think he is!'

As I see her lunge again, grabbing for my grandson, I rush forward and push her with all my strength, the heavy spanner dropping from my hand with a loud clang as I move. I don't want to hurt Keeley. I don't want to do the same to her as I just did to Drew. She is as much a victim as the rest of us. She's been manipulated, deceived, just like Sarah was. I just want to stop her in her tracks.

I watch her fall backwards, her back hitting the end of the wooden bed before she lands on the floor. Lying spread-eagled, she seems to be stunned.

I sprint to the dresser and put out the oil lamp, in the hope I can disorientate my enemies. I shout loudly as I move. '*Run*, Sarah.'

Trying to focus in the dark, I usher my daughter towards the door and out into the cabin. Together, we move through the living area and the thin galley kitchen, trying not to slip as the bright moon outside guides us. As we reach the narrow steps, I take my grandson while Sarah climbs up, then awkwardly pass him to her through the gap, losing my breath with the exertion. As I start to climb myself, I think I can hear something behind me. Movement perhaps, as someone gets up in the bedroom, the cabin now too dark for me to see anything. I feel a jolt of fear. My family is still in danger.

Sarah puts a hand down to help me. 'Hurry, Mum.'

I scramble up the steps, my whole body in shock now, my limbs refusing to function as they should. The boat is swaying with our movement and I'm starting to feel slightly sick. As I come out onto the deck, my foot catches in what seems to be a thick cable, hidden, like a snake waiting to strike, under the dense layer of snow. I fall, feeling a sharp current of pain travel the length of my leg as my ankle twists.

'Mum!' Sarah turns back. Shifting Dylan to her other shoulder, she tries to help me up.

I try to move but my left foot won't seem to do what I want it to. I wonder if my ankle is broken, the pain intensifying as I clumsily roll over onto my butt, my arms supporting me from behind. My clothes are drenched. As I begin to shiver, I pull my phone from my pocket and hand it to Sarah. 'Go, get Dylan out of here. Call Jane Fellows.'

'I'm not leaving you, Mum. I can't. What if . . .?' She looks up suddenly, gasping, her eyes wide.

I follow her gaze. Just a few feet from where I'm sitting, Drew is coming up the steps, his head and arms already through the hatch.

He looks dazed. Thick blood runs over his right ear and down his neck and his words are slurred as he yells.

'You're not getting away from me, Sarah. I'm not letting you go, not ever . . .'

I wonder if Keeley can hear him, if her heart is shattering right at this very moment.

'But first, I'm going to kill that interfering mother of yours.'

He hauls himself through the gap, His movements seem sluggish and he trips as he steps onto the deck, only just managing to right himself. He's holding the spanner I dropped.

I shuffle backwards and the pain the small movement causes makes me feel faint. Trying to focus, I see that Keeley has now followed Drew up the steps. She looks pale, horrified at finding out that she's been tricked. Perhaps she now knows how Sarah feels.

My son-in-law lurches towards me, like someone who's very drunk.

'I mean it, Claire. I'm going to kill you. In the most painful way I can think of. And I'm going to make your daughter watch. After that, she can watch me kill that brat of hers as well, and her best friend. In for a penny . . .' As he speaks, his eyes roll into the back of his head and drool spills from his lips. The blood from his wound seems to be flowing faster now. It drips onto the snow at his feet, large red splashes marring the white.

Behind him, Keeley, now on the deck, looks as if she's frozen on the spot. Her mouth hangs open, her eyes wide, as if she has no idea what to do.

Drew tries to focus on me. He steps forward, one arm outstretched as he attempts to swing the heavy spanner at me.

Trying to ignore the pain in my ankle, I shuffle backwards again as quickly as I can, my hands on the deck behind me, numb with cold. I watch as Drew moves, as his own foot catches in the same cable that caused me to trip. A look of horror crosses his face as he loses his balance. He's going to fall right on top of me.

In the next few seconds, the only scenario that can end this whole sorry mess plays out in my head, like a film on fast forward. *If I can just manage to move myself*, I think. *Just a few inches.*

I lift my legs and shift myself to one side, just in time. Drew falls towards me, the spanner still in his hand.

My son-in-law topples over the side of the boat and disappears into the freezing water.

Keeley screams loudly and pushes past Sarah, leaving the boat. I watch her disappear down the dark towpath before leaning back and looking at the sky, my breath coming in spurts. My ankle feels as if it's about to explode. I hear helicopter blades somewhere in the distance. Could this nightmare finally be over? I think. At long last?

I look at Sarah and see how pale she is, how shocked, her skin as white as her bleached hair. She needs me to take the lead. 'Take Dylan below deck and put him on the bed. We need to call the police.'

Chapter 40

Guy now

Guy stands in the living room doorway and watches his daughter. On the far side of the room, Sarah is kneeling on the rug in front of the fire. Boswell is lying to one side of her, his eyes barely leaving her face. Dylan sits facing her as he pulls wrapping paper off one of his gifts and Sarah claps her hands at the toy her son has unveiled. She looks better now. In the past couple of weeks, she's put on weight. Her face has filled out and regained some of the colour it used to have and her letter S necklace is back around her neck. The clothes she's wearing today – a top and trousers she found in her mother's wardrobe – are a little more like what she might have worn three years ago. In her old life. Not quite the same, but a little more Sarah than the threadbare sweaters and tracksuit bottoms she wore as Amy. Guy wonders if she'll grow her hair long again, welcome back its natural dark shade to match her brown eyes. It might seem strange after all this time.

He thinks back to the first Christmas they had to spend without her. It was a grim affair, two weeks after the police had told them that Sarah appeared to have been murdered by her husband.

Of course, he and Claire knew better. Knew what had really happened. What they'd all done and would have to keep to themselves forever. Not wanting to spend the day at home, they'd gone into Gilbert House, taking Dylan with them, just a year and a half old then. While they were there, helping dish out turkey and Christmas pudding, they'd both spoken to Amy, wished her all the best, encouraged their grandson to spend some time with the person he didn't recognise as his mother, even after such a short time. What they'd both wanted to do – hug her, bring her home, shower her with gifts – they hadn't been able to. Might never be able to again. Until now.

Sarah is back. She's home, where she belongs.

He pokes at his right wrist, trying to scratch it as far as he can beneath the plaster cast. The sling that holds his arm close to his chest has been annoying him all day, the rough material catching at the back of his neck. He's had two pins put in, one in the upper arm and one in the lower. The doctor who came to speak to him, after the operation, said that no one could predict at this stage whether Guy will ever regain full use of the limb. He doesn't mind all that much. He's left-handed anyway and at least he's still here. With his family. That's all that matters at the minute.

He rubs at his full stomach. Cooking Christmas dinner hadn't been easy with only one functioning hand. He and Claire had worked together, Guy stuffing the turkey as she prepared the veg. His ex-wife's injured ankle is much stronger now – just twisted, rather than broken, as she'd first thought – and she's walking almost normally. It was fun to be in the kitchen together, just like old times. Kind of.

He looks down at Claire now, as she sits on the nearby sofa, next to her mother, the two of them smiling as they watch Dylan open another present. His mother-in-law hadn't been happy when she'd found out the truth about Sarah, angry that they hadn't trusted her enough to say anything sooner, but she's coming round now. Soon, he imagines, their family life might be somewhere

256

near to being what it was before. Not the same – it will never be that – but maybe similar. Although he's not sure his own mother will ever speak to any of them again.

He'd thought it might seem strange, being back in the house, but it doesn't somehow. After what happened at the bedsit, neither Claire nor Sarah had wanted him to return there, and it seemed natural for him to come back here; be part of the family again. Sometimes, he feels as if he never left. Even though he's sleeping in the spare room, the one he used as an office when he used to work from home, his razor and toothbrush look as if they're back where they belong in the bathroom upstairs. He has no idea what the future will bring, but he's happy to wait and see.

He looks down at Claire again and clears his throat. 'Do you fancy a little walk, to burn off those two helpings of pudding? Might do your ankle good to get some exercise.'

Claire looks up at him and nods. 'Sure. It would be nice to get some fresh air.' She stands and joins him in the hallway, her limp only slight now.

Sarah runs her hand over the dog's fur as she looks at them both. 'Be careful, you two.'

'Why do they need to be careful?' Claire's mother's voice is overly loud as always. 'Isn't all that behind you now?'

Sarah looks at her grandma. 'I just meant because there are still some journalists hanging around. Just because it's Christmas doesn't mean they'll get bored quite yet. Not until the next juicy story comes along.'

'We'll be fine.' He smiles at his daughter.

He helps Claire with her coat before wrestling with his own, putting his left arm in the sleeve before suddenly deciding to pull off his sling. *Fuck what the doctors have said.* His arm is feeling a lot better and only having the cast, being more mobile, will make life a lot easier. He drops the sling to the floor and awkwardly pulls on the other sleeve of his coat before they both head out of the front door.

Outside, one lone reporter and his sidekick photographer are still lingering at the end of the driveway, trying to get a story that will soon be old news. As soon as they lay eyes on Guy and Claire, they immediately move forward. The reporter holds a small voice recorder towards Guy's face.

'Mr Wallace, could I just ask you . . .?'

Guy stops and shakes his head. 'You do know it's Christmas Day, don't you? Go home. Spend some time with your family. You never know if you'll get chance to do that again.'

The reporter ignores him and turns his attention to Claire. 'Mrs Wallace, if you could just tell me how you feel now that Drew Allison seems to be out of your life for good?'

Guy takes Claire's elbow and they both turn away.

'Any news on the search for Mr Allison's body? Mr and Mrs Wallace? Do you think they'll ever find him? How does Sarah feel now her abuser is dead . . .?'

They carry on walking, across the street and to the end, the sound of the reporter's voice fading behind them. The weather is still cold, an unprecedented amount of snow having fallen over the past couple of weeks. The ground is icy now. A hard white layer covers the pavement.

He takes Claire's hand. 'Just so you don't slip.'

She smiles. She doesn't pull away. 'I keep thinking. About the trial. How we watched him get taken away, to prison. Knowing what we'd done.'

He nods. 'Have you ever regretted it?'

Claire seems to think for a few seconds before she shakes her head. 'No. Not once. We did what we had to do. I have absolutely no doubt that we wouldn't have Sarah at all now if we hadn't done what we did. He would have killed her and not even blinked.'

'I agree.'

'The hardest bit was watching the police search for her. Knowing they'd never find her. Knowing it was fruitless, but not being able to say anything. It seemed never-ending.'

'They found what we wanted them to find.'

They cross the main road and enter the estate on the other side. The police hadn't been able to find Drew either. Despite the efforts of the diving team, submerging themselves for hours on end in the freezing, dirty water, it seems now that Drew Allison has disappeared without a trace, just like his wife did before him.

They walk in silence. The streets are mostly empty, anyone with any common sense likely curled up indoors, in front of the TV or playing Monopoly. A cold-looking dog walker passes them and nods – *All the best* – and a family trying out new bikes zips past. Then they're alone again. Guy's arm throbs with the cold.

He thinks about his daughter. Sarah has been through so much. Her body has scars that will never go, from the beatings and the burns, the cut on the inside of her thigh that she'd done herself so they could plant blood in the flat. Even now, perhaps *especially* now, Guy worries incessantly about her. His family have always meant everything to him. That's why he agreed to Sarah's plan without hesitation. Ever since he first met Claire at uni, all he's wanted to do is build a life with her. And now they both just want to stop that life from falling apart, crumbling into dust, because of the actions of Drew Allison. Not to mention Sarah's so-called *friend*.

Even though she doesn't talk about it much, Sarah is devastated at what Keeley did to her. The police soon caught up with her, they'd told him and Claire, shortly after the incident on the boat. After she'd run away from the marina, Keeley had been found wandering the streets in a daze. The shock of what she'd done, of being made to look a fool by the man who'd coerced her into thinking she had to do everything he said, had hit her hard. Now Sarah's former friend is facing charges of aiding and abetting an offender. Rumour has it she'll get a suspended sentence. Keeley is a good person really, Guy thinks. Just like his own daughter, she was lured in. As if Drew Allison was some kind of cult leader who cast a spell on women.

He squeezes Claire's fingers as they make their way down the hedge-lined lane towards the marina. Of course, Keeley isn't the only one looking at a possible court appearance. He and Claire have spoken to the police and told them everything. Everything they did three years ago: how they framed Drew, how they planted evidence, lied to the authorities. They've both insisted it was all their idea. That they persuaded Sarah into it, such was their worry about her welfare. At the time, their daughter was vulnerable, they said, not capable of thinking straight due to the mental and physical trauma she'd been through. Dan has also confessed his part in it, from his hospital bed. Has told how he distracted Drew while Guy set up the scene in the flat, how he then denied his brother an alibi. Like Guy and Claire, he's insisting that Sarah is completely innocent. That he is much more to blame than she is.

Claire looks at him, as if guessing what he's thinking about. 'There's no point in worrying. We can only wait and see what happens.'

Guy nods. Their solicitor is attempting to get the charges reduced, perhaps get them all off with a fine or community service in the long run. In the few days after the story broke that Sarah was still alive, social media was in uproar. Hundreds, maybe thousands, of women jumped in to defend his family. To denounce the violent culture they've had to put up with for so long, the drastic measures they've always had to take to avoid getting beaten, raped, killed. #JusticeforSarah, Guy has read on Twitter numerous times. #IstandwiththeWallaces. The clients of Claire's helpline have been especially vocal.

He puts his head down against the cold wind as they cross the bridge over the canal and cross back again until they're on the towpath. The area seems desolate now, only the geese and ducks huddled on the water, protecting each other from the cold. As they walk, he thinks again about Dan. Two or three times in the last fortnight, Guy has helped Sarah leave by the back gate, to avoid the crowds of journalists at the front, so she could go and visit Drew's brother in the hospital.

He looks at Claire. 'Sarah says Dan is improving. He could be out by the new year.'

Claire looks at the snowy scenery around her. 'Fingers crossed.'

'We couldn't have done what we did without him.'

'No, he's a good person.'

They slow as they approach the boat, not the *Lady Sarah* this time, but one further along the canal, even more run-down. The name of it is too faded to read. The hull is damaged and worn, wood splintered and metal rusting. He looks around. There isn't another soul in sight. The divers are gone now. The search for Drew has long since been abandoned, the presumption that he's been swept away in the murky depths. A length of crime scene tape snakes by, caught by the wind. It must have escaped from the original boat, the one where Claire and Sarah found Keeley and Dylan that night, two weeks ago.

Guy looks at Claire. She nods.

Still holding hands, they step over the gap onto the deck of the very shabby vessel, trying to keep their balance. The wood beneath their feet is icy as Guy glances around again and then moves to the small hatch door. Bending, he inserts a small key into a shiny padlock, turns it and pulls the door open. He stoops as he makes his way down the narrow wooden steps before turning to help his ex-wife.

They stand together in the cabin, the weak winter daylight coming through the portholes as they both hold their hands to their noses. The boat smells rotten. Leading the way, Guy walks through the empty kitchen and living area to the stern, only pausing briefly to pick something up from by the very old log fire, something that he carries with him in his good hand. The smell gets stronger: shit and urine and decay. He stops in front of a ramshackle cabin bed and tries not to retch. Beside him, Claire coughs into her hand.

Drew Allison stirs and looks up at them, his face as white as the snow outside, his features almost skeletal. He's lying on his back, his wrists and ankles bound to the bunk beneath him with thick tape, another ream of it across his mouth. His clothes are drenched with his own waste. He looks like a fish that's been dragged from the water and left to die.

Guy stares down at him. 'Not smirking quite so much now, are you? Are you not enjoying the game anymore, Drew?'

Drew tries to move, but his muscles are weak from lack of use and his attempts to fight his bindings are futile. He makes a strange noise behind the tape on his mouth, like a strangled cry. Perhaps a bit like the noises Sarah used to make when he put his hands to her throat.

Claire speaks to her son-in-law. 'Maybe now you know how frightened Sarah felt every time you attacked her. How your ex-girlfriends felt when you killed them.'

There's no doubt now; Guy and Claire both know for certain that Drew is a murderer, that he would have killed their daughter if he'd had the chance. Despite the fact that they'd framed him for Sarah's *death*, they know that what they did was right. That someone had to stop him before he did any more damage. Not long after the fugitive they were chasing disappeared into the water, the police had found Hannah's body. She'd been visited at home by her ex, it seemed, shortly after he'd succeeded in getting out of prison, and thrown into a wheelie bin not far away. Keeley had apparently driven him to Hannah's house and had waited outside in the car, completely unaware of what was going on inside, that the man she thought she loved might have killed her at some point.

Directed by the estranged family of Drew's previous girlfriend, the investigation team had also found a second body, buried deep beneath the wasteland at the back of Drew's flat. Skeletal remains they'd somehow missed when they were looking for Sarah. It had soon become obvious why their son-in-law had looked so nervous when going through airport checks, as Sarah had later told them he had, why he'd chosen to live where he did, despite the money he had. No functioning security cameras, barely any police presence, a vast area of undergrowth to hide his crimes. The cases of both women had now been closed, their killer missing and presumed drowned.

Except he isn't.

Drew is here, in front of them. Still alive, or just about.

It had been Sarah who'd dragged her husband from the water. After Keeley had run away and Claire had told her daughter to call the police, Sarah had spotted Drew, scrabbling by the bank, almost unconscious. It had been a huge effort to pull him out, Claire doing her best to help on her swollen ankle, but they'd managed it between them, Dylan still sleeping in the bedroom of the *Lady Sarah*.

It was only after they'd dragged Drew to this boat, the one with no name, that they'd called the police. Told them how Drew had disappeared. How one minute he'd been on the snowy deck; the next, he'd gone under the water. It was a risk; they both knew that. But it hadn't seemed to occur to the search teams to look in the other vessels, so damaged, they were hardly seaworthy.

He looks down at the pathetic excuse for a human in front of him. Sarah knows that he and Claire have been coming to visit Drew almost every day, keeping her husband alive with the occasional sip of water and the odd scrap of food. Letting him think about what he'd done to her. Stew on his actions.

And their consequences.

She knows what the plan is. Why they're here today. How this is going to end.

It's time.

He glances at Claire before reaching forward and roughly pulling the tape from his son-in-law's face.

Drew winces. 'Don't hurt me.' His voice is hoarse, his throat probably as dry as sandpaper, his whole body dehydrated.

Guy grits his teeth. What Sarah doesn't know is, this isn't the first time her father has been in this exact position.

Standing here, with Drew in front of him, dribbling and snotty, Claire at his side, he suddenly finds himself transported back to a time over thirty years ago. A time when he stood over a bed in the grubby student room of someone he hated as much as he hates Drew Allison. When he'd first set eyes on his future wife, Guy had loved her instantly. He would have done anything for Claire, right from the day they met. She'd only wanted to be his friend at first. She was seeing someone else at the time, an arrogant kid who'd hung around with their crowd. Guy didn't think Tom was good for Claire. He instinctively knew when someone was bad news.

He remembers once eavesdropping on a conversation between Claire and Sarah, as they were washing and drying dishes together in the kitchen at home. Claire had been telling her daughter about a friend she'd had at uni, a girl who'd lost everything, become isolated from her family and classmates due to her abusive partner. So the girl had ended the relationship. *And that was that,* Claire had said before inviting Sarah to watch some TV with her.

Except that wasn't that, because Guy knew the truth. And he knew Claire wasn't talking about one of her friends. She'd been talking about herself.

He'd been livid when he'd seen the woman he loved turn up to classes with black eyes and split lips. Her beautiful face marred by what that bastard had done to her. And, when Guy had walked in on Claire's so-called boyfriend raising his fists to her, one day when he'd been searching for her to discuss plans for a night out, he'd seen immediately that he had to do something to protect her, to end what was happening to her once and for all.

He sees himself, standing in the doorway of Tom's tiny room, the student building they lived in more or less empty now, everyone else having gone home for the summer, just a handful of them having stayed behind. Tom was in the process of trying to convince Claire to spend the next few weeks with him and him alone, to forget her friends. That he loved her, despite everything he'd done. Except his way of convincing her was to beat her to a pulp. When he'd seen Guy push the door open, catching him mid-punch, mid-kick, Tom had flown across the room, suddenly directing his violence towards his unwelcome intruder. Feeling a tidal wave of rage wash over him, Guy had reacted with more strength than he'd known he had. He'd grabbed Tom and thrown him onto the bed.

He'd done what he'd done for Claire, just like what he's about to do now is for Sarah. His future wife, now his ex, had stood by his side, the same as she's doing now, her face pale and body shaking as he'd grabbed a nearby fire extinguisher and raised it above Tom's head, completely terrified yet determined at the same time. Seeing Claire hurt had simply been too much for Guy to cope with, something he couldn't accept. Just like when he saw Sarah hurt after she married this monster.

Please don't hurt me, Tom had pleaded, his words almost exactly the same as Drew's.

Guy had simply curled his lip, sneering at the snivelling mess in front of him. *Please don't hurt me. Have you any idea how pathetic you sound?*

Why are you doing this?

Do you really need to ask me that? You hurt her. You hurt Claire. The same as you'll do to every other woman you meet, as you've no doubt done before.

Please think about this. Tom was crying now, snot and tears dripping down pale skin.

Think?

It doesn't have to be like this. There's a way out. There's always a way out. For me and for you. We can talk, work it out. Go back.

There's no going back. Not now.

I know you. I know you don't really want to do this . . .

Guy had raised an eyebrow. *You think you know me? Believe me, you have no idea what I'm capable of when it comes to protecting the people I love . . .*

Later, when he was almost done, Tom's body almost defeated, Guy had stood over him.

You really didn't know what I was capable of, did you?

There was no answer. Just a gasp, a dribble of drool. Of thick mucus.

Admit it. You thought I was one of the good guys when we first met. A real good egg. That I would never dream of doing anyone any harm.

A fresh drop of blood had rolled down Tom's flesh before hitting the ground. It had spattered in a star shape.

Funny how appearances can be deceptive . . .

He'd finished him off after that. The police had blamed an intruder, Claire quickly locking the door from the inside and opening the window before they both clambered through the gap. No one had suspected the two of them. They'd got away with it. Claire was finally free.

Like Sarah is going to be from now on.

Guy looks at his ex-wife, thinking about how she told him, a few days ago, that she's been dreaming of it recently. What they did to Tom. How it fills her nights still, but how she doesn't regret it. Guy had helped her, all those years ago, and now he's going to do the same for their daughter. For all the other women Drew Allison might have lured into his web in the future. They all need to know for sure that Drew is gone. Not just to prison. They'd already tried that and he'd managed to escape, to hurt other people. Now they need to know he's gone for good.

Guy takes a breath. With Claire standing next to him, he raises the heavy iron poker he picked up on his way through the boat with his good arm.

He's going to sort this. For his family. And then he's going to go home and tell Sarah it's done.

A Letter from Jacqueline Grima

Thank you so much for choosing to read *My Daughter's Killer*. I hope you enjoyed reading it as much as I enjoyed writing it! If you did and you would like to hear more about my books and new releases, you can follow me on Facebook, Twitter, Instagram and through my website below.

My Daughter's Killer is the second psychological thriller I have released with HQ Digital. I have thoroughly enjoyed collaborating with the HQ team and am so appreciative of all their hard work. If you have time to leave a short review on Amazon, Goodreads or your social media channels, I would be ever grateful. Reviews are crucial to authors and publishers in spreading the word. They also make our future books better! Also, if you enjoyed this book, I would really appreciate it if you could recommend it to your friends and family.

Thanks so much for your time!
Jacqueline xxx

Facebook: www.facebook.com/jacquelinegrimawriter
Twitter: www.twitter.com/GrimaJgrima
Instagram: www.instagram.com/jacquelinegrimawriter/
Website: www.jacquelinegrima.co.uk

Keep Reading . . .

The Weekend Alone

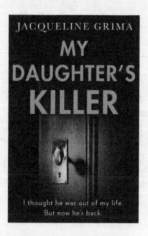

A devoted wife and mother
Bella has the perfect life with her husband Jack and their two children – until the ex who stalked her years ago is released from prison.

A tragic past that haunts her
Now Bella is convinced he's back to hurt her, and sees him everywhere – but no one else can see that anything is wrong.

One last chance to put it behind her
With her family away for the weekend, Bella determines to leave the past in the past – but she's about to discover the danger is closer to home than she ever imagined . . .

A gripping and unputdownable thriller for fans of *The Perfect Couple*, *The Marriage Lie* and *The Housemaid*.

Acknowledgements

When an author writes a book, it is in no way a solo endeavour and a lot of people have had a hand in making *My Daughter's Killer* what it is today. Particular thanks must go to my editor Abigail Fenton. Without you, Abi, I would no doubt be still trying to find my way through my jungle of a manuscript. Your insights and enthusiasm are invaluable and I've thoroughly enjoyed working with you. Thanks also to the rest of the HQ team – copyeditors, proof-readers, cover designers, marketers, to name just a few – for all their hard work, and to my fellow HQ authors for being so supportive.

Thanks also to all my fellow writers for their support, especially my writing 'buddies' Catherine 'Kitty' Murphy, Georgia Davies and Stephanie Rogers. I couldn't do it without you! Also, thanks to everyone in 'the office' for their support and enthusiasm for my writing, including Zoe, Kristie, Gabby, Ang, Andrew, Sara, Lewis, Mandy, Keith, Megan, Lauren (and her granddad), Amy and Mike (apologies if I've forgotten anyone). And here's hoping Amanda Musgrove will be 'in the mood' to read this one ;)

Special thanks must also go to Martin Bloomfield for his insights, knowledge and, in particular, his patience when my plot changed for about the millionth time. Thanks, Martin! Any mistakes are completely my own.

Thanks, as always, to those at home: Dan and Andrew, for always supporting me; Krista for the lunches and tidying so I could lock myself away and write; Mike and Nora for the unexpected smiley arrival who made the completion of this work-in-progress rather interesting, and to my dad for the many, many jobs around the house and for being my number one 'go-to' person.

To you, the reader, for choosing my words to keep you company.

And, lastly, to Taz, for being the best old boy until the end.

Dear Reader,

We hope you enjoyed reading this book. If you did, we'd be so appreciative if you left a review. It really helps us and the author to bring more books like this to you.

Here at HQ Digital we are dedicated to publishing fiction that will keep you turning the pages into the early hours. Don't want to miss a thing? To find out more about our books, promotions, discover exclusive content and enter competitions you can keep in touch in the following ways:

JOIN OUR COMMUNITY:

Sign up to our new email newsletter: http://smarturl.it/SignUpHQ

Read our new blog www.hqstories.co.uk

https://twitter.com/HQStories

www.facebook.com/HQStories

BUDDING WRITER?

We're also looking for authors to join the HQ Digital family! Find out more here:

https://www.hqstories.co.uk/want-to-write-for-us/

Thanks for reading, from the HQ Digital team